PEREGRINE ISLAND

Peregrine Island

Island

A Novel

Diane B. Saxton

SHE WRITES PRESS

Published 2016
Printed in the United States of America
ISBN: 978-1-63152-151-5
Library of Congress Control Number: 2016938635

Cover design © Julie Metz, Ltd./metzdesign.com
Interior design by Tabitha Lahr

For information, address:
She Writes Press
1563 Solano Ave #546
Berkeley, CA 94707

She Writes Press is a division of SparkPoint Studio, LLC.

This is a work of fiction. Names, characters, places, and incidents either are the product of the author's imagination or are used fictitiously. Any resemblance to actual persons, living or dead, is entirely coincidental.

In memory of my mother who believed
in the importance of family.

It is not enough to believe what you see.
You must also understand what you see.

—LEONARDO DA VINCI
1452–1519

CONTENTS

PROLOGUE

*P*eople who live on the shores of an ocean or a sea know what to do when a squall comes in. Lovers of salt-whippy air and fermenting waves enjoy the kick they get from the sudden, short-lived storm.

But not Winter Peregrine, sole owner of a small island, and mother and grandmother of a family insulated by the waters of the Long Island Sound. Never has she waded out to a waiting skull, rowed till she collapsed, nor has she experienced the thrill of hooking a bluefish, a flounder, or a sea bass. Nothing she does allows the sport of the sea into her life. She prefers to observe it—and from her shut-tight windows, she has learned its secrets well. Nevertheless, in a squall, Winter would probably perish.

Unlike her daughter, Elsepath, who relishes risk. Hooking a fish is child's play for Elsie, as she prefers to be called. She enjoys a fight for survival. Water-skiing upside down on her fingertips while ricocheting between rocks at low tide—this is another one of her passions. And squalls—one would assume Elsie thrives on them.

Her daughter, tiny Peda, however, would never hook a fish, never water-ski where crabs multiply and make their homes.

To become one with her habitat and to safeguard sea life from sudden ravages—this, she sees as her mission. Particularly in a squall.

In our mind's eye, we picture the family on the beach: the grandmother on wet sand, her forehead coated with the sweat of icy fear; way ahead of her, the daughter, looking back, knee-deep in a stony tidal pool. And behind them both, we imagine we hear humming, and the skip and splash of a little girl's feet. The three of them together are like inharmonious survivors on a raft, fated to capsize if thrust together too long, we think. But then again . . . maybe not. For what you see, or think you see, on Peregrine Island is seldom what it seems.

Chapter 1

WINTER

*I*n the beginning, when Peda told me that an old man named Jake lived with his dog, Scarecrow, under the pier, I didn't believe her, because, like me, she is a storyteller and a follower of fantasies. In retrospect, I should have paid more attention to her: when she crouched low, as if she were dodging rats that hid in the shadows of the derelict jetty; when she spread her ribbon-thin arms wide to describe the radius between the boulders that formed the old man's living space. And I should have heeded her when, giggling, she announced that Scarecrow was as sleek as Jake was dated, and that with a shine to his coat Scarecrow was a braggart of a dog who led Jake, neglected and bedraggled, around by his belt. Down on the beach of the Long Island Sound, on an island off the Connecticut side where one wouldn't expect to see rats as big as cats living in seawalls.

But no one believed Peda, least of all me. Not about the rats, or about Jake, or about his smooth, silky dog, Scarecrow. At least, not in the beginning. At that time, even the girl's mother,

1

Elsie, dismissed Peda, lamenting that her daydreams were unnatural. Because after spending time with Jake, Peda would often repeat riddles she claimed had fallen from the old man's tongue. Once, she said blithely, "There's nothing that concentrates the mind like the prospect of death." Naturally, I, Winter, as the girl's grandmother, was quite concerned. Still, after keenly watching my granddaughter, who sat at my knee, I determined that she possessed a precocious imagination, is all. Or maybe I merely misinterpreted her words.

So I nodded patiently while I passed yet another afternoon resting on my chaise, and I directed my attention, instead, at the painting on the wall in front of me. A small girl like Peda couldn't hope to compete with *my* fantasies—the people in the painting who were often in my dreams—or with the artist's quiet, clear colors, muted toward the sky, where the lighted street lamp casts shadows on the cobblestone lane below, which runs adjacent to the sea. The painting's saga, its elapsed time and gone-by place, seemed much more appealing to me than did the stories of my granddaughter.

Unperturbed, Peda would prattle on anyway, pretending that Jake and Superman were one and the same: a godlike individual with rare, miraculous powers who, with one divine swipe, could erase the hurdles that prevented us from having the warm and loving relationship for which, I learned later, she so yearned.

At the time, however, I didn't realize the extent of my granddaughter's sensitivity—or her loneliness. I thought only of myself. Of my own sensitivity and my own loneliness. You see, whenever I caught Peda staring at me, I tried to envisage looking at someone such as I through her eyes. Sometimes, after she chattered on about her imaginary beach friends, she would just watch me. It made me uncomfortable. I would wonder, *who* does she see? You understand, of course, that inside I, too, am still a girl. To this day, I glance behind me when someone yells out, "Missus, Missus," searching for the old lady who walks behind me.

So, you see, although I wanted to help the child, at the time I simply didn't know how. Thus, when Peda stared at me, I studied my painting that hangs over the small fireplace. Immerse myself in art, I told myself. Immerse myself in the conversation of those strollers, people who seem to move about more comfortably in their early-evening twilight than I do, people of maybe sixty or more years ago. If there is no discussion with Peda, I decided, then there is no problem. Ignore her fantasies, was my motto. Delve into my own. Eventually, she'll have to join the real world. Look at me as a real person, the young girl behind the powdery skin and the sticky fluffed hair and the old-lady aura. And forget her raggedy man with the slick skinny black dog who chases super-rats in seawalls.

As I recall, when our story began, it was the first day of summer. I was on my chaise, as usual, stirring from an afternoon nap, when a tinny sound slipped into my consciousness. I thought I heard, "O . . . mum, O . . . mum," like a faint, recurring water drip. And then again, the tinny sound, leaking through the thick, beveled glass of the window. I listened, cocking my head toward the Sound.

There, playing on the beach, squatting on a sand dune, was tiny Peda, with eyes the color and consistency of honey and a forehead marred by a magnificent bruise, purple, its indent a scalding yellow. Healing, all right, but such an imprint on such a small person. Before her, she had gathered bunches of pure green seaweed, like stacked firewood ready to be lit, their necks tied by closed, stuck-together clams. Fingering the seaweed strings, she alternately held them up and waved them at me, the figure in the window, her omum, to whom she called while she picked and pierced the moist, bulbous pimples on the voluptuous seaweed. The skin, I saw, was similar to a toad's—wet to look at but surprisingly soft, I imagined—and I believed she wanted to tell me so. Her voice, though, kept fading into the salted wind, and finally, annoyed with the futility of her calls, she leaped up from her seat on the dune. Grasping her booty in one hand, she ran to the water's edge and threw the vibrant bunches of seaweed back to the ocean, to save them, I guessed, from the fate of their dried-up kin on the upper beach.

"Winter?" My daughter interrupted my reverie. "Winter? . . . Mother? Are you in there?"

Her presence, I remember, filled my senses like a heady perfume one can't avoid when crammed into the close confines of, say, an elevator or a crowded subway. Potent and relentless. Life rippling from her pores, seeping into mine. Helping me to breathe, I think she believed. Unaccountably, I sank backward against my chaise. Squinting against the glare of the day—which almost obliterated my view of the jetty and the stone-strewn beach at the entrance to the harbor—I wished that I could escape her vitality.

"Clay is here," she announced coolly, always in charge, outwardly always in control. But to my mind, after the shock of her homecoming three years earlier, after half a decade of silence and accompanied by a child of whose existence I was unaware, Elsie had taken on the aura of a warrior, impregnable and ready for battle. Spirited, too, but scared, I felt. And so closed up. Worse, she was unwilling to talk about it, at least not to me. Very different from the young, effusive Elsie, blooming and full of hope, who had returned home to her father and me the summer after her graduation from Vassar.

I watched her carefully now for a giveaway, something

to betray the scene I had observed after lunch from the pantry door. Over the last year, Clay had stolen covert glances at Elsie—this I knew—but I never paid much attention. He'd make a point to slide his gaze over her bare back whenever she ran to the sea, to rip the suit from her bottom with his hot stare. In one graceful swoop, those long, rippling muscles in her legs thrusting her trunk into the waves—it was lovely to look at. But Elsie had ignored him. Maybe by confronting him in the way she did now, she expected to be done with it. I shrugged, curling into my thoughts. From the little I had seen, I thought she had manipulated him admirably. But then, of course, I didn't see everything. He was insatiable, and for one brief moment I experienced a sharp inclination to shield my daughter from the hot wind of his penis, a burst of feeling so unexpected it quite startled me. My daughter is hardly the vulnerable child who needs my protection—anyone's protection, for that matter. Though she exited from my womb, flatulent and flabby as it is now, she has truly become a child of steel.

"Hey, Winter," Clay said, slipping from behind Elsie when he entered the conservatory. "I figured you'd be napping."

I'll just bet you did. My fingers followed him, acknowledging him, as he moved into the circle of faded afternoon light thrown from my window. When he reached me, I extended my cheek for his kiss. "Hello," I said sweetly.

"What time are those curator fellows due?" Clay sat down, too familiarly for my taste, on the foot of my chaise, perching on its edge as if he wanted to make a quick getaway. He looked nervous, wound up, but then, this was his way. Bending down, he moved my ankle to make more room for himself. How did he know about my experts? My meeting with a curator? I raised my eyebrows at Elsie.

Disregarding me, Elsie lay down on the nubby-knit green sofa, careful to arrange her bare legs so that they covered the entirety of it. Pink on green. Though she pretended to close her eyes while Clay and I discussed the painting and the museum, I noticed that she kept one eye slightly ajar, and with it she regarded the painting, studying it closely while we talked, so much so that furrows appeared on her forehead like tracks on wet sand.

"Hadn't you better see to little Peda?" I asked. "She woke me, you know—"

"So?"

"She could use some attention, don't you think?"

"Why don't you go if you're so concerned?" Elsie didn't budge, just rolled her eyes at Clay, who turned and stared out at the sea, shading his eyes against the glare while he made a show of searching the vista for her daughter.

I sat up and with much sighing puffed the cushions, as if to leave, but Elsie jumped up first. "Don't bother," she said, "O . . . mum."

She made Peda's name for me sound old, senile and silly. Something out of a nursery rhyme. Not cool enough for my daughter, who would rather my granddaughter call me by my first name. I had vetoed that idea immediately. I'm not her playmate, I had said when she broached the subject. Shrugging, she had walked away, leaving the youngster with me anyway.

Clay shifted in his seat and scowled at me from under his bushy eyebrows, while Elsie, in her long stride, stalked from the room. Neither of them, I decided, was worth my aggravation, and I pulled my attention back to my painting, the one the museum experts were coming to see, where it hangs in the middle of the faded cherry-paneled wall.

A misty, dreamy scene by the ocean, the Long Island Sound, near here, I supposed, on a quay off an old, cobbled road, rough waves slapping at the stone wall. People I have stared at all my life: A woman in a fitted, ankle-length skirt holds the hand of a child. A few feet away, a man in a fedora bends over the railing and gazes into the water. People who seem to belong more to my past than my own. Early evening interpreted by shades of gray and a lit brass lamppost with an ornate over-hang. Even so, the colors of the half-light remain remarkably pure, for every line, every shade and curve, is delineated. Every stone, every wave—you can see that it is high tide—each grain of sand, each section of seaweed, the mother's slight smile, the gloved hand of the man with the hat. Clear and haunting in the pale, diffuse light.

I looked out the window. It could be this evening but for their dress and the time of year. The figures are familiar to one another—even the suited gentleman in the near distance whose hand is raised in greeting, a small, curly-haired dog at his heels. I feel as if I know them all, and well. The smell of the Sound: a reek of fish mixed with brine; the damp coolness in the air; the wind that blows my hair and scrubs my cheeks. I put my hands up to my own cheeks and held them there for a moment, mesmerized by the probing black eyes of the young woman in the painting. . . .

"I never asked you," Clay said. He pushed my foot. "What-ever possessed you to call the Getty? It looks to be such an ordi-nary picture." He got up and moved to the painting, blocking my view of the figures.

"I didn't call them," I told him. "They called me." I paused, trying not to look at the hairs in his neck. "It's an honor, you know," I said softly.

It *was* an honor, and some part of me longed to have oth-ers learn the grandeur and sublimity of my painting. In my heart, though, I wondered whether I had forfeited my privacy by allowing people to come here to analyze and dissect a paint-ing I had grown to love. The thought so upset me that I had to restrain myself not to jump up, shove him out of the way, to restrict his view of the painted figures.

Whatever induced me to befriend you? I wanted to shout at his affected back, that languid pose: his hand draped nonchalantly over his jutting hip, his other hand just so, pushing aside his navy-blue blazer, resting in his jean pocket, and on top, the tiny ponytail he sometimes favored and styled with such pride, dyed, I knew, by my own hairdresser. I snickered into my teacup. For here stood my lauded landscape architect, the man responsible for replacing my Burberry bushes with windswept pines, my Kentucky bluegrass with tidewater grass, both meant to bend under the weight of salt and high winds. Here, we had first met, on my worn-out, dried-out, filled-with-crabgrass lawn, aged, just like me. The lawn that runs down to the rocky beach of the Long Island Sound. A horticulturist, an arborist, a lawn doctor, a man who came highly recommended, Clay had been there when my grounds needed tending, when I needed fixing up, too, someone to call upon when Daniel left, a tonic, someone to stroke my wounded ego.

Alas, what did Clay see in me? But I knew the answer, and I didn't like it. I ticked off the reasons in my head, like so many points one needs to win a nomination for political office. He enjoyed associating with someone who lives in an inherited, albeit run-down, island waterfront home; he admired my style; he relished Elsie's youth. He liked being admired, cajoled, catered to, pampered, and paid for.

"Well . . . ," he said, with a sudden ferocity, his face still to the wall, "what time are your guests expected?"

The grainy, hoarse voice that had attracted me at one time now sounded petulant, and it annoyed me. *He* annoyed me. He wanted to home in on every aspect of my life; he reminded me of mistletoe, an alluring parasite that inevitably sucks the life out of its host. Hence, on this occasion I decided to stand on my own, get rid of him before my guests arrived, and hoped, for once, to stay firm in my decision.

"Dinner. They're coming for dinner," I snapped. "A curator and an archivist, I'm told." He turned to look at me, arced his eyebrows. "Who just might want to borrow it for an upcoming show," I added proudly. *Although I hope not*, I thought privately. To forfeit my painting, even temporarily, would be a severe blow.

We were interrupted by Elsie, followed by the elfin Peda, who blew into the sunroom from the stone-mildewed loggia—built by my great-grandfather, who, though he had never lived in Europe or even traveled abroad, had sections of Venetian palazzos copied from paintings he favored, tacking pieces onto his home as if with sticky glue, with no rationale except that he admired them: a too-long arm, a round eye to go with one that squinted, a loggia, a terrace, a stairwell, three fireplaces planted in a Victorian hodgepodge.

Peda came fast on Elsie's heels with the purposefulness of youth, the door behind her swinging on its hinges. Galloping toward me, she whipped up the air in the room. Like so many particles of dust, cool humidity settled around her when she planted herself at my feet. I wanted to heave a sigh of relief, for this time in her wake no porcelain figurine crumbled, no patch of salt water marred the Oriental, and no sand scuff dented my satin shams, as is generally the case when she enters. While a remarkably small child for her age, she is unusually active—probably to compensate. She also has an overly active imagination.

"I'd like to stay," Clay said, ignoring Peda's intrusion. He faced me with his hands on his hips.

I shook my head. "There's no room. I'm so sorry."

He looked toward my daughter. "Elsie?" he said.

As if she could help.

Peda put her small, chapped hand over mine. "Can I come?"

"Of course," I said. "You're my granddaughter."

"What am I, chopped liver?" Clay glared at me; his fists were clenched.

"You're a good friend," I said, "but this night's for family, and I didn't know you'd be here." I was talking too fast, and my excuses sounded pitiable.

"I wasn't invited."

I stood up and smiled at him, role-playing. "Next time," I said. "Okay?" And I opened my hands to him, tantamount to/ no better than a vacuous and flirtatious teenager. I hated myself.

"Oh my God," I heard Elsie say from behind me. Dragging out the "oh . . . my . . . God" as if she, too, couldn't stand me. "Come on, Clay," she said. "I'll walk you out."

She slid past me and grabbed his arm, then propelled him from the room. Clay's fists evaporated into a wave, and, with a weak grin pasted on his face, he leaned toward Elsie. I saw him breathe deeply, taking in the scent of her hair. Elsie glanced quickly at me, then looked up at him and, attempting to cover her mouth with her palm, murmured, "We need to talk." I frowned, straining to hear their conversation as they passed through to the foyer. They had lowered their voices, and their whispers fueled my aggravation. Their shuffling of feet, their procrastinating.

Peda took hold of my hand and swung it.

I stared down at our loose-hanging arms, and mine felt disjointed, as if it didn't belong to me.

"Tell me again about your name," she said in between breaths. Her long lashes batted at me, pale as wave froth beneath sand-colored bangs, which are straight and fine as spun silk.

"Not now," I said, and gently disengaged my hand.

Her sweaty little fingers struggled to retain their hold.

She raised her voice. *"Please?"*

"O . . . kay," I said, at length. "O . . . kay." It was easier to give in to her than to argue. I leaned down and patted the pillows on my chaise, which she at once settled into delicately, belying her tomboyish reputation. Grinning at me with the satisfaction of her victory.

I sighed. "Well, I was born in the winter, right here in this house. Upstairs." I pointed to the ceiling, and her mouth fell open, and she peered up to where I pointed. "A quiet time, it was the season my father preferred; he used to say there were no distractions then." She looked at me quizzically, prompting me, and with my fingertips I touched her cheek. Then I edged her over so that I could sit down next to her, leaned back on a cushion, and closed my eyes. "On cold winter days he'd sit before the fire and stare at a favorite painting or a piece of porcelain or a cherished photograph. Sometimes for hours."

"What for?"

"It was a sort of self-hypnosis. He'd travel to another place." I sat up to glance sideways at her and said, "Not physically, of course. But in his mind." I thought for a moment, trying to remember my father's face, the look on it when he concentrated on the rhythm of his breathing. Peda would never comprehend the significance of it, even I had a hard time. "Certain monks, I'm told, do the same thing by meditating: concentrate so hard that they're able to leave their bodies—fly away, escape the everyday."

I hummed in a drone, tented my fingers as if I were praying, and then bowed, bobbing up and down, until Peda cracked up. Bobbing too, she grabbed a praying hand and laced her fingers through mine. She bent over the other, quiet for a moment, and examined the lines that run through my palm.

Embarrassed, I gave a little laugh. "Anyway," I said, and tapped her chin, "he named me Winter when all this time-traveling occurred. In the summer my father reverted to the stodgiest of men, disciplined and stern, never too much fun."

"I wish I had a father." Peda leaned forward and stared at me intently. "Sometimes I pretend that Jake is my father, but he's too old—even if he is magical—and he smells like clams. My father, if I had one, would be young and handsome and smell . . . like what, Omum?" She screwed up her nose. "What would my father smell like?" She pulled at my sleeve.

"How would I know?" I sucked in my breath. How indeed would I know? Elsie had never married, had been deliberately evasive about her child's paternity. Maddeningly so.

I waved my head, tilting it toward the door, and averted my eyes until she got up—she knew I meant business. "I need to rest now," I said. There was no way I'd get into that one— not an hour or so before the Crandor experts were due. Not before I climbed the stairs to dress, organize my outfit, shoes, stockings, earrings. God, it made me tired. For what purpose, all this? This struggle to keep up appearances? To blink away tiny Peda's pretend games. To absorb Elsie's sins, bury them under a feigned cloak of goodwill. To stifle the throes of my own mush-rooming fears? My fantasies? My rapidly deteriorating sense of self-worth? Would the world's recognition of my treasure be sufficient recompense?

But Peda refused to move; she just stood there, biting her lip, while the two of us listened to the slow tick of the Seth Thomas clock. I massaged my forehead and stared outside at the branches of my favorite willow tree, which, pushed by a surge of wind, swept the ground repeatedly. "Never mind," I said after a minute, and started when one of the branches broke from the force of the wind. Feeling guilty, I spread my palms. "I don't have time for a nap anyway."

Peda looked down at me. "What's wrong, Omum?" When I grinned weakly at her, she placed her hand on my forehead. I looked outside to where the broken willow branch scurried across the grass, closed one eye, and squinted at it when a stump caught it around its tail. In the gusts it squirmed so that it looked almost alive. "Remember when we had to evacuate?" Peda asked. She pointed at the tree, whose remaining branches hit the ground now—*thump, thump*—with a vengeance.

It was a hurricane I'll never forget—we were totally unprepared, the three of us, with no evacuation plan and no shelter available to us in case of emergency. I remember I refused to act until it was almost too late, but when the rising waterline reached the house and the eroding soil uprooted the huge willow closest to the foundation, we actually feared for our lives. So, risking the fury of the winds, the rain, and the swollen tide, which threatened the outdated bridge we had to cross to reach safety, at the last minute we abandoned the island to the elements.

After landing on the mainland, safe but cut off and helpless to prevent our home from flooding, we watched—bare-faced and then through binoculars—as, piece by piece, the bridge collapsed behind us. Today I had the same feeling of impending doom that I had had the night before the storm hit. It was so strong that I shivered and waves of goose bumps crawled up my head from the stem of my neck.

When I felt a sharp draft cross my shoulders as well, I quickly raised my hand to Peda's for a helpful pull-up. I needed to hurry, prepare for the dinner party. Because the sooner I understood the motives behind the imminent arrival of the Getty archivists, the better I'd feel. *This* time, I told myself, I intended to be prepared.

Chapter 2

ELSIE

*A*t seven o'clock promptly, the doorknocker sounded. I knew this because I heard the knocker at the same time I heard the chime of the seventeenth-century gilt-edged gold clock, which sits on the attaché in the upstairs landing, the Venetian one I wanted my mother to sell to raise cash.

"Get it, will you?" I heard her shout. "You're dressed."

No bell for Winter. Too déclassé, she had always told my father. I proceeded slowly down the stairs. One foot in front of the other—with immaculate grace, I fantasized. I loved the way I felt when I moved. I would have liked to have been a dancer. Too gawky, too big, my mother had always told me. I heard the caterers juggling pots in the kitchen and noticed in the living room that the candles were lit and, in spite of the spring weather, a fire started. I rubbed the curved post of the banister with my thumb and pictured my mother at her dressing table, combing, rouging, powdering, and these days girdling as well, with her paints spread around her, like an actress about to walk onstage.

In the foyer, the thick oak of the front door vibrated from three prolonged knocks, so insistent this time that I grabbed the brass handle to stop it from shimmying, then fingered the smooth, heavy metal while I deliberately stalled. I leaned back after counting to sixty, tossed my hair from my eyes—annoying me with its fine, flyaway texture, all static and squeaky clean— and opened the door.

Two old men. In dark suits. One tall and stooped and thin, like Rip Van Winkle, awake but just. I laughed to myself. The other one short, stocky, sweating in the cool of the evening. But behind them, that was another story. A good-looking guy, late thirties, maybe forties; average height, well built; with dimples, dark, oiled hair, and chiseled cheekbones. A suit worth well over a thousand bucks. Too slick for me, but still, I felt my muscles tense. In my form-fitting slacks, I have the figure, I think. I perked up. Not so dull an evening after all. I stood aside to let them in.

"We got a phone call," the older, sleepy one said as he crossed the threshold.

The other two crowded behind him, the small, sweaty one peering around his friend's shoulder into the foyer. In the bright light, his face assumed the consistency of soft yellow pudding.

"You're with the Getty?"

"Not quite." The good-looking guy gave me the once-over. Not as friendly as I had hoped. "They sent us, yes. But I'm not affiliated. Never met them before an hour ago." He gave the two men a sidelong glance and sniffed, moving away from them as if to disallow any connection.

"Who are you, then?" I stepped backward, stopping them with my right hand. "Two guests from the Getty for dinner, my mother told me. If not you," I repeated, "who, then?" I tapped my foot.

The good-looking guy put his hand on my arm, and I shucked it off.

"Winter said you flew in from California?"

The older men stared at each other. In unison, they shook their heads. "No, we took the train," said the shorter, nervous man. "Him . . . ?" He threw his thumb at the younger man. "Before today, we've never laid eyes on him."

"Who's Winter?" The younger man had moved into the center of the stone floor and before the Florentine mirror was rearranging his tie. He looked at me in the mirror. I stood behind him, wondering how I could throw him out. Thinking that my mother had done it again. One of her crazy schemes. She didn't even know these people.

Once before, Winter had invited a radio announcer, his assistant, and the weatherman from a radio talk show. Hadn't they just shown up, too? For lunch, and what a farce that had been. The weatherman, his fat roll covered over by a T-shirt he had picked up at Disney World. Winter had handed him a jacket, which, when he struggled into it, fired eagle-stamped brass buttons onto the cherry dining table like bullets. They exploded with *pops*, I remember, and they scratched the table's smooth surface, defacing it with faint skid marks that to this day we can't erase. And the other guy with him, Jesus, what a loser. Short of breath, short of teeth, but high on words like *motherfucker*, which Winter had either ignored or bitched about behind closed palms and clenched teeth. To escape, I had finally excused myself. Winter later explained to me that she had wanted only to educate herself, learn about the subjects they discussed on the radio. I didn't blame my father for getting the hell out. My mother was a kook. Who would ever have thought we were related?

"My mother—your hostess," I replied, and then, watching the young guy closely, said, "Why are you here if you don't know who she is?"

The man held out one navy-blue-worsted, well-clad arm, his hand open, fingers spread, begging me to take hold. *Accept me*, he meant. *Shake my hand.* I obliged, because his gray eyes flecked with red specks were hypnotic. With them he held on to my own—as if the red specks were darts of light, lasers that had attached themselves to my brain. I was reminded of Peda's Jake, the Superman of the waves, and wondered if he indeed resembled this Mr. Slick of the Getty.

"Allow me to introduce myself," he said. A hint of a Southern accent. Slurred vowels. A deliberately slow, low tone that I had to strain to hear.

I wanted him to continue speaking and concentrated, mentally willing his darts, his laser look, back to him. I forced myself to drop my gaze, but I took his hand. He held it gently, not moving, as if he were cradling something of great value, something delicate and rare. I snatched it away then, as if I had been burnt.

"I'm Hamlet Crandor, grandson to the painter, Simon Crandor." He was sure of himself. Pleased by his announcement. His face was fixed on mine, waiting for my astonishment. When there was none, he said again, "Hamlet Crandor. Startled you, did I? You can call me Ham; everyone else does."

I nodded, thinking that he had the most beautiful lips I'd ever seen on a man, as full and as contoured as a Greek statue's. I turned to face the other two. The old men, waiting, waiting. I thought that the younger, stockier one smelled like days-old garbage and cringed when I shook his hand.

"Barry Zinger, expert on the artist, I'm afraid," he admitted, with a slight apologetic grin. "The only one, I'm afraid. So I get a call. Thought I'd know what to look for, if you know what I'm saying."

I smiled slightly.

And then Rip Van Winkle, the one with the worn-out hat, the drooping eyes, and that bent-over stoop. With a shock, I realized that the poor man couldn't straighten up. He stared at the young Mr. Slick with distrust. "Simon's grandson was invited? What for? I know about Crandor. Who needs him?" He snorted. "Hell, for a while we even shared the same woman." When Hamlet stiffened, the old man waved his hand at him and inclined his head toward the small, sweating man beside him. "Didn't pay much attention to his art, though," he went on. "Zinger here took care of the business angle." Still bending, he swung toward me. "Miss Peregrine, I take it?"

"Call me Elsie," I said. "Miz Peregrine is what people call my mother."

I didn't feel like being polite. It was Winter's place to deal with these people, not mine. She should have been here to greet them, instead of anchoring herself to her dressing table like some sort of femme fatale.

I shrugged and, enjoying myself, said, "Maybe Miz Peregrine can shed some light on the mystery." Though I sincerely doubted it.

I led them into the living room, where, from the corner next to the bar cart, I said abruptly, "Sit down" and yanked hard on an old needlepoint bell pull, hoping that it still worked. Puffs of dust motes immediately filled up the light halos under two lamps next to where I stood. I fingered the fabric of the bell pull, afraid that the needlepoint would disintegrate, and felt my cheeks flush, after which I sent up a silent plea for Winter to come down. After all, she was the one obsessed by the painting.

But why, for the life of me, I couldn't figure out. Value? Maybe. But the painting was no Sargent or Monet. On the other hand, these people had Getty connections. Obviously, there had to be others besides my mother who were attracted to the picture hanging in the conservatory. I wondered why her visitors hadn't mentioned it yet.

As if a mind reader, the bent old man asked, "Would it be possible to see the masterpiece while we wait?" He stood up and looked down at me where I had settled on the ottoman, and for just a second, his drooping eyes appeared sinister to me.

"You said you weren't interested in your friend's artwork. . . ." I was such a smart-ass.

He turned away then so I couldn't look at him, but his labored breathing told me that he had sat down again and was rearranging his rusted joints on the wing chair. When I finally glanced his way, he was staring out the window, and briefly, I felt a stab of remorse, because his hands, I saw, were frail and twig-like: mottled and twisted together in his lap.

"I thought it would give us something to do while we wait for your mother," he said.

I looked through the door, hoping to hear her footsteps, and thought back to the fourth grade, the hostility of my teacher when he realized I wouldn't obey his rules. How my mother had hated me, hated the phone calls from him. "Who *are* you?" my picture-perfect mother had once said to me, when to protest Mr. Mofey's injustice I had refused to go to school—because for one whole morning Mr. Mofey had locked a kid in the supply room to punish him for stealing an eraser. To study alone, he had told him. "Why can't you listen to your betters?" Winter had demanded when I went on strike. And then dragged me to Mr. Mofey's office to apologize, to spend *two* whole mornings in the supply room in place of the boy, with no key and no way out—or so I thought when I was a kid. And Winter had been supportive of the old bastard. Betters? What made Mr. Mofey better than me?

When I considered how I had retaliated, I didn't even have a guilty conscience. I had hit my mother. Slapped her full in the face, so hard that a flaming red streak—my handprint—had settled on her cheek for a good two days, and she had had to wear sunglasses and extra makeup.

Did I love Winter? I wanted to . . . but I wondered whether

I knew the meaning of the word. I was fond of her at isolated moments, I suppose, but I certainly had no respect for her. Returning to live at home had been a matter of convenience. No rent and someone to look after the kid while I was out selling yachts, sailboats, and Whalers to mainland yuppies. I could even make my own hours.

I pressed my forehead between the tips of my fingers. I hoped Winter's ways wouldn't rub off on Peda. I thought not— Peda was too locked away in her own fantasy world. But then, come to think of it, so was Winter, staring up at that painting like she did, for stretches at a time.

"Good evening," my mother said, when at last she entered. Her hand was extended in greeting: the benevolent dictator, sweetness through and through.

After introductions were made and drinks poured, I managed to take Winter aside. In a hushed voice I whispered to her, voicing my skepticism about her guests, giving her a quick rundown on each of them. I felt pleased with myself, her knight in shining armor, as I provided descriptions, replete with adjectives, of her visitors—the self-proclaimed experts on the artist: Mr. Good-Looking Grandson, Zinger, and Droopy Horatio Guardi. Blinking madly as she listened to me, she furtively cast looks at them where they were ensconced around the coffee table in front of the shelves of Limoges figurines. At length, she plucked at my arm and insisted that we join them.

Because of her perfect manners, we made small talk for at least half an hour. I know because I timed it, glancing at my watch at five-minute intervals. She asked about their trip, their health, complimented their graciousness in visiting her, inquired how long they were staying. Their answers strained to reach two syllables, so you can imagine how many conversational chasms she had to negotiate.

Finally, the younger man said, "Aren't we here to discuss

the painting? To see it?" Like I was, I guess he was fed up with the formalities.

"My grandfather painted well but rarely," he continued. "As far as I know, most of his important pieces are in the hands of the Selfe and the Kobein families, the rest spread between the Met, the Whitney, and one or two lesser museums." He paused and caught my eye. I looked away, embarrassed by his attention, by his lips.

"No others that I'm aware of, except for one or two images my father swore he remembered seeing, even dreaming about"—he laughed—"when he was a child. And I have only one of his works, and a minor one at that. So where does this one fit in?"

"That's precisely why we're here," said Barry Zinger. "To find out where it fits in." His eyes, shining behind his glasses, darted around the room. He waved his drink and stopped his hand before his droopy-eyed colleague.

The man nodded. "All of Crandor's paintings have been cataloged," he agreed. "There are no other pieces."

Though he sounded definitive, I heard an element of doubt in his voice. "You told us before that you knew nothing about his work," I reminded him. I stared at the slack mouth, which quivered under my gaze, and sat up straight, tucking a strand of hair behind my ear.

"I know nothing about the style," he said, "the paints he used, the subjects he painted, but I know who owns his work. I make it my business to know."

"Didn't you say that Mr. Zinger handled the business side?"

Droopy looked confused, and Winter came to his rescue. "Elsie, how rude," she said. "Of course this nice gentleman knows about the paintings. He was the artist's best friend. You told me so yourself."

She must have been in seventh heaven after hearing that

her guest was best friend to the artist. I gave her a withering glance and set my attention on the other one, the sweating, short man, whom, when he walked in, belly jiggling, I had pegged as the real expert anyway.

"If indeed he *was* the artist," said the small man, emboldened by his lovely hostess's approval. "None ever left Simon's possession, not without my knowledge. So I'd bet that this painting you own is a copy." He caught Horatio Guardi's eye. "Don't you agree?" The old guy returned his look impassively. "*Right?*" Zinger persisted.

Jeez, that sleepy old man was a cold fish, no two ways about it.

Winter looked at Zinger and wrung her cocktail napkin. Her left lid had developed a nervous tic, and she had forgotten to pass the salmon canapés, had just left the tray on the table, the fish congealing in oil and soggy toast. "How will you prove it?" she said. "How can you prove it?"

Louder, I wanted to yell. Her voice was always so soft, so patrician.

Zinger couldn't stand it. "May I have one?" He pushed his meaty hand in front of her and reached for an hors d'oeuvre with hairy pink fingers.

I had heard that gorilla hands were gourmet delicacies in the Kenya marketplaces and pictured his hand for sale next to the apes'.

"How thoughtless of me," Winter said in a tiny voice.

"Maybe we're wrong," said Zinger, swallowing. "It's better to say nothing until we've seen it."

Fearing that the dinner would be a repeat of Winter's radio-lunch disaster, I longed to skip out on these people. Except that I found myself glaring at the greedy little man and forced myself to stay put, at least for a while.

"So let's go take a look," said Mr. Good-Looking Grandson. He got up, and the other two rose as if on cue, as if he had raised his hand for the benediction.

Zinger bent over and grabbed two more canapés, shoveling the first one into his mouth before he straightened.

Though Hamlet had never been in the house before, he led the older men to the conservatory—passing me by as if I were an annoyance or, worse, something insensate and therefore unseen—where the three of them grouped around the painting and examined it. Yet none of them, I noticed from the doorway, seemed very surprised by what they saw.

Which disturbed me. A jab of an elbow, a nod of acknowledgment, *anything* would have been better than their deliberate lack of communication, which in the prolonged silence seemed fishy to me. And, also for me, blasé as I was back then, unexpected—and strangely unsettling.

Chapter 3

WINTER

*A*s the hostess, I stayed behind to add a table setting and quickly reshuffled my good family silverware, worn thin in spots, I discovered, as I picked up a teaspoon. Feeling faint, I then moved the Lalique goblets and the gold-rimmed Tiffany plates. I felt clammy, and on my upper lip and my forehead cropped up bumps of cold perspiration, which I blotted with the back of my hand. An invasion, that's what this was—an invasion of privacy. And to think that I was using my best china for these people. I had meticulously glued many of the chipped pieces myself, so I was proud of the job, and I had a fond feeling for the old pattern.

But I had no illusions—this dinner party was of my own making. After the mysterious phone call from an archivist at the Getty requesting information on my Crandor painting, intrigued, he claimed, by the subject (my friends who lived in its tableau), I had invited him for dinner, stirred up by his interest. How was I to have known he would bring an entourage with him? Now I wished that I could discard the lot of them, for I felt their hostility as sure as pelting, salted sand in a windstorm, stinging my eyes and blinding me. Scaring me.

Thankfully, images of the beach and the sand also brought to mind Peda, which prompted me to forget my morbid reflections, finish up my table arranging, and call her, along with the guests, into the dining room.

At dinner, I indicated the seating: "Peda, you'll sit at the foot of the table." I turned to Elsie—"You don't mind, do you, dear?"—and searched her face for a sign of anger. What I saw was a supercilious smile instead, and I sighed and wondered if I was afraid of my own daughter. She seemed so taken with Ham Crandor, the grandson, that I thought it might be nice to seat them together. In my opinion, she needed to socialize more.

The first course was served: cold tomato aspic with slivers of parsley and cucumber. Hot bread sticks and goat cheese. I watched Mr. Zinger slurp. Orange specks flew off his spoon onto the white satin scalloped tablecloth.

"We'll have to put it under the rays," he said between mouthfuls.

"Is that really necessary?" Ham asked.

"We have to make sure it's authentic," Horatio Guardi said. "The colors look almost too fresh, as if it were worked on yesterday." He enunciated each word, as though speaking to idiots.

I tried to smile. "That's because I've taken good care of it."

The sweating, slurping little man acted as if he hadn't heard me and turned to his colleague. "It has his imprint." Avoiding my eyes, he wiped sweat from his forehead with his napkin.

"A forgery, perhaps?" Mr. Guardi delicately spooned his soup and mopped up the plate with his bread stick, painting the bottom of the bowl with crumbs. He raised one eyebrow.

"No, I think it's probably his," Zinger said.

Clearly, he was taking the role of the trusting partner in response to Horatio's pose as the doubting Thomas. In my married days, I had watched too many TV detective movies not to notice their thrusting and parrying, which, I imagined, was for our benefit.

"We have to be one hundred percent certain," Guardi said. He shrugged. "I have a feeling . . . if it's his, I wager we'll find something hidden in the back. Simon used to leave dates, remember? Inscribe messages. He liked to leave something personal—"

"I don't know anything about a date," I said.

He nodded. "There's also a nondescript inscription we think we identified on your piece, but it's fuzzy. We'll have to do more tomorrow, take the painting apart. With your permission, of course."

I felt faint again. I wanted to tear their throats out but bit my lip and stayed silent. After the call from Mr. Zinger, I had quite looked forward to his visit. Strange, though, that he would telephone with no warning. Nothing. Just his phone call claiming to represent the Getty, and of course I was flattered. But who had told him I owned a Crandor? The museum had no record, no knowledge of having acquired the information. *Someone* must have informed them. Deep in my heart, I believed it to be Elsie, who thought available cash was the answer. That's why I had decided to invite these people to dinner in the first place, not realizing it was to be three. To satisfy her. But to satisfy my own ego, too, I suppose.

Barry Zinger sat back in his chair and stretched out his short legs. He might have been relaxing at his favorite club. The sweat had dried on his face, but I could see the remnants: faint white, salty lines.

"The inscription reads: *To George,*" he said, "*with continued luck on your quest for self-fulfillment. And with hopes for the future, Simon.*"

I was shocked. And so was Elsie, I could tell. Because she had been with them when they examined the painting, and, as far as she could see, no one had found an inscription. She told me they hadn't even taken the painting off the wall. I stared at the two men, who watched each other smugly. They obviously knew the painting. Why the act, then? I felt like a character in a charade, or maybe a Kafka play. I straightened my skirt so that it covered my knees, and patted my hair—not a curl out of place, so smooth I could have posed for *Vogue*—and was filled with an inexplicable urge to mess it up. I swung my head, and I could see flakes of dandruff, which floated gently to the floor like new snow.

"No one saw an inscription," I said.

Elsie looked up. "That's true," she said. She frowned at Mr. Zinger. "You didn't look for any inscription."

He leaned forward. "No?" He smacked his lips. "Perhaps I made it up." He leaned over and, smiling, produced a magnifying glass from his hip pocket. "Go see for yourself. On the bottom, on the very edge of the canvas, you'll discover fine writing, as if someone scratched a verse in pencil and then erased it. Why don't you go look?"

The waitress entered and began to clear our soup plates. I excused myself, and Elsie followed me.

"I never saw him take out a magnifying glass," she whispered when we reached the conservatory.

It had turned dark outside, and her face, peering over me, was in shadow. I could smell her, though: a pleasant odor, soapy and whistle-clean. But her nearness offended me—she was trespassing on my space—and I bent my head away from her. I felt the residue of her warm breath on my cheek and touched it with my index finger.

"You could have been preoccupied."

I peered at the edge of the canvas, and my nose touched the pitted wood of the frame under it. I knew where it was, of course. All these years, I had assumed it to be nothing more than a scratch, a smudged erasure of the artist. The magnifying glass fogged up then, and I bent over to wipe it, tried again, squinting, blinking. My eyes teared when I espied the faint inscription—from emotion or the strain, I couldn't tell which.

"He was right," I said, resigned because the little man knew too much. He had delved deep into the painting: the lives of the people I look up to, the people I went to sleep by and woke up to.

Imperceptibly, Elsie cupped my elbow—I felt like an invalid—and together we returned to the dining room, where Peda, small but commanding at the foot of the table, entertained our guests with stories about Jake and Scarecrow. All eyes were trained on the child, but droopy Mr. Guardi glanced over at Zinger, who, waiting for our reaction, was grinning into his napkin. Both of them eyed us as we sat down, but I didn't give them any satisfaction, and Elsie—good for her—wouldn't look at them either.

"I know where Scarecrow came from," Peda said, "and how old he is, because Jake told me. He found him tied to a pier." She looked around, trying to hold everyone's attention.

What a surprise; she was normally such a shy child.

"With a piece of rope that had shrunk right down on his neck—because of the salt, Jake told me. It was choking the life out of him. If the tide had come in, Scarecrow would of drowned; he would of floated like a straw scarecrow because he's so skinny."

Hamlet Crandor smiled self-consciously. "I see," he said. "What else does Jake talk about?"

I supposed he was making small talk with the child for the mother's benefit. It was obvious that he found Elsie attractive.

Peda screwed up her nose. "Time. . . . He melts time like caramel candy. He stretches it, winds it around his tongue." She stuck out her tongue and wiggled it, staring at the rosy tip until she went cross-eyed. "When he talks to me, we're, like, the same age."

I could see that no one knew what to say. The men glanced at each another, and Ham stifled a grin.

Watching them, Peda fell silent and then eased herself deep into her seat, until only her head appeared over the table's edge. As if she had worn herself out. Or maybe she was trying to hide from her mother's disapproval.

Because Elsie, from across the table, was glaring daggers at her daughter. "Peda, *please* . . . ," she said, and then turned to the young man. "You'll have to excuse her—she's always making up stories, and she'll go on forever if we let her. Speaking of which, Mr. Hamlet Crandor . . . Your name. You can't tell me you made that up. Did you?" She peered at him and gave a quick, nervous laugh.

"Excuse me?"

"Ham? Hamlet?"

I felt my face flush—the impertinence of her. "I'm sorry, Ham. It's none of my daughter's business."

"Quite the contrary. I think you'd all be interested, because, coincidentally, it was my grandfather who named me."

"So, *Hamlet* was a favorite of his?" Elsie said.

"It was more than that. The young woman in your painting . . . You know the one?" He surveyed the table, then fastened his eyes on mine. "Do you know her?" he pressed.

"Yes." I pulled in my breath.

"She was adored by my grandfather . . . and your father, too, I believe . . . and Simon by her, apparently. She admired Shakespeare, especially *Hamlet*. Her name was Beatrice, pronounced

Bay-ah-treece, in the Spanish fashion." He didn't blink, and I felt for a second as if the two of us were alone at the table.

I gaped, holding my butter knife in midair. My mother had also been a lover of Shakespeare; at least, that's what I had been told. And that my father had known Crandor—had maybe been friends with Beatrice, of the Spanish inflection, as well—was strangely exhilarating because it opened up a chapter in his life about which I knew nothing.

Carefully, I placed my knife on the butter plate and looked away from the young man, this too-good-looking man with the smirk pasted on his even features, who was blatantly amused by my discomfiture. The waitress, young, with a pert, freckled nose, bent over me, her breasts skimming my arm as she lowered my dinner plate. She smiled coyly at Ham, and I wondered if she had been listening.

But I forgot all about her when Ham said, "It's obvious, anyway, that the painting should have belonged to me."

The clatter of silverware ceased abruptly.

"That young woman, Beatrice, she named me, after all. . . . My brother, too: Sebastian."

"*Sebastian?*" Elsie looked as angry as I felt. What games were these people playing?

"Sebastian. My brother . . ." Hamlet stared at Elsie and widened his eyes.

I wondered if he practiced his expressions in front of a mirror.

"*Well?*" said Elsie.

He raised his eyebrows.

"Did you know about the painting before you got here? The subject?" Elsie spit out the words that I couldn't form. I wanted to hug her.

"My father talked about a favorite painting of my grand-father's that he never saw, I don't think, or if he did, he didn't remember—just heard so much about it that he relayed the details of the painting on to me. He had no idea what had become of it, which always seemed to bother him, much like those childhood images of his. . . . I don't know why." He smiled apologetically. "Until now, I never knew its whereabouts, or even if it really existed."

Most women would have melted at his smile. Not I. I just felt sore.

"And I have a feeling that you just know it's this one." When Elsie was mad, her eyes had a tendency to almost close, forming slits like a lizard's.

In that too-calm voice of his, Horatio Guardi said, "This is a lovely dinner, isn't it?"

I gazed at him, nonplussed. When we had been introduced—it seemed hours ago now—I had been a bit startled because somehow the name Horatio Guardi didn't fit sleepy, droopy Rip Van Winkle. Horatio implied wisdom and confidence, whereas the old man exuded melancholy and artifice.

He swayed toward me. "Tell me, Mrs. Peregrine," he said, "or is it Masters? How did you come by the painting? Did your father give it to you? Kept it for the inscription to him, did you?"

"Please start," I said, trying to keep my temper. Frankly, I didn't care which name he called me—my maiden or my married—and neither did he, as far as I could see. My painting was the only issue here; there was no place for small talk.

"For as long as I can remember," I said, "the painting has been in my family, hanging in the same spot. So I guess you could call it a family heirloom."

"Would you consider selling it?" In little more than a whisper, Droopy dropped the question, leaning in to me in his loose-jointed way.

Why their avid interest? "I'd like to know who told you about my painting in the first place," I said, my tongue relaxed by the wine and the tension I felt so acutely.

The tall, bent old man thrust his jaw at me, so close to me that his face blurred, his pitifully thin beard melting into cheeks I had noticed earlier were tracked with burst capillaries. And I knew as surely as I felt the wind of his wine-flavored breath that he had *never* been best friend and confidant of the late Simon Crandor. Indeed, I wondered whether he had even known him.

"The Getty called us," he said, with great forbearance, as if he were speaking to a child. Patronizing.

Elsie bristled. "It doesn't make sense. Who wants to buy it?"

"Why, the Getty, of course."

"Why would the Getty take a sudden interest in my mother's painting?"

"There's a resurgence of interest in Crandor."

I felt like laughing. "More lamb?" I asked. "More wine?"

The waitress hovered over Ham Crandor with the wine decanter; she drained the bottle, and I motioned toward a larger one, sitting on the sideboard. The sound of pouring wine makes me pensive—it's soothing, almost hypnotic—and I let my eyes fall into the burgundy rays as the drops that had accumulated on the crystal sparkled in the soft light.

How could I live without my friends in the painting? I needed money, all right, but did I need it that badly? And as far as Ham's claim went, I wouldn't even entertain it. I had come to love Crandor's lady and child, the loner with the hat, even the faraway gentleman who approaches them. Keeps his distance, he does. Never infringes upon their privacy. I was fascinated by these people in my picture and spellbound by the lull of lapping water, which their eyes, too, rest upon. I knew their faces intimately, their stories, their habits; I could smell the salt in the picture's air, feel the humid wind on my skin; I could talk to these painted people about myself. They recognized me for who I am—and they *liked* me.

Little Peda slid down from her place and made her way

around the table to my side. Fingers twined, she formed a funnel with her palms through which to whisper to me and placed them, with her lips on top, to my ear. Whiffs of her breath tickled me, and in the candlelight her eyes looked enormous. On tiptoe, she hissed through them, "You *can't* sell your painting, Omum." Then she teetered on her patent sandals and her heels scraped the oak floor with the friction of a fingernail dragged across a blackboard.

I winced, shook my head. She was right, of course. Touched by her loyalty, I pushed her away and turned to face my dinner guests, tight-lipped. My heart hammered painfully. *Take their advice about art, Winter. Educate yourself. Discover their motives*, I told myself.

"Do you collect your own pieces of art?" I asked. My voice felt thick and sounded foreign to my ears. "What period do you prefer?" I directed my questions to Mr. Guardi, so abruptly that he would have to take notice, have to stop his line of questioning about my family. Elsie had thrown off the queries of our three visitors like a fencer on the rebound. It was time now, I decided, for a few thrusts of my own.

Chapter 4

ELSIE

*T*he next morning dawned bright but chilly, with shafts of luminous sunlight in which there was no warmth. I felt as if Winter mimicked the weather in the way she treated everyone around her, including me. She averted her face when addressed, but, forever the lady, she allowed the "Getty" men— ha!—access to her conservatory and the Crandor painting. She told me that she had promised them, after all, and she wasn't one to go back on her word. So she stepped gingerly around them, tiptoeing in stockinged feet, as if she didn't belong in her own home. When Peda disappeared onto the beach, I, however, anchored myself to her visitors. For all I knew, they were going to steal the damn thing and switch it with a fake. But Winter snubbed me in the same way she snubbed the men, not realizing for a second that I was doing her a favor.

I was used to it, though. Having lived on my own for years, enduring cold, unending winters, so white the glare scorched your retinas, swallowed up by the earth, which had been my intention all along, I could take what my mother had to dish out now. During those long Vermont seasons, I was near crazed by April—by the weather, my work . . . my life. I was fed up with making little stick figures to sell at premium prices to fat, squawking tourists dressed head to foot in shiny polyester tracksuits. Mid-February, ten miles or so from Woodstock, Vermont, Robin and I had spent our ten-degree daylight hours smoking pot and making up stories about our clients while we blackened our fingers fabricating homespun Vermont dolls out of pinecones and sticks. But who knew? Maybe our clients really couldn't find any other clothes to fit.

Robin. I sank my eyes into Ham and thought of Robin, father to Peda. I seesawed on my haunches. He had known about the painting, too, been extraordinarily interested in it at the time, staring at it for long stretches at each visit—those times only, of course, when Winter was out. Once a compulsive shopper, she was often gone for eight hours a day; hence, trespassing became an easy chore—one that I never got used to but that, in the end, was necessary when we were hungry for a meal or a comfortable bed. Eventually, I guess, I would have introduced Robin to Winter. But drugs had finally taken their toll on him, taking his attention away from me outright, nailing him before I ever got a chance to show him off. My woodsman from the North.

I had come home then because I had no choice. Hotdogging the child beneath my arm. A squalling brat who got along better with the old lady than she did with her own mother. I shrugged. They were alike, my daughter and Winter. Pale and wispy, tiny people without appetites. I took after my father; I felt like a wolf in a herd of midget deer.

"Hey, would you look at this?" The bent old man was hopping from foot to foot, so excited he danced on his toes. "There are *two* paintings here, maybe three!"

I stared at the painting, at the flat palette knives arranged as carefully as doctor's instruments next to it, and caught my breath when Zinger took up a particularly sharp one and started gently to pry the entire backing from the frame, wondering if he would mutilate the piece, or if he even cared.

I moved over to the French doors and opened them, hoping to catch sight of my mother or Peda. Strangers working on Winter's painting, by which she set such store, yet she was nowhere to be found. Why did she always run away from confrontation? Sea breezes flowing from the open door rotated some dried flowers and long grass stalks that she had arranged in a tall vase; the wind forced some of the daisy petals from their stems, and they fell to the table and disintegrated. Squinting, I tried to follow the path of the flower particles, but they vanished into the air. I swallowed and squeezed tight my eyes. *Where the fuck is she?*

"Got it," Zinger exclaimed, and, leaning back, held out a picture he had removed from behind Winter's painting.

The image was dynamic and, for me, unusual, because I'd never seen anything like it. A marketplace of people from another era, faces unremarkable all, but most recognizable. Even to me. Grouped together according to religious affiliation, race, and political persuasion. The few I didn't know were bathed in a kind of celestial light, as if they, and not the famous people, were the lucky ones who had found the answer to a perfect life. Kind of like tripping. Things that you'd never expect to see or experience, awash for a moment in a golden light. I peered down at the picture; the condition was flawless, as if it had been painted yesterday. The colors were bright and clear, and as lustrous as the rays of sun that poured in from the door and the overhead window. Lining the cheeks of an elderly man were dots of hoary moles—*The Judge*, I read on a label affixed to the side with tape. He was probably from the McCarthy era, an especially heartless individual, I assumed, who had put a lot of innocent people behind bars for not squealing on their colleagues.

I squatted next to Hamlet, who had removed a tiny camera and recorder from his breast pocket.

I stood up. "Who gave you permission to take pictures?"

He tilted backward and stared up at me, smiling slightly. "What harm is there?"

From the current of his movement, I could smell him, and I felt myself hankering toward him. *Shit.* I shrugged and turned away, toward the old man, who was studying the image with a magnifying glass and taking notes. I guessed Ham was right—what harm *was* there?

Barry Zinger, meanwhile, finally removed the canvas from the prying eyes of old Horatio Guardi and placed it next to the original painting, petting it as if it were alive, before he finally let it go to pick up another palette knife, a lighter one this time, and resume his digging into the backing. It occurred to me that the gesture seemed oddly inappropriate for the rough-tough, gangster-like little man, and the implication reinforced my belief that the visitors were not who they claimed to be. Mr. Zinger seemed to me to be the most alarming. Glancing at the indomitable Mr. Crandor, I saw him stare unblinking at the back of the canvas—the double, triple thickness of it—with such intensity, I imagined I could count the beats of his heart.

It was like watching an excavation at a dig. *Screw my mother!* I grinned. This was a hoot—an hour or two when I wasn't able to control the outcome. I think I actually missed night hiking in Vermont's frigid temps, especially when Robin and I would get lost. The outcome was chancy, yet it was invariably exciting. I threw myself on Winter's chaise, smiled at the three engrossed men, and offered to make them sandwiches and a drink.

"Not in that order, I hope," said Ham, with a sidelong wink. "Bloody Marys—do you know how to make them?"

"If we have Mr and Mrs T mix. . . ."

He lifted his shoulders—"Whatever"—and gave me a half grin.

"Sure. . . ." I rose, pleased that they had included me. As the fourth cog in their investigative wheel, I hoped to get a handle on their true intentions. "Don't find anything before I get back," I ordered, and waved my right forefinger in a silly, schoolgirlish way as the door banged behind me. I felt my head wag in time to my wagging finger.

Robin would have hated my antics, I thought. As I dug through rows of dusty bottles thrown chaotically into the first pantry cabinet, a true-to-life vision of him appeared before me, so real I blinked, and a greasy container of petrified olive oil slipped though my fingers and rolled onto the counter. My New England woodsman—the Earthman, I used to call him. Bearded always. I was afraid to move, afraid to blink the mirage away. And then I got pissed. Who the hell was he to just appear? I moved about, collected glasses and a bottle of Absolut, some of which I threw in with the Mr & Mrs T, and didn't give him another thought until I filled the ice bucket. He was still there. Not in the flesh, but real just the same. I clenched my fist, remembering his rugged appeal, his tenderness when he touched me—the ache between my legs, the hunger on my lips, and the tips of each finger and each swollen nipple. Sweat broke out over my upper lip, and I tried to ignore it. I sliced some lemons, placed them in a dish, and carried the tray with the drinks and condiments into the conservatory.

Just inside the open French doors, Peda, her hair sprinkled with sand, stood next to Winter, who was holding her hand. "Mom . . . see what they found?" she said.

Grandmother Winter, stationary as a statue and just as expressionless, looked sick. Why didn't she *do* something, say something—voice her objections, at least?

I turned to look where she looked, and saw that, from the dug-out slot behind the painting, incredibly, another painting had slipped out. In addition, there was a thin, crumbling packet of what appeared to be crinkled letters written on tracing paper, and at which she now gawked. Zinger had risen and, looking down at his trophies, was systematically rubbing his hands, the sound ricocheting from the high ceiling so that when his palms clashed, the sound magnified to a hollow clap. Droopy was sitting Indian-style, rifling through the packet, while his glasses wobbled on the tip of his nose. With the long middle finger of his right hand, he balanced them, his brow puckered, his eyes half-closed to see through the fogged lenses.

I searched the room. Where was Hamlet? Given all the excitement, he should have been with the other two.

Unexpectedly, Peda screeched, and, embarrassed, I turned around to yell at her. She dropped her grandmother's hand and ran to the painting, behind which Hamlet materialized as suddenly as my vision of Robin had appeared. I hugged my goose-flesh arms.

"That's enough—all of you," Winter said. Her voice was barely above a whisper. Still, it was the urgency of her tone that made the men look up, stop their activities as if they were frozen mimes. Then, with all the authority that I remembered distastefully from my childhood, she said, "Leave the papers and those canvases you found. . . . I want to look at them."

Hamlet stretched and smiled winningly at her, but his mouth appeared twisted somehow, and I wondered how such a perfectly molded mouth could change so quickly. I put my arm around my mother, who, surprisingly, let me do it, even seemed to welcome it. Actually bent her thin, wired, and inflexible body right into mine.

Droopy dropped the packet, but his papery hands remained suspended over the thicket of translucent papers, all of which blended admirably—the hands and the papers—and in the breeze from the doorway, the outstretched fingers and the letters trembled. I wanted to laugh. Zinger's expression was belligerent; his mouth dropped open, and he glared at my mother, daring her to say more. Which she did. And I was proud of her—a unique but somehow satisfying experience for me.

"Step away. Now," Winter ordered.

She moved in their direction, and her walk was menacing. Her perfect hairdo was torn up but more of a crown for her fine features than the sprayed, coiffed crown 'do the hairdresser worked on once, sometimes twice, a week. She smoothed it back, but the wisps of white-blond tendrils ran through her fingers like so many strands of heavy yarn painted with paste. Stiff and unmanageable, but natural for a change, so that, along with the pink in her cheeks, colored by the wind, it made her look healthy and formidable.

"Hand me the envelope and papers." She held out her hand to old Horatio, who obligingly placed them in her outstretched palm.

He kept his eyes averted, but he scowled and compressed his thin lips; in the bright light, they looked purple. "You'll return them for analysis?" he said. "Today?"

She nodded. "But they're not yours to keep."

"Of course not. You'll get them back as soon as we determine their age and authenticity."

She didn't look at the papers, just held them at her side. "Show me the painting," she said, indicating the largest one, whose front was hidden from view. "That one first." She bent over it protectively, blinking and absorbed. And then she smiled broadly—so broadly, in fact, that I wondered if her face might crack.

It was a painting of a family around a dinner table. All of them smiling, too, just like Winter, but these people looked genuinely happy. From another century—no, from around 1910, maybe 1920 or 1930. Wonderful food in front of each of them. Clear, primary colors of broiled, buttery fish; small quail eggs; beans; crispy rolls; chunks of meat and ripe cheese. A lady at the table—Beatrice? And laughing children and one of the two gentleman from Winter's painting, though he appeared younger. A marvelous image, a slice of life from long ago.

Without turning to face us, smiling still, I could tell, she said, in a gentler tone, "And the next one, please." I felt genuinely sorry then, for my cruel thoughts, and had a yearning to apologize to her.

Too late, thank goodness. Zinger stooped to retrieve the second canvas, and unfolded it. It boomeranged with a whistle of wind. He snatched his hand back, then tried again, this time anchoring the corners with palette knives.

The colors on this one were fresh and sharp, too—fresher. I could almost smell the turpentine. A work of nature that reproduced the ocean, each wave so clearly outlined that the depths of the sea acted as a mirror, the sand beneath the water so pure and light-filled it created a religious quality. Until the viewer looked more closely . . . and then, to his or her shock, realized that the painting was a collage of tiny bric-a-brac, with the exception, that is, of a large boat's destroyed motor, rusted and neatly cracked, almost in half, a testament to garbage: melted, moldy parts of smashed-up Victrolas and radios; rusted, sharp-torn metal pieces of knives and guns and ice picks; rotting, eyeless, open-mouthed fish wedged in anal crevices of human torsos, their staring, lipless human heads and chewed-up gray matter pegged by burst syringes and flaccid condoms; perfectly preserved animal and human and God knows what other kinds of waste; bloated, headless cats and rats; even a pig or two caught in the blades of the motor, their hairless bodies, gashes to their genitals and their gnashing teeth. These things were eternalized by the salt of the sea, but more, of course, by the artist, his painting's detail: flawless, awesome, and truly horrific.

Hooked by the image, we congregated behind Winter, who was grim-faced once more, bowed over her simultaneously, and stared down at it, all of us: Peda, the three men, and I. And so powerful was our reaction that we were tongue-tied. Instinctively, Winter backed up against us. She threw her arm protectively in front of Peda, just as if she were driving in a car, because Peda, in the passenger seat, had flown forward on impact when Winter slammed on her brakes. And the rest of us, well, we did the same. Stuck out our right arms. Under the neck of each neighbor, we provided a protective arm bar. To withstand the sight of that sea canvas. But with a seeming mind of its own, the canvas recoiled at our movement and rewound with a peculiarly live but vicious finality that none of us at that moment wished to disturb.

Chapter 5

WINTER

"*H*ello! Hello in there. . . ." The echo of Clay's voice resounded through the house.

It recalled us to our senses, and we snapped to attention—except, perhaps, for Peda, who, not as stunned as the adults by the painting's implications, was still mesmerized by the illustrated story under the sea.

"Where is everyone?" Clay called.

Elsie twisted to face me. "How did *he* get in?"

I shook my head.

"In here," she shouted.

Zinger pointed to Horatio Guardi, whose tousled appearance seemed magnified in the morning glare, unscreened as it was by drapes, shades, or blinds. "Have you noticed something strange?" Zinger asked him.

The older man was shivering in the sharp draft, and he moved out of it, disregarding Zinger, shuffling as if he wore slippers.

"Let me close the door." My daughter's long stride seemed almost an insult to the old man. "What should we have noticed?" she asked Zinger. She stared down at his thick tufts of side hair.

The squat little man looked up at her, then turned back to Horatio, whose sad appearance almost made me feel sorry for him.

Zinger flapped his hand at the tubed picture at our feet. "That ocean scene looks like it was painted yesterday. I mean, there aren't any age marks; it's wound up too tight. Just look at it—it's never been stretched, and the colors are too vibrant, too real, no cracking . . . nothing." He paused, glanced at Peda, and lowered his voice. "Moreover, syringes and condoms were a rare sight in Crandor's day."

"Yeah? How do you know?" Ham asked. "Were you there?" He looked Zinger up and down and grinned broadly. "Anyway, that's not true—there were plenty of addicts back then."

Zinger flushed and went on as if Ham hadn't spoken. "On the other hand"—he straightened and sucked in his stomach, leveled his gaze at Horatio—"if the canvas was never exposed to light or air, maybe *that* explains it."

Hamlet smirked, not a nice expression. "That would be worrisome, wouldn't it, fella?"

"What are you talking about?"

"I think you know." He caught Elsie's eye, gave her a conspiratorial wink, and beckoned her to his side.

She might as well have run. My plan to place them side by side the night before at dinner had obviously worked. But now I wasn't so sure that I wanted it to work. There was something about Hamlet Crandor that bothered me—besides his obvious cupidity, he was too sure of himself, his charm not altogether wholesome. Though, to be fair, my unease was unqualified and, furthermore, uncalled for, since Elsie was not altogether wholesome herself.

Hamlet put his palm to his mouth and leaned into Elsie's face, whispering. I could hear the hiss of his *s*'s, telling secrets to my daughter while the room looked on. She wore a silly, vacuous grin and, staring into his eyes, nodded rapidly. For someone who reveled in her emotional indifference to men friends, she seemed quite attached to *this* young man.

"What's going on?" asked Clay, announcing his presence.

Elsie automatically backed away from Hamlet.

But Clay didn't notice. He fixed his watery gaze on Zinger and Horatio Guardi, who shut up when he appeared.

I took a step closer to Clay. Did this slight, effete man with the thinning reddish hair and the crepey pouches under his eyes have the power to disrupt a room of people? I swept my gaze about the room and realized that the problem was with us, not Clay: it was our crackling nerves that had created the tension. Apparently, Clay had picked up on it, too, because I noticed that his usually pallid complexion had become red and mottled. As if he had caught a robber in the middle of a holdup.

Elsie cast her head in the direction of the painting, which lay facedown on the floor, its back slashed and torn apart, the wound stark in the white glare, its gaping holes filled with tacks, lots of them scattered in the mangled incisions. It looked as if the experts had performed a sloppy operation, and when Clay focused on this aberration, botched from a lack of scruples or greed or both, so did I, and I panicked, alarmed all at once for the welfare of my painting. Clay and I moved to turn it together, and for a moment I experienced a rush of warm feeling for him, his face achingly familiar in this welter of strangers who occupied my home.

I examined the piece while the experts, my daughter, and the artist's grandson looked on. "It's okay," I said with relief. I felt their eyes upon me and wondered if they read correctly the intensity of my feelings as I gazed down upon the upturned and

welcoming expressions of my friends: Beatrice, with the watchful eyes; her child; the dapper man, forever walking toward
them; not to mention . . .

The old man coughed. "We'll fix it, of course."

I placed my hands on the back of my neck, raked my fingers upward through my hair, let it fall slowly, like a waterfall.
I could see Elsie eye me critically, as if only young girls were
allowed to play with their hair. "I'm sure you will," I retorted,
and my sarcasm surprised me.

"Do you know anything about these two paintings? The
folder?" Horatio Guardi gazed at me with a heavy-lidded dignity, that moist-eyed face with the thin beard.

I wondered how I should answer him, this man who
seemed to carry a perpetual burden on his narrow shoulders—
and the reason for his stoop, I theorized.

I felt like a criminal. Of course I knew nothing about the
paintings . . . or the packet of papers. How could I? But would
anyone believe me? No doubt the Getty men suspected that the
hidden canvases were rare, priceless pieces. The thought of the
money didn't interest me. How they had gotten there, and when:
those were the real questions. I thought about my father and the
odd people that he had collected. And my spine stiffened when
I realized that Simon Crandor—Beatrice, for that matter—had
been members of my father's habitual cold-weather club. The
beat of my heart was audible deep inside my ears, and I was
mildly surprised that I noticed it. I remembered his avid interest
in me, especially when I described things like my beating heart
(which he believed was a receptacle for the soul). He would peer
at me then, with his glasses shoved above his forehead, and give
me his undivided attention, as if I were the most important person in the world.

And, as if in answer to my thought, Guardi said, "Maybe
your father placed the canvases behind the painting?"

The hairs along my arms stood straight up. Was he psychic?

"Maybe he helped Crandor?" he went on.

"Nah, impossible," Zinger interjected. "They're too new."

"The papers?"

"Of course not—the paintings. But we'll get everything analyzed as soon as possible. Who knows? Maybe the paintings, protected from the atmosphere, really did withstand the erosion of years. Maybe Crandor was like Jules Verne, a man ahead of his time—broken syringes, condoms, and all." He slapped his thigh. "What a coup if that were the case!"

I stared down at my mutilated painting and, with a bravura I didn't feel, retorted, "Not without my permission, you won't. Get it analyzed, I mean."

They looked at me with pity then, as if I were an intruder or a displaced person: my daughter, whom I barely knew; wedged against the grandson of the painter whom he never knew; across from the Getty people, who weren't with the Getty at all; and my adopted landscaper, who had forsaken landscaping, he said, because of me. And I wondered what these people were doing in my conservatory, in my house, for that matter, and I silently apologized to my father, berating myself for having orchestrated this situation, or, at the very least, for having allowed it to happen.

Chapter 6

ELSIE

∽

"*C*an you imagine anyone in their right mind naming you *Elsepath*?" I sat across from Hamlet, under the mantel clock in Grandfather George's study, which ticked with the persistent, irritating rhythm of a metronome. (When I was a child, Winter insisted that I take piano lessons, which I endured for a year, regularly falling asleep to the click of the metronome that my bad-breathed teacher, Miss New, kept going. After all was said and done, however, I still couldn't play anything except scales, and those not well.)

Next to me, Clay Earshow perched on a moss-green leather chair, balancing himself on its ornately carved mahogany arms with one hand, and with the other stroking the nap of his too-cool two-day beard while he angled this way and that to catch his own cool look in the dark reflection of the room's glass-paneled door.

Opposite him, sunlight fell through the panes of the triple-hung windows onto the patterned carpet, creating a luridly bright block of whiteness, and I shaded my eyes against it to better catch Ham's expression. But, installed behind George Peregrine's high-backed desk, he was engrossed with the envelopes that stuck out of every pigeonhole, papers that matched the one he played with in his breast pocket, the lone paper Zinger and old Horatio had missed when Zinger opened up the painting.

"I wouldn't do that," I warned. "Winter hasn't touched my grandfather's desk since he died."

"Then it's about time."

"You can't just rip the desk apart."

He shrugged. "I wanted to find your name in that book of sonnets you seemed so hot on. *El-se-path.*" He swirled the syllables around with his tongue.

"It's easier just to tell you about it." I gave a quick laugh.

He spun the desk chair around to face us, Clay and me. "Fine, then." He sounded miffed.

I imagined that this was how George Peregrine must have looked when he worked from the old roll-top: somehow invulnerable, especially from the protective cocoon of the wrapped desk arms.

Clay dropped his hands into his lap. "I *like* Elsepath," he said. "Prefer it to Elsie." He mock-shuddered—"It's so cowlike"—and rolled his eyes, so that only the whites showed.

Watching Hamlet continue to check us out, me and the slim, tense man with the light gray eyes and the stubble, I knew he wondered what I saw in him. Well, it was none of his fucking business.

Then he laughed.

At which I took offense. So I said, "They used to make up 'Elsie' jokes about me in school. You know, rhymes, that sort of thing. They weren't funny then . . . and they aren't now."

I stared at him, shook my head, and started to chant a ditty the kids had sung about me: "Too much milk, too much cream . . . Too much puddin', 'n' so she couldn'."

"I think it's kind of cute," Ham said. "The name, not the song." He grinned . . . and I tried not to grin back.

"Well, I think Elsie's dreadful," Clay said. "I think I'll call you Elsepath."

"No, you won't."

Ham raised his hand, palm forward. "We've got to talk, Elsie. You, too, if you want to stay." He fluttered his fingers at Clay.

I felt my cheeks redden. "I'll be the judge of who stays and who goes," I said. Who the hell did he think he was, this arrogant man whose scent drove me to fantasize about God-knows-what? I sniffed behind my fingers, trying to pick up a trace of his sandalwood musk.

Then I got up to leave.

"Please. . . ." He looked at me earnestly. "I have something to show you, ask your advice about. Yours, too, Clay." He smiled, trying to appease me.

I backed up and slowly sat down.

"Thank you." He saluted with two fingers and made a sort of kissing noise. "Don't want the so-called 'experts' to hear. Can we lock the door?" He glanced toward the double door that separated the study from the conservatory. A steady drone was barely audible, but he inclined his head toward the sound anyway. "See what I mean?"

"No one can hear us." I was getting tired of his game playing.

But a knock on the door proved me wrong, and Clay jumped up to open it when he heard Winter's voice.

"May I join you?" she asked from the threshold, and then moved to the nearest chair without looking at us or waiting for an answer. "I see you've introduced yourselves." She carried a mug of steaming coffee, topped with what looked like a skein of hot, curdled milk. When she saw Ham and Clay staring at it, she said, "I'm sure Clay would be delighted to bring in the pot and more cups."

Always the hostess—she could never forget her role.

Both men shook their heads. "No, thank you," Clay said, and averted his face.

"I've had enough of the excitement in there." She waved in the direction from which she had just come. "Tell me, have any of you—"

But Clay cut her off. "Did it ever occur to you," he said in a low voice, "that we might be in the middle of a conversation?"

She pressed the coffee mug between her palms.

I heard the disdain in Clay's voice, as we all did, and, watching my mother's face, I felt bad for her, felt the blow to her pride as surely as if it had been dealt to me, as if I had been forced to play my scales in public—worse, in front of Ham.

"Oh, I'm sorry. Was I interrupting?" She looked from him to me, then put her hand to her forehead as if she were ill.

"Of course not, Mother. Hamlet was about to reveal something of great importance; he'd welcome your input, wouldn't you, Ham?" I could tell that Ham was embarrassed, and I enjoyed his discomfort.

"I'd be honored, Miz Peregrine," Ham said. "Anyway, the subject pertains to you directly." His slight Southern accent gave him a kind of heroic appeal, I thought.

Which made Winter relax, made everyone relax. She leaned back in her chair.

"Come close," said Ham, "so I won't have to raise my voice."

I let out a laugh; he sounded so serious.

"Wait until you see this. . . ." And from his breast pocket, he pulled out the paper.

Winter half-rose when she saw the artist's handwriting. "Doesn't that belong to me?" Her voice sounded peevish.

"*This* is what I wanted to talk to you about."

She resumed her seat, erect on the edge of the cushion. "Go on," she said, and tucked one ankle behind the other.

He bent his head toward the voices in the conservatory and in an undertone said, "This note is from my grandfather to George Peregrine, *your* grandfather, which makes me think that Crandor—"

Clay made a faint noise of protest. "I really don't think I should be here," he said, with unexpected rancor, "if it's a family matter."

What the shit was he talking about? He had never seemed to care before. He avoided my eyes and glanced at Winter, who, bathed in the light that came flooding in through the window wall, looked like a pale and pathetic old woman. And who, I expected, would later get Clay for his outburst.

It had come to me recently, after watching Clay interact with Winter, that I knew what makes a dog growl—in fact, I felt through all my pores how a dog feels when he is ready to bite. At first, like I did, Clay *wanted* to serve Winter Peregrine; he did it willingly. He *liked* soaking up her polish. But Winter didn't feel obligated to be nice to him anymore. He was like an old shoe: someone she took for granted, someone she used, someone she could discard. It fell to him to do everything: serve the coffee, fix the stuck window, tape the windows before storms, untape them after storms, babysit, grocery-shop, mow the lawn, plant the tulip beds, provide companionship, provide solace . . . and on and on. Yet when it came to a dinner invitation, and there weren't many to be had, she cut him off like a dog. And he was hurt. Well, he had a right to be.

Only last week, he had let on that he had a few things up his own sleeve. For instance, neither Mom nor I ever suspected that he had a roommate, and that their relationship wasn't exactly platonic, either. I didn't care, but I wondered about Winter's reaction, especially when she learned that he had apprised this roommate, *in detail*, about all the goings-on here—things that took place on her run-down old Peregrine Island.

So, naturally, today when I looked over and saw his mouth compress into angry folds, it didn't surprise me one bit.

"You enjoy being dramatic, don't you, Clay?" Winter asked. She stared at him, blinking. "You're always here, it seems. Why leave now?"

Clay sucked in air, then let it out slowly. "Whatever you like."

I turned toward Hamlet. "Can I read the letter?"

"I'd rather summarize it, for the sake of expediency." And he brandished the paper in the air. "As you can see, it's a letter dated in 1955 and written to George Peregrine by my grandfather Simon. In it Crandor details his suspicions about his longtime agent, Barry Zinger, and his longtime friend—yes, *friend*—Horatio Guardi." When Hamlet saw our expressions, he gathered himself and took a deep breath. "But Simon says outright, right here"—he pointed at the paper with his pencil—"that he thinks his life is in danger." Ham stared at us for a moment, letting the import of his words linger, and in the reverberating silence I swear I felt the tension in my fingertips. "Upon his death," he continued, "Crandor claims, the value of his artwork will increase tenfold, and because the two men, he writes, with his son, Jonah, have, and I quote, 'recently incorporated to harbor the paintings selected by museums and other institutions for acquisition,' end quote, in a far-fetched scenario, he alleges that the three of them would become multimillionaires if he died before his art was delivered."

Ham drummed his fingers on the desk. "You want my interpretation?" He didn't look up, but he cleared his throat. "If the corporation holding the paintings demanded outrageous fees after Simon Crandor's death, well, I suppose the museums and organizations that couldn't afford the works could back out, leaving the corporation free to sell to whomever it pleased, at whatever prices it wished to tack on to the artwork. And which, I assume, is exactly what happened."

His voice thickened, and again Ham cleared his throat. "I'd like to question Zinger and Guardi. . . ." He looked up, studying each of us in turn. "Wouldn't you?" He tapped the paper with his forefinger. "Ironically, Simon writes here"—Ham scrutinized the faded scrawl—"'If you can't trust your friends and your family, who *can* you trust?'"

He smoothed the letter flat on the desk. "Sadly and prophetically, my grandfather disappeared very shortly after this letter was written. I'm positive that it's his handwriting, although I think we should get a handwriting expert in to verify it." He frowned, then swiveled around in his desk chair to pull an old magnifying glass out of a far cubbyhole, after which he bent down over the desk to examine the writing himself.

In a breathless voice, Winter said, "You're *accusing* your own father."

Hamlet raised his head to look her in the eye. "The letter, I believe, was written by Simon Crandor, *not* by me." He was silent for a moment. "He and my father weren't close, you know. As a young child, I saw my grandfather maybe once."

Clay and I looked at him skeptically, and he glanced away to stare out at the distant waves.

I looked at what he looked at, imagining that together we heard the slap of the waves against the wet, rock-strewn beach. A seagull passed in front of our wavering vision, and then another on its tail, and I saw his eyesight founder and he looked down at the floor.

"My roommate, who has a master's in twentieth-century art history, works for a noted contemporary art dealer," Clay volunteered. "She could help out."

I noticed Winter glance at him with vague surprise but she

didn't say anything. Neither did anyone else. *Another purported art connoisseur? That's all we needed!*

Clay pursed his mouth when no one reacted, and sank back in the big green leather chair. And I stood up, then went to stand over Ham and peered down at the letter, which a puddle of light on the desk accentuated. Somehow, its slanted, loopy cursive seemed a bygone art yet because of it surprisingly poignant.

"What do you want to do?" I asked.

"Reopen the case. Find out the real cause of Simon Crandor's death."

"Isn't that a little extreme?"

"I don't think so." He looked up at me. "My grandfather disappeared in a boating accident during a storm just a year after he wrote this letter." His eye swiveled back to the paper. "No one ever found his body." His words seemed to shimmer and then melt into the haze that hung over the window.

He hesitated. "No one ever found his letter, either. Not until today." A furrow appeared in his brow. "You think I'm nuts, what I'm implying, don't you?"

I dug my nails into my palm and looked down at the pattern in the rug. No one answered him, because to voice his thoughts aloud—*foul play, foul play, foul play*—would be to validate them. The silence, therefore, and the haze, and the deep thinking, seemed to go on forever, until Ham twisted away from us so that he faced the desk.

"That," he said, "or the person who stashed this letter, along with the rest of the retrieved documents, is playing a terrible joke on us."

Chapter 7

WINTER

$\mathcal{B}$y late afternoon, the benign waves from the morning were long gone: their gentle lap upon the shore had turned fierce and beat at the land violently. A fickle mistress indeed was the sea that ruled the way I lived, the way I slept or didn't sleep. Even my late-afternoon nap that day was a disaster. And because I am a nighttime insomniac, I *need* my afternoon nap, which today was sabotaged by the weather and circumstances beyond my control.

I was already disturbed by the morning's occurrences. After leaving Hamlet Crandor to his own devices, I had tried to persuade the Getty pair to take their leave—without my painting, of course, and the letters or the paintings that they had discovered hidden behind the canvas. Eventually, without thanks or even an explanation, the men left grudgingly with Clay, who had volunteered to escort them to their hotel. With the packet of papers, I might add, that I magnanimously allowed them to take and study. I knew the papers would be returned to me, however, since the two men made sure that I understood their departure from Peregrine Island would be temporary. They even hinted at recruitments, strength in numbers and all that, as if to say I didn't have a chance, inasmuch as they had the Getty guns at their disposal. Still, after considering their predicament, mine as well, I came to the conclusion that their threats were empty; the painting, after all, was mine, and so were the other three found in its casing. Threats were a waste of time. How could they take my art away from me? I worried, though—and my fear that day was unflagging.

Therefore, to alleviate my anxiety after lunch, I decided to walk on the beach—for me, a rare event—and, initially, I enjoyed myself. The silence engulfed me, and it seemed as if I might walk forever. The water was moving slowly, and the swaying of some marsh reeds produced tiny bubbles that caught the sun, so that the top of the water seemed to flicker with light. At the edges, beyond the reeds, the water was transparent and near smooth under a vapory white-clouded sky. I had just bought new sunglasses, which I wore while I studied the sea. The colors of the waves were a teal blue and the sky a pale slate, delineated by the horizon. Everything looked perfect, and I breathed in deeply, relishing the salty flavor of the soft breeze and hoping that I would catch sight of Peda, who had not returned for lunch. Who could blame her for staying away, amid the uproar in the house?

Close to the seawall, I stopped while I contemplated my granddaughter. I took off my sunglasses, and they hung like an appendage from my fingers at my side, and I stared out at the Sound and was mildly surprised to see that it had turned dark and the teal had disappeared into waves that suddenly looked forbidding. Even the sky looked menacing, the vaporous white-colored clouds replaced by clouds of weighted graphite, which rolled in toward me. A storm seemed imminent. Just like that it had come up, without any warning at all. One moment, perfect; the next . . . just like my life. I slipped my sunglasses back on to protect myself against the glare. I knew they were a crutch, another facade to keep my life at bay—I didn't want to face the storm. And my recurrent unsettled feeling, a nagging thing, an itching, a need to call my father—and my mother, whom I'd never really known—both of them dead all these years. I considered my nightmares; some mornings they left me with the same sort of vague feeling. What if they weren't nightmares? The dead rise and walk about in timeless fields of thought, I'm told.

The wind struggled with the wide brim of my hat. Strands of streaked yellow-white-gray hair blew across my mouth, and I drew them away with my fingers. The motion reminded me of Peda. She liked to drop her hair across her eyes, as if by doing so she could look out but the world would not be able to look in. She would be safe and hidden, as protected as a woman covering her smile with a hand, or a girl looking away so you can't see her eyes, or me wearing my sunglasses. I pictured her then. At sunset, bending over as she examined her shells, her hair so pale it seemed to glow in the darkening shadows. I shivered. The sky was darker now, and there was a brief hush, presaging rain. I held the top of my cardigan closed on my chest against the onslaught of the wind that I knew would follow. And when it came, as I feared, it created an inflated balloon effect—crescendoing, then deflating, then building up again—the wind so constant at one point that I no longer felt alone with my thoughts. And so stiff it made my eyes water. *Where are you, Peda?* I wanted her with me. So that I could cradle her under my arm while we ran into the shelter of the house. I swiveled on my heels, making dents in the sand, and I started calling her by name, my hands cupped to my mouth, hoping my calls would resonate and funnel in between the wind gusts.

PEDA

When I turned into the wind, I felt its full force against me, pushing me the other way. Looking for Jake and Scarecrow. The sky had grown angry, and the sea was no longer clear but was boiling and black under the gray, marching sky. Carried along by the strong, charging wind, I was all but flying as I ran along the tide line. How long would it be before high tide? I didn't have much time to make it out to the breakers where he sometimes hid.

To Jake, time meant nothing, whatever that means. Following it was a pointless exercise, he once told me, and then he whispered in my ear that he could never understand the importance given to it—except, of course, the hours, the minutes, the seconds it took to meet and travel, which he said he had stopped doing years before. It was as if he were telling me a story. About himself. He had always liked to watch and to listen, he said, from screened, secret places; the secrecy made him aware of himself, stirred him as nothing else did. And so he would stay for hours, often more, in one place and follow the path of the weather, of the seagulls, and now, of me. I didn't understand everything he said, but I loved the sound of his voice.

So he saw me turn, I'm sure, way before I spotted him, and he called out to me. He had a low, echoing voice, as if he were calling from inside a hollow barrel.

And I heard him and ran in his direction, into the rocks, under the breakwall. His overflowing eyes watched me, and I slid next to him on the dark, heavy sand. A bone-skinny, white and gray–haired old man with caved-in eyes and large, moving hands. He limped off to settle himself under one huge boulder, then motioned for me to join him before the rain fell.

One of his legs was a little shorter than the other—a war injury, he had told me. But I never knew from which war. He loved me, I know, and he said he wanted to shield me from the vices of the modern world, whatever *that* means. "When we are little we are vulnerable, like soft-shell crabs," he would tell me. "Kids, like soft-shell crabs, have nothing to protect them. Once, long ago, when I was in the sixth grade," he remembered, "for no reason at all, a boy, a doctor's son, attacked me and beat me up so badly I never forgot it. It must be a vibration I give off. That's why I feel more comfortable here." And then he patted the stone that he sat on. And he grew tears. And I thought that he must be thinking of himself as a child still. I loved him for that. And for his stories, which were filled with words that made me feel pretty, as if he were blowing gold dust onto my eyelids.

He raised his face so that his chin pointed at me and his eyes dug into the darkest gray streak of the boulder's ceiling above us. And Scarecrow, his shiny black dog with the red clay-slick collar, sniffed the side of the rock where water from the tide was beginning to show itself, then lifted his leg and peed a foamy yellow stream.

I stood then, and leaned next to my old man. Cold spray from the tide and the rain wet our faces. I thought about how he thought of me: pale and wide-eyed as a fish. And "this is the way you stand," he once said, copying me in between his own sprays of laugh-snorts, "sort of with your weight on one leg, like me, the left one as if you've stopped yourself in the middle of a hop." He said he wished he could paint me that way too ... with my red Band-Aid of sun across my nose.

WINTER

Not far from where Peda, Jake, and Scarecrow waited out the storm—not that I knew it then, of course—I moved through the sudden wind gusts, and the dry cracks of lightning, and the clouds that had gathered, and the rain that then began to fall heavily, driven by the high winds. I tried to protect myself with my hat, and I pulled down the brim over my cheeks, fanning it back when I shouted for Peda. *"Peda, Peda, Pe . . . da!"* I yelled. In my mind's eye, I pictured the conservatory, warm and protected, with the rain falling aslant, running against the windows in thick rivulets, and I willed warmth into my wet flesh. But I couldn't return to my house, my room, my painting. Not with the tide rising, the winds so forceful, the lightning and now the thunder—great claps of noise so invasive that, childishly, I tried to shut out the vibration with my fingers. I ran, probably around in circles, I don't know, and I yelled until my vision blurred and my blood rang in great waves deep inside my head. *"Pedaaaaa, please . . . ,"* I called. *"Come back!"* I was frightened by this time, truly scared that something had happened to my granddaughter, and I considered going for help. But there was no time, and anyway, these summer storms are usually brief. Though the black clouds had blotted out the light from the sun, I could see easily through the sheets of rain and in the near-translucent and eerie fog that the storm had produced. It was almost like taking a shower. How long I walked up and down my beach, I couldn't say . . . for hours, it seemed at the time, although I doubt that it was much more than fifteen minutes.

Because my memory faded when I glimpsed the man, the dog, and the child before me, walking up my beach as if they had walked out of the sky. Or a Renaissance painting. A chill began in the center of my back, just between the two wings of my shoulders, then raced along the skin and down to my hands. I squatted to control my shaking. and I squinted into the pelting downpour. I felt weak, suddenly, as I waited for Peda, Jake, and Scarecrow—for I knew, as surely as I stooped there, that this was who they were—and when I rose, I felt my vision blur. And I folded then, like an accordion.

Just a second it took, for me to get my bearings, and then I felt Peda's hand on my forehead, a gentle touch. As she bent over me, rain dripped from her face down onto mine like tears. "Where is Jake?" I asked, as natural as can be.

She shook her head. "He couldn't stay, you know," she said. "But he told me that you have a Victorian face." She smiled at me then. And the downpour ended abruptly, as if at some signal.

On our way home, we held hands and we studied the wet ground, which had begun to exhale wisps of fog as the air cooled . . . and I pondered the words of Jake.

Chapter 8

ELSIE

rom the kitchen window, I watched my daughter and my mother walk up the beach in the drizzle and felt a hollow sense of relief. The sky was gray, leaden, with a bank of low clouds, but the downpour had stopped, at least for the moment, and although I heard distant claps of thunder, my family was safe from the imminent danger of lightning. I looked around at Hamlet, who sat at the battered pine table, on top of which lay the rice-paper letter he had stolen from the packet behind the painting. He was studying it so closely that his nose almost touched the pine knots and the scribble. I glanced back toward my mother, whom I watched smile, remove her hat, and pat her hair, and I realized with a familiar pang that Winter had once been young and she thought herself still beautiful. I tilted my head to one side, narrowed my eyes. My mother's sense of herself, her self-absorption, I felt, had been the source of a lot of my own unhappiness.

Behind me on the kitchen counter, the radio softly played a fifties song by Ricky Nelson, and, inadvertently, I tapped my toe to the rhythm. I hated the music from the late forties and early fifties—my mother's era—because it all sounded the same, with the same beat. It was *boring*. It hypnotized people, turned them into robots; it was for *fat* people, that one-two beat to which my toe tapped as I watched my mother and my daughter. *Like crickets drumming*, I thought, and flexed my foot, sweeping it against the kitchen tile.

I edged closer to the window, leaned my forehead on the cool pane of glass, and closed one eye to better see Peda. The girl clutched her grandmother's hand and raised her eyes to Winter's, and then she said something and they laughed, totally engrossed in each other. Against the glass and through the fog, I peered at them like a stranger, like a peeping Tom. I noticed Winter stop, lower her head so that the two were at eye level. They whispered together, and their foreheads touched. Then Winter took hold of Peda's other hand and lightly she swung it, as if she were about to folk-dance with her. An intimate scene, and one that I was envious of.

Peda annoyed me just as much as Winter did. Maybe more so. Asleep, the kid looked innocent and mummy-like; she slept in the fetal position, yet her fists were usually clenched and she wore a look on her face that said, *Get the hell away from me.* When we first moved back here, she drove me crazy. I wondered if her mood swings changed according to her environment and her audience. She should have been an actor. Recently, the child had gone about with a pebble in her shoe. Literally. A week or so earlier, I had found a pile of wet, sandy stones in her closet. I swept them up, only to find a new pile there a couple of days later. Again I removed them, and again they reappeared—always a fresh and dirty supply of them. When I finally asked Peda about them, the girl faced me with her hands in her pockets and told me, *her own mother*, that my efforts at housecleaning were useless. I couldn't believe it. You see, in a monotone—very unchildlike, if you ask me—she explained that from her pile every morning she chose a jagged stone to place in her shoe, so that when she walked she would know what it felt like to be uncomfortable. Do you *believe* it?

In front of me, a moth drifted by in the fog and lit upon the windowsill, where in slow motion it flexed its peppered wings under the light drizzle. Keeping my eyes fixed on it, on the delicate spots of purple dotting its white wings, I didn't turn around when I heard Ham move from his kitchen post at the pine table and leave the room. This was not the life I was meant to have. My real life was somewhere else, but where, I had no idea. I felt like I was outside the orbit of my fate, hurling haphazardly through the cosmos, and I rubbed my eyes to erase the image of Robin, Peda's father, my long-gone, long-ago boyfriend, of whom I had dreamed the night before. In my apron pocket, I fingered Robin's light woolen scarf, which I had dredged up from my closet after the dream.

"Look . . . the sun's trying to come out," Ham's voice said behind me.

I leaned back against him and looked up through the highest panes of the window. Overhead, through filaments of gauzy gray clouds, a weak, perfect sun had emerged, covered by the haze. I exhaled and found that my heart was pounding against my chest. I put my hand on it to still it, and I could feel Ham's leg jiggling against my thigh. And his heat. From his hair as it swung against his cheeks—no oil kept it in place now—came the scent of stale smoke. I pressed the back of my head against him, and, with his two hands, he cupped it firmly and turned me around so that I faced him. Then, with one long finger, the tip of which he dabbed with saliva from his tongue, he traced a moist line down the side of my face and pressed into the hollow of my throat to stop the pulse. I couldn't look at him because my breath was coming so fast that I thought I might suffocate. With the other hand he came up against the inside of my thigh, holding me there, in place, forcing my legs apart, hurting me. But I didn't care. He smiled slightly. I could smell the musky sandalwood scent of his skin again, the smoke, too, and I wanted to burrow into him, wanted him to burrow into me. I looked up at him, into the eyes that uncannily in color matched those of Robin, fresh from my memory of the night before. Which instinctively caused me to back up against the window. Away from him. And when he released me, my head hit the glass with a vicious bang.

"What is it?" His voice was very low and controlled, but now, listening for a hint of the remembered lilt in Robin's drawl, I could also make out a tremor of rage running through Ham's.

"Nothing." I shook my head. "Peda will be here soon, and my mother. Did you forget Zinger and Horatio? Clay, too. You wouldn't want them to walk in on us."

"Bullshit."

I tucked my hair behind my ears, willed the quiver from my voice. Felt my false bravura leaking out of me like a bad odor. "I can't do this now."

He shoved me against the window. "Why the hell not?"

"You remind me of someone."

"So what? Shit . . . I should've known it. You're just like every other little cock teaser." He leaned away from me and eyed me while he held his hand taut against my chest, pinning me against the window frame. "Not so little, though." He gave a nasty laugh and drilled his fist into the ribs below my breast.

I gasped. "Fuck you! And get the hell off me!"

"Not so fast."

He thrust his knee up into my groin, and a jab of pain hit me so completely that I staggered against his open palm. Sweat broke out on my forehead, and I had to force myself to breathe normally. "You bastard."

When he let go of me, my knees buckled. I wiped my brow

with my elbow. "What's the matter with you?" My voice caught in my throat.

"You want it as much as I do." He waved his hands in my face, and I flinched.

I didn't answer him. Trying to compose myself, I got up and edged an orange-juice container from the back of the refrigerator. I poured myself a glass, drank it quickly, and slammed the glass onto the counter.

"Where is he?" he asked after a while. "The guy I remind you of."

"How should I know? I haven't seen him for years. We used to live together in Vermont. He was a nice guy, though— not like you."

He snorted. "Nope, not like me, then."

I stared at the dregs of my orange juice. "He couldn't hack the world, so he did drugs. Marijuana at first, then the hard stuff. Well, I couldn't hack that, so I split."

"Why the sudden attack of conscience?" He regarded me in the same lingering manner, but with a strange dispassion now, as one might look up at a plane in the clouds, invisible except for its drone.

I shrugged. It was a fair question. "I don't know, I honestly don't."

He studied me, biding his time while he controlled his temper. His eyes had dilated to black pucks.

"Truce?" he asked after a few moments. He nodded at the letter that lay in front of him on the pine table. "There's a mystery here, maybe one for the police. We could work on it together."

His dark eyes dug into mine, and I dropped my gaze, drove my thumbnail into the meat of my palm, wanting, against my will, to go to him, do what he wanted.

But I realized that I didn't like him, for that matter liked myself less. I wanted to slap him. He'd most likely slap me back. And probably do more than that. Still, I had an almost unbearable urge to hit him hard. As I looked at him, it came to me suddenly that what I really felt was no more than a sexual yearning.

He sat down in front of the paper and smoothed it. Sat up straight—back to business. As if our encounter had never happened. Pressed both thumbs to his temple. "Those letters Mr. Guardi took are about my father. One is addressed to him."

"Not really." I could feel heat coming into the back of my neck. I watched his mouth. "The one you read is written to my grandfather," I said.

He pointedly looked away. "Those paintings are rightfully mine. . . . Mind if I have some orange juice?" He nodded at the container.

I felt as if he had punched me. "Yeah, I mind." I shook myself, ridding myself of my itch. I tried to sound normal. My throat felt sore. "That painting has been in my family forever; it belongs to my mother."

He came around to where I sat at the table and, behind me, began to knead my shoulders. Nothing sexual this time, just his way to bring me into line.

I cringed and bucked myself free of his groping hands. "No," I said.

He dropped his hands and moved toward the orange juice. "May I?" He gestured toward it and reached for a glass.

"Go ahead," I said darkly. "What's this about the police?"

He poured. "Well, besides that letter's content and its very serious implications"—he nodded at the table—"something else is going on here." He turned to look at me. "You and your mother know more than you let on."

I smiled curtly. "You're crazy. My mother loves that painting." I hesitated. "Crandor's figures are so realistic." I looked away. I sounded idiotic.

"That's not what I mean, and you know it." His voice was angry now. "How did that canvas end up secured inside the back of the painting? Or the other ones? Not to mention the packet of letters. Your mother didn't act very surprised."

"No, she wouldn't." I paused, and our eyes locked. "Nothing much fazes her these days."

Winter's voice usually sounded tired, but recently there had also been a peculiar uniformity to it, as if something were seriously off. With no inflections whatsoever. She had always been detached, but now she was farther gone than ever.

I glanced out the window. The fog had lifted, and the sea glittered, undulating, the light catching each crest. I narrowed my eyes against the glare. "What gives you the idea that any property in this house belongs to you?"

"Not to me personally. To my family."

What gall. "You don't have any family. You told me so yourself."

"I have a brother. And I'd like to call him. Bring him down here, since the case involves him, too."

"How is that?"

"That's a foolish question."

I had the urge to strike him again. Clenched my fist instead. "And the cops? You intend to call them in, too?"

"I don't know yet. That depends entirely upon you. This case would be a hell of a lot easier to solve if you cooperated, worked with me away from the prying eyes of those two old men. By the way, who contacted them originally?"

"Who contacted *you?*" I asked with a sneer. Who did he think he was, questioning me like this?

He stared at me and smiled. "*They* did, of course."

"You said you didn't know them." I frowned, suspicious of his contrived answers.

"Did I? Maybe." He shrugged. "Well, I didn't really, did I?"

I reached for my glass, slugged the last bit, licked the flakes of orange from my lip. "It was Clay, I think, who called them first."

"But why?" He looked puzzled.

"To stir things up, I think. I'm not sure, exactly; I just assumed as much."

"*You* did it, didn't you?" He winked at me, and I felt small, as if I had been found out for something I hadn't done. My heart beat painfully. Punished again. Locked up in the teacher's closet. Ashamed of myself.

"No, of course not. Why in the world would I?"

"Money?" he asked, and, smirking, raised his eyebrows knowingly, staring down at me, punishing me for something I hadn't done.

Chapter 9

WINTER

∽

I was scared, of course—and shocked—by the recent events. As I walked into the conservatory with my second glass of wine, slowly, because I was tired after the storm and my beach confrontation with Peda, I juggled in my pocket pieces of smooth glass that I had found on the wet sand. One by one I removed a few of them, set them out on the walnut envelope table, which sits next to my chaise. With one eye closed I bent over them, peering at them with the other as if they were smaller and more precious than they actually were—jewels, rather than glass pebbles stolen from the sea. Slate blue and round in color; bottle green and pointed but gradual; pancake-flat golden and light; translucent white, long and narrow like a worm. Between my fingertips I massaged the rest, then rolled them over my palm as I sipped my wine and stared at my mutilated painting, which lay on its side against the fireplace wall, the faces of my friends turned inward so that I was unable to see them. I choked back tears, ashamed of my sentimentality, and told myself that

I needed no one, least of all my painted faces, and then I went for the Sancerre on the mantel, thinking that if one had to have a vice, gum would be preferable to wine. Although, after picturing Elsie's overburdened shoulder bag with her melted sticks of cinnamon Trident on its sticky floor, the blood-red dye seeped deep into its pliable Italian leather, I shuddered . . . and refilled my wineglass.

My stones, I placed on the table as if they were pieces of my heart. I took a step back and felt my knees quiver; then I folded the way I had on the beach, one bone at a time, carefully letting myself down until I was sitting, exhausted, on my chaise. With my left hand, I rubbed the bulbous veins I felt on the backs of my thighs and fervently hoped that I wasn't moving my blood into the wrong places. I've read that anything is possible with phlebitis. Move your veins around too much, and you die.

Against the light of the late afternoon, I closed my eyes, elevated my legs, and collapsed into the softness of my lace-framed pillows. The windows were open; I heard the faint drip of a dying runoff from the roof—residue from the rainstorm—but the French doors were closed and the windows' latticed shutters were closed tight so that the room was dim. Only narrow bars of light came through the chinks in the lattice and fell in random patterns, striping the chaise and painting faint spirals on the walls.

I thought about the acrid smell of the Sound, the brackish quality that seeps into my pores, the humidity and the salt that saturate my hair, giving it the consistency of cotton candy, the sustained slap of the waves, unremitting as the wind, which is almost alarming in its relentlessness—the things that signify the potency of saltwater life. I thought of Jake in the same way. Alarming, potent, obdurate—his features wouldn't disappear from my mind; they were imprinted in my brain as if I had been hypnotized. *He has pale eyes, almost colorless,* but maybe it was the light from the storm. It was as if they were bleached, and they were set deep in his head. The frame of his body was big, but he looked wasted, either from illness or from underfeeding. He was standing unnaturally still when I saw him, with the immobility of someone threatened, despite his obvious arthritis, which was painful, I imagine, because of his somewhat bent posture. *Is he real? Am I fabricating him from Peda's fertile imagination, her descriptions of him? Am I crazy?*

Am I someone who is, technically speaking, insane, because I see significance everywhere, a purpose and a design in everything, think that trees are responsive entities and seagulls, dolphins, bears, and bees hum in conversational song? Am I out of my mind because I communicate with painted people in a canvas world that only I, with their creator, the painter, understand? My world intertwines with theirs, you see, and we people use a common language, a thread that crosses over the line of reality. A few months ago, I read about virtual reality in a periodical, and, strangely enough, I understood it. Before that I rarely understood anything modern. The young people's music these days is deafening and obtrusive to my eardrums, not a concordant chord in it. I hate it. Yet virtual reality is something different—modern, but as old as memory, and something I am sure I would feel comfortable living in. Sometimes, like now, when I am drifting off to sleep, I wonder if I am already in it.

When I woke it was evening, the air thick and warm. I leaned over and opened the shutters and peeked outside. Across the seawall, down on the damp sand, I could see the dusky ocean with fringes of white as the waves crashed in and left their foam behind. The inner harbor was swollen with high tide. A light, which was slashed by a yellow band, ran along the horizon, and I stared at it, spellbound. Eventually, I swung my feet onto the tile, and, despite the warm air, the chill of the floor struck through my silk-soled slippers and I shivered. On the table there was a note from Elsie, which she had slid under the wineglass: *Clay brought dinner—on the kitchen table. Have gone for a walk with Ham, Peda, Clay, and his friend. Back soon. E.* After I glanced at it, I dressed and walked outside to find them.

As I made my way across the grass, my high heels drilled holes in the ground, and I hopped on the soles of my feet like a breast-heavy dove. In the light cast from the window, I reread Elsie's note.

What friend? I looked down at my watch; the dial glows in the dark. I had slept the day away. Past eight o'clock, and here I was, wandering around in the shadows. The clouds hung low and thick. I doubted there would be a moon tonight and decided that the night would soon be as murky as the bottom of the sea and it was foolish to walk around in it. Though no rain was falling, moisture hung dispersed in the air, dampening my hair and my face. I patted both and rubbed the condensation from my hair between my fingers, and thought again that I should go inside. From where I stood, directly in front of the sand and the breakwall, I felt as alone and as afraid in this bleakness of black as I ever had, and I wished I had a person to whom I could relay my fears.

How auspicious, I thought, when Clay unexpectedly appeared. *How ironic.* I sniffed. It was as if he had heard my silent plea by turning up the control on his homing device, the one made to cater to little old ladies. Wading through the moist night air still heavy with the heat of the day, I made my way toward him. The silk sheen of my dress shone in the dim light like seaweed underwater, and I stroked the skirt as we came together.

"Where are the others?" I asked nonchalantly. I didn't want to let on how glad I was to see him.

He hunched his thin shoulders. "Maybe they went in. I don't know."

I studied his face: the smallish eyes, pretty enough because of the gray color but hardly there, not his best feature, though his lashes were curling and thick. The face of a philosopher or a thinker, or a nineteenth-century opium addict with TB: pale, indented cheeks; a high forehead; and a narrow mouth, glossy pink, probably because he wet it so often with his tongue.

I linked my arm through his. "I hear you brought dinner. Thanks. I was planning to scrounge for leftovers; there was quite a surplus." I smiled conspiratorially.

"I wouldn't know." He raised his eyebrows and looked out toward the water, but not before I caught the corner of his I-told-you-so grimace, which reminded me that I had excluded him from my dinner party the night before . . . and that lack of food had been my excuse.

Ah, but he can be a nasty SOB when he chooses. It is my definite opinion that it was *he* who called the Getty people—most likely he and Elsie together. They were the culprits. Who else? For the money, I assumed. But why would either one of them think the funds would be directed *their* way? Unless the two of them killed me, of course. I frowned, thinking all at once that maybe the idea wasn't so far-fetched. I mean, why this sudden solicitude for me?

I stopped walking and, twisting this way and that, leaned over to free my heel from the dirt. "What happened to the Getty men?" I asked.

"They're coming back in the morning." He held me steady while I wobbled. "Why do you wear those god-awful things? Nobody's here to see you."

Because I have always strived for perfection, I wanted to say, *because I have been a compliant daughter and have tried to live my life in the same fashion. You would never sneer at Elsie,* I wanted to say, *my daughter, and your lover, too, who has always enjoyed opposing me, has always reveled in the outlawed and the contrary.* I freed myself from his grasp, stumbled, and caught myself. *Maybe,* I brooded, *it's all the same kind of predictability in the end anyway.* After all, I tried to do everything I could to suit my parents, while knowing that it would never be enough.

"How do you know no one's here to see me?" I said. I'd never admit to him that I had found the shoes shoved under the chaise because I was too lazy to go to my closet.

I felt argumentative, probably from the relief of it all. From his hand, which had firmly taken hold of me again. He had appeared—I blew out a whistle of pent-up air—when I needed him, and he *was* a man, even if he was only Clay Earshow, whose store of sayings, from which he selected to suit the occasion, irritated me unbearably, sometimes, I admit, out of all proportion. Because it was as if he weren't honest with me most of the time. I scowled, thinking about it.

And, annoyed, he shook his head, scowled back at me.

I watched him, saw his disgust. I knew what he thought of me. My stiffness reminded him of dead things: washed-up fish lying curved and stiff on the rocks, flaking like old wax crayons and plastic pieces of wind-up toys. I felt my eyes brim with self-pity. I pushed his hand away.

"Tell me," I asked, peering up at him in the dark, "have you ever seen a tall old man walking on our beach? With a black dog in a plaid collar?" I fingered the silk of my dress, which was so springy it felt alive. "The man looks kind of arthritic, and he has hollow eyes that look through you."

"Oooooooh." He laughed, then picked up my hands and pressed them between his, stroking my fingernails, mine just as manicured, it occurred to me, as his own, though cleaner. He found a hangnail and played with it, then abruptly dropped my fingers while lightly continuing to hold my hand.

Did he *know* how annoying he was?

"Can't say as I have." He watched me with a sardonic grin as if he thought I was batty, hopped from one foot to the other as if he was impatient to be gone from my company.

The poor little old lady who doesn't have much upstairs anymore, except for the inflection in her voice of her forebears, the privileged has-been generations, for which he has an unwilling respect and a regrettable envy. Does she wear purple slippers and a purple pointed hat? He was looking at me strangely, and then, out of the blue, he started to perform a wild, bawdy jig, making lewd signs with his slender fingers.

I scowled again and started to make my way back to the house.

"Sorry," he called. "I was only kidding." He caught my arm and pulled me toward him, crushing my shoulder against his linen jacket.

For a second I was tempted to remain there, relax against him, his spare, pale face resting on top of my damp, cottony hair. I closed my eyes and breathed in his sweet cologne, which, as I ran my fingertips lightly over my breasts, struck me as being remarkably similar to a woman's scent.

"I've brought someone to see you."

He stroked my back, and I felt liquidy-soft.

"My roommate, the art dealer. Remember? I told you."

I arched my neck to look him in the eye, and he avoided my stare, but the black center of his eyes caught the mirrored rays from the water. "I didn't know you had a roommate. What's his name?"

"She . . . What's *her* name? Don't you remember?"

I was taken aback. I was fairly certain he was carrying on with my daughter, or trying to, and, for that matter, wasn't he my frequent companion, my eager escort? *And* he had a girlfriend?

"It's not what you think; we're just roommates. I've known her forever. She's good, you know. She knows her art. You'll want her advice, her opinion, about the Crandor paintings. Now, before those Getty people return tomorrow." He smiled slightly, proud of himself, as if he had just handed me a priceless gift.

How dare he? Quite intentionally, I had excluded him from my dinner the night before, and now, without asking my permission, he had brought his friend into my house. Invited her to examine my painting. *The* painting. It smacked of collusion, and it made me believe emphatically that Clay had engineered this whole thing with the Getty experts. What had he planned? How did he hope to acquire funds, social standing, and recognition from this debacle? Because, without a doubt, I believed that Clay Earshow's motives emanated not from greed but from a desire for social acceptance for born-on-the-wrong-side-of-the-tracks Clay Earshowtsky. I would humor him, I decided, see what he was up to. I could be wily, too.

I felt my adrenaline pump. I jumped, and my heels slid out from under me. From the ground, I laughed giddily. "How stupid of me," I said, looking at my legs, which were at odd angles in the grass. I tried to wipe them dry with my hands and noticed that the damp earth had stained the silk of my dress; I accepted Clay's ever-present handkerchief to blot it.

He hunkered down beside me. "Come on," he coaxed. "I left everyone else to find you. Sophia's so anxious to meet you." He hesitated. "No . . . *excited* is a better word. Especially after we drove over your bridge." He squeezed my arm and gazed into my eyes. This time, his look didn't falter.

I turned away. His supercilious behavior nauseated me.

"We could use some native flavor, don't you think?"

Implying that my Getty experts were foreign criminals up to no good. Well, he was probably right on that score.

I made a face and hoped he couldn't see my expression in the dark. "*Of course,*" I said sweetly, "the locals are always eager to get a glimpse of us island folk." I saw him look at me queerly, to see if I was joking. "Help me up, please," I said, even more sweetly, and held my hand out to him.

As he pulled me up, I thought about the girl I was about to meet. The girl from the mainland: overindulged, new money–saturated Fairfield County. The roommate *had* to be "new money"; "old money" would never be impressed, much less *excited*, by my island home. Old money would rather die than admit to such a thing. They *knew* about it, understood it. Had always known about it and didn't care one way or the other whether my island existed or sank into the sea. The others, they were a different matter. They would pay almost anything to acquire my run-down, oversized overbuilt home, because they coveted bigger, which to them meant better. Not to me, of course, but my home was just that—my home. And when my grandfather added on to it, he did it from fantasy blueprints. He had fun. And that is more than I can say for them. Those corporate types soaking up their conglomerates' bottomless incomes, the foreign explosion trying to home in on the action, and then there were the thirty-eight-year-old entrepreneurs, their money made from the market and the dot-coms—no substance there whatsoever, just like their wives of no past and no taste, new snouts and new cooks. Ironically, few of them know how to wield a fork—that's what I'd been told, anyway—but, then, neither did Clay until I taught him. No wonder Elsie avoids them like the plague. True, most likely I'd make a fortune if I sold my home to one of those freshly made multimillionaire mainlanders. But then where would I go?

Chapter 10

WINTER

*W*hen Clay and I entered the conservatory, a lamp was poised high over the three canvases, which were spread flat in the manner of laid-out corpses. In between the lamp and the paintings, Hamlet and Elsie were bent over the pictures, studying them, Ham's polished light-brown head so close to her dark-blond ponytail that no air seemed to separate them and they appeared to me as one. Both heads glistened under the intense beam of light and highlighted their coincidentally matching auburn tints. Over them, Sophia's dark head stood out in shadow, for me an ominous presence somehow, hovering and controlling their light—the only light in the room, it turned out, with a switch that she held in her hand.

We stopped in the doorway. My leg started to jiggle uncontrollably, and I felt beads of sweat gather on my forehead and under my arms and then dribble down my ribs. My eyes, I think, must have glazed over, and I stared down at my hands in a sort of stupor. I felt Clay close his palm around my elbow while at the same time he edged away from me as if my breath were bad. I looked up at the high wainscoting and ceilings that were, literally, lofty and reminded myself that he needed me. Some of the floors in the house were narrow wooden boards, and some of the flagstones, like those here in the conservatory, were varnished but uneven. The house had a subtle leaning toward its past, and Clay loved it, I knew, craved its history, because he had none of his own.

Still holding on to my elbow, he guided me into the room. I heard a pause, like an intake of breath, and then the conversation resumed, barely rippled by our presence, and I felt another tug of irritation. Someone turned on the small overhead chandelier, and I blinked because it was blinding after staring with my eyes wide open into the near darkness.

Elsie straightened at her post above my painting. "Well, look who's here," she said.

Both Clay and I winced, and I felt a rare stab of camaraderie for him. Until—smiling so broadly that his fleshy gums showed—he introduced me to the roommate: the lovely Sophia, the woman who was *so excited* to rub noses with the grand dame of the island.

"Mrs. Crandor?" she said, holding out her hand. "So nice to meet you in person."

"No," Clay said quickly, "Ms. *Peregrine*."

"Of course—how stupid of me."

What else would it be, if not in person? I thought. She didn't smile, just raised one perfectly plucked brow over an eye that unnerved me, the way it checked me out. Deliberately, from my heels all the way up. As if she were interviewing *me* for a position, as if *she*, not I, were in the driver's seat.

My voice shook. "Have you discovered anything new?"

Out of the corner of my eye, I saw Ham stand up, unwilling, I figured, to let another minute go by without taking part.

He had watched Clay, whom I knew he dismissed as a dandified upstart, lead me into the room. Now he turned his attention to the roommate, whom he frankly and rudely appraised.

"I'd like to explain," said Sophia.

"Do you have credentials?" I asked.

"Of course she does, Mother—she's an art dealer." Elsie glanced over and made a face at Ham.

Who, in turn, after inching close to me and to the woman, placed his hand over mine. "She's an expert in modern art, Miz Peregrine. Eh, Clay?"

As if the woman weren't there, right smack next to us.

Ham squeezed my hand lightly. "You of all people," he said, "you've got to admit that we could use an independent appraiser."

This was getting away from me. *Who*, after all, was Hamlet Crandor? Hadn't *he* come in as the expert? And why was *Clay* bringing in a third party? Who had given *him* permission?

Elsie watched me yank my hand out from under Ham's. My left eye twitched, and I was sure that she felt sorry for me. She had told me that in my photographs I always look down. As a rule, my head is lowered, too, she claims, but my eyes look up, blinking, as though I am scared of something. I supposed she thought the same thing now.

"It's okay, Mother," she said in a low voice, as if she were speaking to a child. "Sophia here has put two of the paintings under the black light. When she's through, I know she'd like to give you a verbal, as well as a written, analysis."

"For how much?" I asked. I felt mean.

The girl-woman had the nerve to shush me up then. "Nothing, of course. It's a privilege to be here." She dismissed my objection with a flick of her wrist and an ingratiating smile aimed at my forehead. "To study Simon Crandor's paintings firsthand . . . How else would I be able to work on museum pieces of this caliber? Besides, you're a friend of Clay's."

I swiped at my brow with my fingers, as if she were a gnat, and to brush her smirk away from my line of vision. "Do you have references?" I asked. I wondered what made her such an expert if she couldn't get near the museums that displayed the Crandors.

Hamlet shot me a hard look. For some reason, he seemed to want the appraisal done in a hurry. "Miz Peregrine, what more do you want? The girl's doing this for nothing. I'm sure that what she'll find is no different from someone else, who'll charge an arm and a leg. If you want my opinion, she's more qualified to do a good job just *because* she's so receptive."

"I *don't* want your opinion," I said.

Ham's neck turned a deep crimson. "Please don't forget that I'm Crandor's grandson. And besides, you invited us here to give advice."

"*I* didn't. Not *you*."

"Then who did?"

"Let's not argue," Elsie said, cutting in. "Come on, Mother, you know this isn't Ham's expertise."

"How should I know that?"

Elsie looked at me and hugged her shoulders. "Come and see what Sophia has discovered," she said.

I narrowed my eyes. "If you'll remember, that's what I asked her in the first place."

"*Please*, Mother."

She propelled me over to the straight-backed Shaker chair, in which I sat reluctantly and where I then busied myself turning up the sleeves of my navy blue silk.

Ham crouched down in front of the canvases and touched the newest, brightest picture with his pinky. The others squatted down around him, deference coating their faces like butter. Sophia grinned at him flirtatiously. She tossed her hair, cut fashionably short as a boy's except for a wedge hanging in one eye, and flicked the light switch twice so that within a moment the room darkened again and the eerie radiation-blue tinge of ultraviolet rays spread finger shadows onto the pictures. One by one, Sophia examined them while she took prodigious notes. She also conferred with Ham, whispering to him behind her cocooned fingers.

"Can we hear, too?" Elsie said after a short time.

Sophia's dark blue eyes regarded the other woman like two hot-tar eddies—nothing much underneath them, I thought, except artful rapacity and, with Elsie, scalding hostility. "You'll get the report soon enough," she said.

Why had Clay brought her?

After a good five pages' worth of penciled notes, she finally flipped the lights on and stood up. "Finished," she announced. "These three paintings are the finest Crandors I've ever seen." She turned to me and smiled brightly. "You're sitting on a gold-mine here, Mrs. Peregrine. Each one of them would fetch half a million at auction, I think. We could name our reserve and still end up with a bidding war."

I grunted, digesting the information. Mosquitoes hitting the windows sounded like grenades exploding from far away. "How do *you* know?" I demanded. This woman was delusional, a liar, or just ignorant. The Crandors in the museums were worth barely half of her estimate—$250,000 apiece, *if* that, and that was a documented fact.

I saw Ham bite his lower lip in the ensuing silence. Clay and Elsie seemed afraid to talk.

I pointed to the painting. "Stick to the facts, please, miss. Only the facts. No opinions, please."

"Well, they're all opinions, now, aren't they?" Ham smiled winningly at me, but I didn't acknowledge him.

Clay looked up. "She didn't mean anything." His voice sounded weak in the high-ceilinged room.

Sophia leaned over a canvas. "Shall I continue?" She looked in my direction, but I leveled my gaze over her head.

"The first one and the second," she said, "Crandor's early piece and his family dinner, are representational, moody, atmospheric, a study in light, the second one with brighter colors."

"That's nothing new," I said.

Sophia tossed her wedge of hair and resumed her appraisal as if she hadn't heard me. "And the third one," she said, "the political piece—Crandor's initials, by the way, are camouflaged on the jacket of one of his subjects, which is typical of him and very clever, I think—is an allegory, extremely well done, in my view, with a subject so powerful and subversive it should *absolutely* hang in a public place."

"I asked you to keep your opinions to yourself."

"Of course." This time she didn't even glance at me. "But the fourth one—that's the one I consider *really* thrilling. Sorry," she said to the ceiling. "The subject is disturbing. It's obviously surreal, again subversive, its message clear in that it is illustrative of undermining or overthrowing power. Irony—that's the thrust behind the last Crandor."

She took a deep breath. "But it's not signed anywhere; it has none of his usual marks—no date, no initials, no message. Which leads me to believe that someone is posing as the master. Maybe someone has interpreted Crandor's style but has gone even further with it. If Crandor had lived, this would probably be his matured style. Possibly an interpretation of a student? You could think of it in the same vein as a sequel to *Gone with the Wind*, perhaps written by a disciple of Margaret Mitchell. Or in the vein of Rubens' later works, painted with the help of one or more of his students." She looked at Clay, who nodded his encouragement. And then at Ham, who was so anxious to hear what she had to say that he couldn't take his eyes off her. And I wondered why.

"To summarize," she said, smiling at Ham—she had obviously misunderstood his avidity for a flirtation—"there's no doubt in my mind that the fourth painting, the disturbing one, was executed long after the others. It's either a magnificent fraud or an original Crandor."

"Of course. We *all* know that," I said.

"But I think the others are original Crandors—they're similar in style to the earlier works represented in the collections. If you don't mind, I'd so much like to bring in a colleague to corroborate my assessment."

"Not on your life," I said. "Didn't Clay explain to you that this painting—all *four* paintings, as a matter of fact—are the property of my family?"

"No one would take them away."

"It's none of your concern."

"Don't you see? She's doing you a favor," Clay said.

I shrugged. I wasn't intimidated by him—or by her.

"Why would someone place the canvases behind the early-period piece in the first place?" Sophia asked, determined, I saw, to ignore our bickering.

My vision blurred, and I could feel the blood beat at my temples. I wanted to tell her to get out.

"Someone took such great care," she went on, "and did it so meticulously, it had to be time-consuming. At the very least, the police, I think, should be called in. There's too much money at stake here."

I stared at her, focusing on the extravagantly thick eyelashes that exaggerated her every blink. "Didn't Clay bring *you* here to answer these questions?"

Clay shook his head. "I brought her here to do the analysis on the paintings, not to solve the mystery."

Ham punched his right fist into his left palm. "See what I mean, Elsie? It's either my grandfather, risen from his watery grave, which is highly unlikely, or a student of his, or a forger, or both: student *and* forger. . . ." He paused. "Your *mother*, I think, is hiding something. Or someone."

I could see Sophia smile.

Elsie stared at him in disbelief. "Don't be an ass."

"Why don't you ask your mother why she objects to sharing the discovery with outside parties? *Objective* parties? Other than those two old men from the Getty. One would think she'd *encourage* our efforts. And, like Sophia said, whoever put those pictures behind the frame needed time." He shrugged, and his well-clad jacket moved up over his shoulders. "A forger? My deceased grandfather? The old men? What difference? Your mother was the only one in the house besides you. And does she not spend most of her time in this room? How could she *not* be implicated?"

"Why would I do that?" I said. My heart was thumping so hard, I thought *heart attack* and began to panic. "Why would I harbor anyone? Help someone to desecrate my painting? For what reason?"

"A good question, Miz Peregrine. Why indeed?"

They all looked at me. Closely. Silently. And for the first time, I understood the power of mob psychology. Even Elsie peered at me, doubt suddenly spreading over her face like a bad case of the chicken pox. Unless it was an act. Her eyebrows met in the middle, I noticed, which was awkwardly apparent when she held a frown such as now.

I stood up. Imperiously, I hoped. "I need some air."

I turned and walked—regally, I hoped—to the door. A nightmare is what my dinner with the Getty experts had turned into, a bad dream from which I couldn't wake up. I felt tears well but stemmed them; I felt like a felon. At the doorway, I forced myself to face my accusers. "I won't defend myself, since we all know it's a ludicrous charge. It's also insulting. Ham, you'll leave immediately; you, too, Clay, and take your lady friend with you."

Never before had I behaved so uncivilly—or felt so distraught. To be accused was unconscionable, but, worse, if Ham was right and my suspicions were confirmed, there was a good chance that my daughter, or Clay, or both—with or without Sophia's help—were indisputable suspects and truly plotting against me. Which I'm sure must have occurred to Hamlet Crandor. Plant the paintings; call in the Getty people. Discover the half-a-million-dollar or more canvases. Collect the money. Live happily ever after. Whoever was the culprit, or culprits, however, hadn't counted on the grandson.

Anger displaced my fear. A fresh feeling for me, but one that didn't much matter right now, because after all this stress, the only thing I *really* needed was to be left alone for a good night's sleep.

Chapter 11

PEDA

I think in smells. So when a couple of cops pounded on our door the next morning, I thought I smelled bologna. Cops at the door with their nightsticks and red cheeks, one with a big beer belly. And their guns. Bologna-sandwich cops, who were neither young nor old, with no memorable features. They weren't hostile, exactly, but they weren't friendly, either. At least not toward my mother, who disliked bologna almost as much as I liked it.

After a while, I could hear the three of them on the patio, their voices shrill, the wind chopping off the ends of each of their words like a sword, so that their sentences—even their questions—sounded square, what I imagined marionettes sounded like—no curves, just up and down, with cutoff endings. Like the wind. Take a breath, blow it out. I stood on my window seat, and, with my nose pressed flat against a high windowpane, I studied them down below, as if they were ants, until I heard the knocker again and wondered who would go for the door.

For a moment I hesitated; then I skipped to the stairwell, where I saw dust bunnies swirling under the big triangle of stained-glass window, the colors of which changed quickly with the light coming through its red, gold, and green wavy panes of glass. Turning once to glance down the stairs, I twirled on my heels and bounded to the bottom, holding my breath like I imagine the wind does. A beautiful wind-woman, I pictured, her cheeks puffed out, her lips puckered, air flowing through her rounded mouth, blowing it out softly when she felt sad, harder when she was happy. Just like me. And I let my breath out good and swift, blowing at the front door before I opened it wide, making a gust, a student of the wind-woman, to see who knocked.

"Morning, Peda." Hamlet bent down and pinched my cheek, and I sprang back, wriggling around him to see who was with him. My grandmother's two art experts talked quietly behind him. I wanted to shout at them, ask them what they wanted, tell them to go away and leave my grandmother alone.

"My mother's on the patio," I said instead, and, peering up through my lashes, whispered, "With two policemen." I pointed toward the back of the house. "My grandmother's still asleep. If you want, I'll get her." I pirouetted like a ballerina.

But Ham caught my shirt, pulling at my puffed sleeve with the elastic that pinched the skin under my arm, and it hurt so much that I knew it would leave red marks. I tried to yank away, hoping he wouldn't tear it.

"Show us out to the patio," he said, and he held me still until I stopped struggling.

I wished I could tell on him. Only the boys in school got treated in this way—the mainland kids who lived in neighborhoods, who trick-or-treated together—lucky them!—who punched each other and bumped their hips together hard until someone stopped them. But this was different. Ham was mean, and I wanted to tell my mother.

I led him, with the old men following, all the way around the house, along an overgrown stone path through higher-than-me azalea bushes. Laurel and myrtle grew to the right, and on our left, full of chattering sparrows, grew a hedge of wild roses, whose thorns tore at our shirts and shorts. Annoyed, the two men held their arms high above their heads, as if they were prisoners, while Hamlet snuck beside me, passing me finally at a jog.

As he squeezed in front of me, he pointed when he saw I was barefoot, then shook his head and guffawed. On the rough ground, pebbles and overturned rocks stuck out. I knew he thought I was crazy, that it was a dumb way to travel, but I loved the feel of old stone under my feet, or warm wood or carpets of grass and beach sand. I hated anything sticky and swerved when I came across a patch of sap fallen from pine needles, which spoiled, especially on stone, the feeling I had in my toes. But I would never tell him how I felt. I believed he was after my mother was all.

On the other side, the water side, the path emptied out onto a bigger path made of large, round but uneven millstones that led down to the beach. Above the millstones was a hexagon-shaped terrace—Clay drew it once to show me the shape—protected by a shallow, crumbling stone wall that faced the Sound. Omum had told me that at one time, in its heyday—her exact words—the landscape was groomed and well maintained, and then it was breathtaking to look at. But now the lawn that grew up around the millstones was full of crabgrass, and weeds choked out many of the tender new shoots of grass. Clay complained he could do only so much on a limited budget. At least he had planted the pines that cut the wind and freed the blackberry-hedged lane in front from messes of poison ivy and sumac. For his efforts, which were never fairly compensated, he said, but due to a lack of funds, Omum said, Omum was grateful. She used to tell Clay and me that she felt looked down upon for having so little money, when her family used to have so much. I don't understand that. Because who cares?

I could hear Omum sighing when we reached the upper ledge of the stone wall. She must have joined the visitors while I was at the front door. And when I drew closer, approaching from the terrace, I could see the bologna policemen, their blue suits bright against the gray fieldstone walls and the uneven pattern of cobblestone floor, in a chummy discussion with the two women: Omum, so combed and perfect to look at even at this hour, had wound around her neck a long, lemony, see-through scarf, which the wind had picked up so that it stood out behind her like a sail. My mom was much taller, much larger—she was always complaining about her big bones—fair-cheeked and oh so healthy. Even from a distance, my mother's good figure was there for everyone to see: in shorts, her long legs, bare to the thighs; her blunt-cut, windy, marmalade-colored hair; her eyes ringed by tiny lines that crinkled when she laughed—or frowned, as she did now, and most other times when she looked at me.

All at once the shrieks and whistles and a 100 percent rush of wings drowned out their talking, and I looked up to see a flock of geese, flying jam-packed together. Below them, a mallard duck, squawking right behind his mate, followed the flock, and all of the birds together beat it like one of my thin black ribbons across the sky. I shaded my eyes to see better, and the flash of a squirrel dashed across the wall in front of me, its tail a pale gray broom, and I waved my hand, imitating the squirrel's speed. The breeze from the Sound was fresh on my cheeks, and I felt good, as if a cool washcloth had brushed up against me.

"Ah, but there you are." My mother's hair was parted on the right side, and honey-blond strands came down almost to her shoulders, showing up the mole by her lips.

I concentrated on it as I climbed the steps onto the patio. I had a sudden ache to lean up against her, and so I did, surprised that she let me. She told me often that I was too old and too big to act babyish.

I peered around her at the big-bellied cop and his partner; both flicked gummy grins at me. Sidestepping me and my mother, they moved in front of Zinger, Horatio, and Hamlet . . . and, like hippos, blocked them from climbing up. I never saw their feet move at all.

"Just who we came to see," said the bigger man. His shiny bald head was covered with a few blond hair-threads, the same color as my mother's.

He grabbed Mr. Guardi to help him maneuver the final step, held him around both elbows, and pulled while the old man gazed at him like an old horse. Mr. Guardi's rumpled clothes looked tired as he did, and there was a sweaty smell—sweet as vanilla—that spilled in whiffs from his body. He was so thin and so light, the big cop practically lifted him off his feet, and the old man's short-sleeved cotton shirt puffed up in the wind away from his ribs like one of those bubbles I like to blow.

The smaller cop faced Ham, who stood with his arms crossed and his fists tucked into his armpits. They looked like two boxers ready to fight.

Sensing my mother tense up, I leaned back and stared up at her. When she looked down at me, she pushed me away so quickly that I felt the damp line where our skin had stuck open up to the air, space widening between us fast as my mother went to stand next to Ham. I glared at Ham then, noticing that his mouth and eyes matched the knotty tree-trunk bump that grew up through the patio floor. A large bottom limb had been cut off, and the old wound looked like a face staring out at me, some living, breathing thing, something like ET or an outer-space creature. I stared from the human face to the face on the tree, thinking about the pickle smell that I identified with Hamlet. Then I slipped my hand into Omum's lily-scented hand and strained to listen to the adult conversation through the whine of the wind.

The policeman was attacking Hamlet, and I grinned. "You were the one; you're the young man, the man the lady over there"—the cop jerked his thumb behind him toward my grandmother—"claims called down to the station. A long-ago murder that never happened? A body that was never found? You're also that man . . . right? Who says that lady over there"— he jerked his thumb backward again—"is trying to pull off a multimillion-dollar art scam, a heist with mystery partners? Who're they? The dead man one of them?" He laughed, and his eyes closed, and he bent over and put his hands on his hips, this bologna sandwich of a man with the carrot-red hair and the grinning, wet mouth. Looked back over his shoulder and jerked his thumb again, then his whole hand, at Omum. "Her? Winter Peregrine? You must be kidding." He opened his mouth and threw his head back. His whole body shook. Looked at the other cop, who stood next to stooped old Horatio Guardi, and slapped his thigh.

And it flashed across my mind that people really *did* look down on my grandmother, just like she had said.

The other cop, the big guy, wiped his eyes where his tears had trickled. He smirked, but no sound came out. Bottled up his feelings, I guess, just like I do. Then both men turned toward Omum and smiled at her in a funny way.

She wore a smile of her own that was twisted, and she wrapped her sweater tight around her. After that, she squeezed my hand and I squeezed it back.

"It's ridiculous," she said. "Why would *I* know anything about Crandor, who's been dead these thirty years or more? I don't even *know* for how long." She sucked in her breath with a whistling sound, which I tried to imitate through my two front teeth. "For goodness' sake, before the Getty men came, I knew *nothing* about the artist." She dropped my hand and gave me a sort of helpless look. "As for the paintings they found behind my painting, I have no *idea* how they got there. I wish I did." She spoke softly, and, because the wind was all-the-time and annoying, the group formed around her to better hear her.

"And you?" Red gestured toward Zinger, who stared hard at his friend, Mr. Guardi. "You two. Do you know what this young man is talking about?"

Zinger shook his head, and the baggy, soft part under his chin shook. He reached for a napkin from the service cart, then grabbed a blueberry muffin off the moon-blue-decorated fish dish that held the breakfast rolls.

"The new paintings we found are frauds, I believe, and my friend here thinks the same thing." He nodded at Droopy—that's the name my mother and my grandmother used for Mr. Guardi. "And the framed painting isn't one of Crandor's best works anyway, not compared with his other ones. The museum pieces, that is. You've seen them, I take it?" His lips were dry and stuck together as he spoke. He took a large bite of the muffin, chewed it, and closed his eyes. "You *have* seen them, haven't you?"

Zinger spoke to the cops as if they were stupid men. And, to make matters worse, when his head went from the big cop's face to Red's, spit dribbled down his chin. His scalp shone in the sun, the leftover hair around his ears thick and as mossy-looking as mold on the jetty.

I tugged on Omum's hand and pointed to Zinger's head. "Look at his hair," I whispered. By turning from one cop to the other, he had given the heave-ho to his toupee, which now hung over one side of his head more than the other. Staring at the make-believe hair, I giggled, and Zinger, his mouth full of blueberry muffin, slid the wig back to its rightful place on his head, as if it happened all the time. As if he didn't care what people saw or what they thought.

One cop looked at the other. They raised their eyebrows, and both of them put their hands on their hips. Pooped by now, I guess, wanting to be gone from this place. They stared out at the water, both of them bewitched, it looked, by the dots of sun dancing on the waves.

"Can't say as we have," the bigger one said. "Seen any of Crandor's museum pieces."

"There's no proof, you know," the second cop threw in. "All your stories, they're so different. There's no body, so there's no murder."

"What about Simon's affidavit that I read to your superior over the phone—his letter that I showed you?" Ham said. "My grandfather's ill-fated predictions came true, didn't they? For *some* people"—he looked over at Guardi and Zinger—"Simon Crandor *conveniently* drowned . . . and at an opportune time. That's got to account for something, don't you think? And now *some* people have a brilliant double-cross going. Unveiling paintings by my grandfather that mysteriously show up years after his death."

"*Ennhh . . .*" Dismissing him with a nasal grunt, the smaller cop waved his hands around. "Somebody's playing tricks. Probably one of you. I don't wanna get mixed up in your dogfights. It's not for the police department. Or for the taxpayer. Why'n you just hire yourself a crackerjack lawyer and a PI who'll get to the bottom of this mess for you? Each one of you can hire one of your own." His partner, the big guy, doubled up, but he held his belly so that I couldn't see it shake. Still bent over, he eyed his partner as if to say, *Let's go.*

Hamlet gave the cop one of his if-looks-could-kill stares, but it was Omum's frightened-mouse expression that was scary to me. Once, in a hall closet, I had found a mother mouse with her babies, the mother mouse's eyes so terrified that they had made mine feel hot and crumbly. Omum reminded me of that mouse now, which made my stomach turn upside down.

"Don't you think I've already thought of that?" Hamlet demanded. "*First*, I want you to do your job. Investigate. *That's* the purpose of my tax dollars." He nudged the big guy's arm. "What if the paintings found behind the framed piece *are* originals? What about the rest of the papers? The ones those fellows took. What's in—"

Red interrupted. "Now you're accusing those two of stealing papers? You got a problem, pal." He laughed, but there wasn't a smile in his voice.

"What's in them?" Hamlet said. "What are they hiding?" He looked directly back at Red.

Ham stood straight and tall and handsome, and I watched my mother watch him, study the shiny-dark, curling hair tufts that flowed from the wide-open V of his white shirt, the rolled-up khaki trousers that reached almost to his knees. He looked like a movie star—probably did it on purpose.

Red motioned toward a patio chair. "May I sit?"

Omum nodded and pulled out another chair so that she could sit beside him. I stood behind her like her guard, holding on to the back of her chair.

"We'll get to your papers—don't worry," the cop said. He tipped his chair back. "But there's still no real proof of a murder plot—apart from your word on it. Anyone can write a letter, accuse someone. And who's to say whether the letter's for real— maybe *you* wrote it—and anyway, what difference does it make? Why dredge up all this stuff after so long? Just because some paintings were found?"

Hamlet stood over the cop. His cheeks turned purplish-red, and he glared at the man. "I told your superior everything I know. I read the affidavit to him over the phone—and I told him I'd have it tested to prove its authenticity. What *more* can I do?" He rubbed his forehead. "*Someone* planted those paintings behind the other one. *Someone* wrote a packet of letters. *Someone* placed that affidavit there. Last night we had another expert, a local dealer, who appraised the works independently. As I suspected, she disagrees with these two gentleman." He gestured toward Horatio and Zinger. "She thinks the new pieces are valuable, even more so than the older painting, and furthermore, she thinks that *all* of them are genuine Crandors, except, possibly, for the last. We're talking about a lot of money if these pieces are originals." He cleared his throat. "I want you to *do* something about it."

The big cop turned to him and scratched his ear. "First," he said, "in a court of law, no one can conclusively prove a paper's age or authenticity. They can come close, but it's never definitive. You already knew that, though. . . ." He paused then, as if he were thinking, but I knew he was watching Ham's face for his reaction. "Because Detective Todd told you that on the phone, didn't he? Second, forgeries or originals—there's a big difference. Shouldn't you do your homework before you go any further?"

After a short silence, Ham said carefully, "In this market, Crandor's paintings—even the copies—bring high prices. The old lady here claims she doesn't know anything, yet she allowed *them*"—he shot a hard look at Zinger and Mr. Guardi—"to do an appraisal on the site. It's her house, remember? And as for the "experts"? Well, they took incriminating papers we have yet to see. Never mind the authenticity. Also, *they* were the ones who, coincidentally, *discovered* the canvases located behind the painting." Ham took a deep breath, talked faster, and raised his voice. "Plus, this lady *had* to have given the person or persons access to the Crandor painting hanging in her conservatory. I'm told she often sleeps in there. You realize, I suppose, that if she sells the paintings she'll be worth megabucks." His eyes glittered. "*I'm* Crandor's direct heir. I'll warrant she didn't know I existed when she—and whoever—initiated this scheme." He waved first at Omum and then at Mr. Guardi. "Consequently, if you don't want to listen to me, it'll be *you* talking to my lawyer."

The big cop sidled over to Hamlet. "Is that a threat?" His lip twitched. "What made *you* come to Connecticut in the first place?"

"To see one of my grandfather's paintings. Besides this one, only a few are in private collections."

"Who contacted you?"

"Them." He threw his chin toward Zinger and Droopy.

"For what purpose?"

He shrugged. "That's the only thing that doesn't fit. Maybe to throw suspicion away from themselves? I don't know."

"I understand you told Mrs. Peregrine, and her daughter, too, that you had never met these men before." He leaned in to Hamlet's face.

"I never *had* met them before. Not until we rang this lady's doorbell."

At this point, I think Red reminded himself that there *was* no doorbell, because he scribbled something in his notebook.

The big cop turned to face Horatio Guardi. "Where are the letters?" he asked. I guess he was starting to believe Ham.

Horatio Guardi swayed against the wind and caught hold of the back of a chair. "In the hotel room," he replied. "Haven't actually had a chance to read them yet."

"*Bullshit*," Hamlet said. "You know very well what's in them." He flung out his fist, and my mother flinched.

Red looked at Ham. "Why would he lie? What does he have to gain?"

"Didn't you hear what I've been telling you? Has the wind made you deaf?"

"As soon as I get a search warrant, Mr. Guardi will *have* to give up those letters. So what's the point of lying now?" Red smiled down at me, but I stared into the dirt cracks of the slate floor, which were covered with tiny flowers, and imagined the life popping below the dirt.

In the honeysuckle, which almost covers the bathroom window, I could see out of the corner of my eye bees somersault from the leaves onto the flower petals below them, then dive into the weeds underneath the bushes. I willed myself away, too, so that I wouldn't have to smile back. Zinging toward the back of the honeysuckle with the bees—into the branches that hug the stone frame that surrounds the window sash—I disappeared from his view, so that he glanced away, finally snagging Hamlet with his fly-biting stare. I sucked in my spit then, pretending I was Ham, who stared right back at him, daring him to look down.

"Mark my words," Hamlet said, "those men will do something to destroy the letters. Remember what I said." He looked over at my mother, who had moved back, away from the shelter of his arm. "Write it down, Elsie, okay? With the date."

My mother frowned and twisted her hands. I had noticed that her neck reddened when she was panicky, and now it looked as bright as a crab's claw. "You accused my mother," she said. "That's a stretch, don't you think?"

"My brother will be here tomorrow. Maybe you'll all listen to reason then. Maybe if there are *two* of us to prove there's something going on here. *Somebody* placed those paintings, very carefully, one behind the other behind the other . . ."

I stood up then because my butt was numb from sitting, where I had slid, cross-legged, onto the slate. Circulation returned, prickling. I concentrated on the bumblebees, until Ham took out a picture of Old Man Crandor, who wasn't old at all in the photo.

"Here . . ." He handed the black-and-white snapshot to

the big cop, who waved it under the nose of his partner and then threw it on the table.

"Recognize him?" The big cop laughed, but he looked mad. He had wanted to leave, and now he couldn't. "For a dead guy, he looks pretty good."

It was only a picture of a man in a formal suit, his tie perfect, his dark hair back-combed perfectly, the stripe of his jacket perfect, too, but the man stared at the sky, away from the camera and his dusty, long-ago world. . . . I guess he was someone who didn't want his picture taken.

"Well, would you look at that?" Red bowed over the snapshot so that his blue body covered the small, square photograph.

Its scalloped edges flickered in the wind, and the paper was lifted for a moment, when I, unable to hold back my curiosity, peered over it as the cop backed away. I leaned my chest on the table and rested my chin on my hands an inch away from the photo, so that I was eye level with it. I breathed on it until the glossy texture glazed over with the glare of the sun, and I saw nothing except a small, white, shiny square. I looked up and rubbed my eyes. Nothing there. Looked again and held my breath this time. Did a double take, because hadn't I seen the man in the picture before? In a movie, maybe? It was the way he rested on his hip that made me sure. With the midday sun beating down on me where I stood in the middle of the patio, I felt funny. I glanced over at the bumblebees—one of them hit the window and fell, its bullet body parachuting through space— then darted a look at the experts, first one and then the other, though I was careful not to meet their eyes. Still, the sight of Zinger's shredded napkin, balled up and escaping in pieces from his hand, propelled me, like the bees, like a plane, like Superman, from the table.

I bolted off the patio, zigzagging around the house, until I came to a large azalea bush, scrambled underneath it, and hid under the chopped and broken branches, which I then discovered were wilting in heaps under the outergrowth. In my refuge, I rescued beside me the still-warm body of a bird. Picking it up, though, I found it was lifeless, a seagull, its glassy eye with the look of what I imagined to be a soul. I hunkered down then, cradling the floppy body in my lap like Omum had held her teacup. And I let my tears run in streams into the hole where I dug its grave.

Chapter 12

WINTER

*T*he evening after our confrontation with the police department, a thin haze of mist hung over the water, rendering more distant objects indistinct—Elsie's old wooden boat was half hidden—and the night sky seemed to take forever to appear. For a long time I stood on the terrace in the failing light, which seemed to cast a bluish shadow over my eyes. Into the setting sun I examined, with a sense of pride, my island, set off here on the western side by a sandy but rock-strewn beach, which we tried in vain to sweep clean each spring. Beyond the beach, visible at low tide, was shale rock mottled with oily brown barnacles, which now, at high tide, I wasn't able to see but imagined. These rock outcroppings grew more abundant and more craggy as they moved northeast to the last point of the island, where a blunt-shaped bluff—its screen of wind-bent pine gripping its side as if to stop the earth from tumbling into the water—stuck out into the sea in the manner of a square-bowed Boston Whaler.

From this point it was easy to see how our minuscule island, like a small finger, mirrored the large peninsula (of the same shape), located east of and directly opposite us. Divided by a narrow waterway, we were slung together by fill and by my grandfather's antiquated bridge, which had been rebuilt—not well—time and time again. To peninsula residents, I knew it was at this tip (the arrow-shaped bluff) that my island appeared especially impressive, even comforting. Because where Peregrine Island sits at the mouth of the harbor—and because of its shape—it acts as a beacon for these mainlanders, people of the same ilk as those cops.

Straining my eyesight against the fading daylight—straining to erase their image—I felt better when I glimpsed the nebulous outline of our man-made breakwall, which lies like a long, low cannon along the horizon. On *this* side, I thought cavalierly, there was nothing between it and the Sound, and then the vastness of the Atlantic Ocean, beyond which lay Europe.

I lowered my hands to my side as the wind whipped at my ears and shivered up my skirt, and for a moment the feeling was exhilarating and I was able to forget Hamlet's accusations. Close to where I stood, I noticed two trees tangled together, as if embracing, and I even felt an unexpected surge of gladness. I inhaled the salt air deep into my lungs and exhaled slowly while I watched the sun, which disappeared behind a cloud. The sea then went dark, in a vast bruise, and the bank of clouds seemed oddly but ominously reminiscent of a nuclear explosion. I shook myself to clear my hallucination and decided to go inside. Behind me, the pigeons on the window ledge softly ruffled their feathers when I left, their seeing eyes like blood-red berries against the beveled green-glass windowpanes.

At the door I met Clay but was loath to talk to him when I glimpsed his eyes, gray and darkly lashed, and then his fingernails, which were permanently ringed with black, despite his many manicures to clean out the earth he worked with. I rushed up the back stairway to the comfort of my bedroom and my evening bath. His eyes, you see, reminded me of our past companionable evenings, but, I knew now, those were no more available to me, and those fingernails of his reminded me too well of his new "roommate." Under her clear nail polish, I had seen, as on Clay, thin crescents of dirt, the permanent variety that you notice on kids and mechanics; I wondered if she had worked with Clay at my house, and, if so, how often. I experienced a flash of hot, surprising jealousy, swept my fingers across my face, and winced at the deep, dry age lines so obvious to me now, trying at the same time to wipe out the remembered smell of freshly cut leaves that Clay usually brought along on his person, the outdoors, that clung to his clothes and filled a room. What a contradiction he was—so deliberately urbane yet so outdoorsy—and, despite his fastidious habits, he had dirt-encrusted nails. It was habit, after all, that had brought him here now, tethered to his daily routine, and punctual, as usual. Unfortunately for him, he had missed dinner. Elsie and I had eaten early. Well, Elsie would just have to take care of him for a while, or tell him to leave, as had been her wont recently. He should go back to the meddling Sophia, his alleged art connoisseur.

A bath—that was the answer. The steam of a hot bath would halt my thoughts. No more visions of Sophia and her extraordinary posture—knees cocked, chest high, hips tilted—which had made all the men lose their reason. I turned on the hot-water faucet full blast, hoping the steam would also put to rest my fears about Elsie, who was consorting with the man who had accused me, her own mother, of preposterous crimes. I pictured him flicking his fingers up against her nose, and I took a few deep breaths, which I then blew out slowly. Even the policemen who had known me for years had searched my face, my very words, for hidden truths after Ham had finished with me.

Remembering their expressions made my throat clot, made me feel ashamed. They had talked about me in the third person, as if I weren't there. I wanted to cry, and I held my face up to the water spigot, and that was when I heard the scream. Only the first, it turned out, of the night.

Helll . . . p! and through the windowpanes, *Hellllp!* and then again, but fainter, *Hell . . . ll . . . p!*

And then it stopped and the silence weighed me down so that I collapsed on the coolness of the bathroom tile, my arms wrapped around the slick, wet bathtub. I could taste fear in the back of my throat, feel its weight on my slack limbs . . . and the helplessness paralyzed me. I lay there, for how long I don't remember, swaddled in a great towel like a papoose. I kept thinking I was dreaming my life, while my heart beat in hurtful bursts. Eventually, in the thick white air of the steamy bathroom, I disrobed and crawled into the tub, where I lay until the soles of my thumbs and fingers wrinkled in the fashion of cooked morels.

Helll . . . p!

I flew out of the tub when the scream hit my consciousness again, grabbed the bath towel from the floor, and ran to Peda's room, where sound-asleep Peda lay blanketed in the dark heat. Wet and dripping, I stood over her, feeling like a fool. Maybe the policemen were right. Maybe I *had* lost my mind. Or was in the process of doing so. I massaged my temples with little circular motions, as if rubbing away a bad dream.

And then: *Helll . . . p!*

Very faintly I heard the scream again, but Peda didn't budge. Was I the only one to hear this noise? As I sensed that the screams came in threes, I waited, holding my breath.

When none came, with relief I exhaled and slumped to the floor, where again I wrapped myself in the oversize talcum-white towel. I leaned over to examine my granddaughter's sleeping profile. It came to me that the sound of her voice suggested daffodils, unlike her mother's sarcastic drawl, heard in remarks usually made at my expense. I knew, of course, that Elsie bolstered herself with her attitude of confrontation, a false bravura that leaked from her like oil or a bad odor. In fact, I felt sorry for my daughter. Over the years she had given up her favorite hobby because neither I nor Peda would accompany her on her excursions. From panic? What?

Helll . . . p!

This time the scream was so faint, I wondered if I had imagined the sound. I tried to ignore it and went on with my examination of Peda's sleeping cheek, jaw, forehead—her slight form under the summer blanket. Such a gentle creature. She didn't like to kill living things—worms or fish, it didn't matter; after two or three attempts at a fishing expedition, she had hidden when she'd seen Elsie with her tackle box and creel. But the sport of fishing meant so much to my daughter that she couldn't understand Peda's aversion. Elsie loved to catch bluefish and bass, outwit them with her hook, then reel them in bucking, giving them no slack but keeping them taut on her line, the art of which she had learned from her father when she was about Peda's age. "The good times," she called them, her favorite childhood memory. With him. *Only* with him.

She wanted to know why I wouldn't talk about him, about *our* times together. I remembered Daniel, all right, but I refused to talk about him with her, because at the end, just before our divorce, even my very essence repelled him. In bed he would actually move away from me, away from my indented pillow if I had gone to wash up, and there was a look on his face if I peeked out, of repugnance, as if I were disgusting. I put my finger to Peda's cheek, drew it back quickly, with a guilty flush, and put my fingers up to my own instead, discovering to my horror that it was slick with tears.

I'd be brave, I finally decided. Search the outdoors for the culprit who screamed, who had dared to land on my island to scare me. But I felt my will weaken on my way to find my clothes, as I conjured up scarred, blank-eyed faces of robbers, rapists, and murderers. I tiptoed down the darkened hall. Where *was* everyone?

Making my way down the stairs, I held on to the banister with my sweat-slick palms, one hand after the other, like climbing down a rope, and I hugged the wall with my body. In the kitchen I turned on the outside lights. Long rectangles of moonlight mixed with the lights, fell through the windows onto the tabletop, and were then swept away by windblown branches, which reappeared, then were swept away again—mood-ripe, I imagined, for a murder scene. Scared to step outside, I stood in the doorway, hoping that Elsie would come, and watched the shifting patterns in the same way I watched the waves break on the beach.

When no one appeared, I stepped onto the terrace. Looking up, I was astonished to find that the night sky was choked with stars, which fanned out into the milkier sky over the water. Here and there, luminous clouds hung in patches, a translucent white against the deep purplish-blue of the firmament. A beautiful tableau, I thought, certainly not a conducive backdrop for a *Friday the 13th* movie. I sighed, forced myself to relax, and deliberately strolled along the perimeter of the stone wall. Looking toward the Sound, I saw nothing, because the water lay so still, despite the wind gusts, which, to be truthful, I found a bit disturbing. Then a sudden splash, and I started, and stared at the circles from the splash that expanded until they became too distant to see. My eyes teared from the strain, and I rubbed at them, looked up again, and was nonplused to see a small fire, which sputtered and whose flames occasionally danced when the wind rose.

Without thinking—for I really believe by this time I was beyond all that—I moved toward it on the dark path of round millstones, and the moonlight made a feathery pattern all around me. No flashlight led my way, just the beacon of dancing fire and the moonlight. And then, halfway down the path to the Sound, that sudden stillness again, and I promise I felt a change in the atmosphere, as sharp and definite as a darkening of sunlit air, and I knew with utter certainty that someone was out there.

Still, what if I was imagining everything? What if the screams were merely a figment of my imagination? If Jake and Scarecrow were figments of Peda's imagination, and now mine as well? I wasn't a child; I didn't have that luxury. I turned around on the path, consumed by a feeling of dread. After all, for years I had slept fitfully, shallowly, while during the day I found myself hitting pockets of empty time that would send my spirits plummeting and my fantasies soaring. Maybe this Getty thing had finally finished me off. Or, worse, maybe someone was deliberately trying to scare me, trying to *make* me lose my mind. I felt tears prick my eyes.

Hell . . . p! And again: *Hell . . . p!*

The screams this time were so close to me and so close together and so tortured and piercing that I could actually smell the bitter, brackish odor of my fright. The fine hairs stood up at the nape of my neck, and I trembled uncontrollably. For a second I remained stationary, glanced around at the fire that I was sure still flickered by the sea, and then I started to run, clumsily at first, and then with the speed of Pegasus. Later, I remember thinking that the all-consuming scream had torn a rift in the clouds, so that the moon burned, ringed by a moonbow, its sphere softened, I suppose now, by the humidity in the air.

Did I sleep that night? I don't think so. And, in the morning, pictures of the night before were stapled on my brain and they tailed after me, contaminating my day. I also know that the black-and-blue circles under my eyes stamped my agony like tattoos for all to see.

Chapter 13

ELSIE

~

*I*n the morning, Winter was in a state of shock. And for the first time in my life, I was really worried about her. After breakfast, I watched her right the painting and balance it against the fireplace wall, then pull up the straight-backed Shaker chair, on which she sat silently erect. Then she proceeded to study the painting. For hours. At noon she still sat in the same place, and she still trembled, as if, she claimed, she were a miniature, shaved dog stuck fast beneath a frigid snow. *Jesus Christ—what a thing to say.*

"We *all* heard the screams," I assured her at breakfast.

"Peda didn't," she said sharply.

"So what?" I answered placidly. "It was probably just an animal, a deer that got stuck on a reef and maybe hurt itself."

"You couldn't have heard it . . . then, because you know perfectly well that a deer doesn't scream. It was a cry for help; it sounded human"—there was a manic glint in her eye—"as if someone were being tortured."

"Don't tell me what I didn't hear," I said, trying to sound normal, "I *did* hear it. Maybe not as loud as you, but I know I heard a scream or two."

My mother let out a sigh, of relief, I hoped, but she continued to argue, suspicious, I guess, that I was lying.

"Impossible," she said. "And there were many more screams than two."

I gritted my teeth. "Have it your way. Someone was being mutilated. That's it, isn't it? What you want to believe. Right?" I glowered at her as she got up to clear away the dishes, fighting the urge not to gnaw on a piece of hair that I wound tightly around my finger, a childhood habit I couldn't get rid of.

I stared at Winter and remembered fighting breakfasts from the past, my father's mocking stare, my mother's neurotic, pinched mouth, when she looked as if she had eaten too many prunes. There were some days, worse than others, when I vomited up her eggs at the school bus stop across the bridge. Hid the putrid pile beneath the reeking garbage I dumped out of a metal can. Kicked it then, hard as I could, hurting my toe once, so that for a week I limped.

I turned to stack the butter on the bread plate and caught my mother moistening a fingertip with her little pink tongue and smoothing a scant eyebrow. I wanted to smack her smug face, rub the prissiness out of her.

Later, facing my mother as she sat on her straight-backed chair, my patience stretched, guilt-ridden and worried about her state of mind, I snapped, "Ham's coming over."

"Of course."

"Don't be sarcastic," I said.

She blinked at me. "I'm not." Then she gave me a weird smile. "I could throw him out, of course, but I don't suppose I would." Rational all at once, even talkative, Winter acted as though we were having an ordinary conversation. "Since he's related to *him*." She said it reverently, leaned forward, and, with her index finger, touched the well-dressed figure of the young man in the painting. "Although it amazes me that he can take so much time away from his work. *Does* he work?"

"He's a trust-and-estate lawyer."

"That's right, I forgot. I'm forgetting a lot of things these days. Besides, he can't get my paintings. They belong to me, don't they?"

Sometimes the way Winter talked grated on my nerves. But my ears pricked up as I listened to her worshipful reference to the painter. "What did you mean, about *him*? Who?" Maybe she *was* nuts. "The guy in the painting or the painter himself?" I pointed at the canvas.

"Crandor sometimes painted himself into a group of figures. Zinger said he was in love with the beautiful Beatrice, who is also in the picture. There, right there." She touched the profile of the woman with hair as coarse as a horse's tail.

Though Beatrice's image had the same dreamy aura as the other figures—as in a faded, old-fashioned photograph—if you looked carefully, you could make out the bridge of her nose, which was broad, and big, dark eyes that were virtually pupilless, the whites of them startlingly so. But I didn't see anything beautiful about her—handsome, maybe, but certainly not beautiful. It's just that I didn't have the energy to argue.

Winter leaned back and relaxed a little against the wooden slats of the chair. She smiled weakly at me. "I recognized him from Hamlet's photograph."

"That elegant man? Ham will be happy to hear it."

Winter squeezed her arms together, looked mostly at the painting but gave me sideways glances. "I'll wager he already knows it. He's here to solve a mystery that wasn't a mystery, by the way, until he and his friends arrived—and to get something out of this whole mess, but I can't figure out what it is. Except for my paintings, of course . . . and for the money that he's convinced they're worth."

"You think Ham is a con artist?" I stared at her. "Because he accused you? Because he's trying to figure this whole thing out?"

I fell silent when she didn't answer. "Really, Mother," I said after a moment, "you think someone's being tortured on your property, and you think those two Getty men are concealing libelous evidence. Christ, what an imagination."

"Don't you?"

I didn't answer.

"Don't *you* think that Ham is a con artist and that those two men are up to no good? Let's forget your 'deer' for the moment."

"Of course not." I scowled.

Because, deep down, I knew my mother had a point. Why *did* they stick around? What were they after? *Why* was Ham suddenly so interested in a grandfather he had never known? *None* of them had a real claim on my mother's property. Not really, even if Ham kept on about it. Certainly, they could do an appraisal of the newly discovered paintings without staying here indefinitely. And the letters—they had no right to keep them, either. I felt my blood rise. Could taste the heat of my anger, feel it surface with my heartbeat, the *thump, thump* against my breast.

I fixed my gaze on the medieval engraving that hangs on the wall opposite the fireplace. The gabled houses, pitching over cobbled streets above canals, looked so inviting that for a second I wished I could join up with the people who lived in them. Winter leaned toward me and whispered something, her lips—those pursed-pinched-turned-down mother-lips of hers—so close to mine I could feel them shape the air, and I jumped back. Washing lines attached to crooked walls evaporated from my vision as long as it took me to wonder whether I might be as crazy as my mother. Reality was reality, and nothing more. My mother was gaga, *not* me.

"Sleep is altogether impossible for me," I heard her whisper. Her eyes all of a sudden appeared unfocused.

"So go take a nap," I said, standing over her. *Shit.* I was sick of her whining. I wanted her to leave me alone.

I bent over her and grasped her arm. "Come on, I'll help you."

She's an old woman, I thought, as we made our way to the chaise. I could smell her breath and turned my head away while I propelled her, supporting almost her entire weight.

At the chaise, my mother, the old woman, lay down with a sigh and looked up at me gratefully, so that for a split second I experienced a stab of guilt so strong I almost keeled over. It brought tears to my eyes. When I see caged animals, I feel the same sort of complicity and shame. *How stupid.* I stuck my chin out defiantly, cleared my throat, and backed up, determined to chuck my maudlin sentiments as I walked out of the room.

Consequently, by the time I crossed the hall, my thoughts had already skipped to the hot but headstrong Hamlet, whose knock I expected at any moment. I hoped he wouldn't bring the old men with him this time, hoped that their analysis of the new works was done with, whimsically also hoped that by now they had shown him *all* the letters to his satisfaction, so that his objectionable questioning—along with my own misgivings—could be permanently put to rest.

In the kitchen, while I was beginning to make tea, my eyes followed a finger's width of sun along the windowsill that advanced to an entire wall painted in gold, in the middle of which stood Hamlet, who, already, to my surprise, waited for me. *Who let him*

in? He looked like a mannequin, silent and stiff. It was as if he hardly breathed. As if he weren't real, either.

I felt my pulse race. Although Ham was conceited and a braggart, although he had accused my mother and was here under false pretenses—an accusation I couldn't prove, yet it was a gut feeling and one I couldn't shake—he was *very* attractive, and I was tired of my own sharp tongue. I was lonely. I stared at him and noticed self-consciously that the way he looked at me was as intimate as a touch. . . . And I felt the heat in my cheeks turn to sweat, which I wiped with the back of my sleeve, but the palpitations—I put my hand to my chest—those I couldn't rub out.

"How did you get in?" I handed him a glass of iced tea.

He looked at the windowsill with its jar of fresh wildflowers, where rain had seeped in so that the wood appeared damp; it had also buckled, I noticed, where the paint had peeled. Turning to me, he said, "I pushed the door . . . and it just opened. I knocked first, but no one answered; I even searched for a key under the flowerpot." He swept invisible crumbs from the counter. "The one with the red geraniums and alyssum."

Maybe I had been too rough on him. Not many men knew the names of flowers. "Why didn't you come around to the back?" I tilted my head at the screen door. "That's the door we usually use."

His eyes rested on the crevice between my breasts. X-ray vision through my shirt? He drained his glass. "Come over here," he said, and grabbed me by my waist, bringing me so close to him that the length of our bodies touched completely. Like interlocking pieces of a jigsaw puzzle. Looking down at me, his eyes on mine, he tracked the contour of my jaw with his thumb, then ran his forefinger over my lips while with the other hand he caressed my inner arms.

I shuddered and turned away, smelled the sharp odor of my own sweat and felt prickled and remarkably tuned low below the waist. *What am I doing?* I went to the sink and splashed cold water over my face. "Want more tea?" I tried to sound noncommittal.

Ham shook his head and moved back to the window, where he peered out at the Sound. "I wanted to tell you that my brother arrived last night. Thought he'd come over with the two men." He lifted his shoulders. "It's okay, isn't it?"

"If I say no, how can you stop him now?"

He just looked at me. Didn't see the humor in the situation.

"Anyway," I said, "I thought you were kidding yesterday. What is this, trumpeting for the troops? Strength in numbers and all that?"

"You could call it that." He leaned over the sink and watched a boat, progressing, with the sun gleaming on her upswept prow.

From where I stood, the boat looked winged. "Look at that," I said.

He didn't seem to care. Because when he turned around, his expression was unexpectedly hostile. "I told you, didn't I? It wasn't a joke. Those two men have incriminating letters written by my grandfather; I have an affidavit from him, which you read; your mother has three new paintings, presumably by him. *Something* is going on. *Someone* is impersonating Simon Crandor."

"Don't start again."

He stepped away from the sink. "*Someone* is trying to make a bundle off my grandfather. Probably will, too."

"You *accused* my mother," I said in a low voice.

"Yeah, well, are you so naive? Maybe it's her; maybe it's not. But I'd be surprised if whoever it is doesn't plan to bring out *more* works they claim are Crandor's and sign them fraudulently. I'd like in on the action . . . wouldn't you? Damn smart idea—whoever it is." He looked at me from under his eyebrows. "You can't discount anyone, you know. Including your mother.

More likely it's Clay, though. That Sophia talks up a big game. Claims the pieces are priceless. Makes sense, doesn't it? Clay certainly had access to the painting."

"Why did you put my mother through all that? With the police?"

"I didn't think it would hurt. Thought it would smoke out the guilty party."

He shrugged again, started toward me, to put his arm around my shoulder, but I backed away from him into the counter, put my hand up to steady myself, and inadvertently swept a glass onto the linoleum, where it shattered.

I ignored it and, unblinking, held his eye. "What if the cops suspect her after your charges? What if they actually *believe* you?"

"That's not likely—even if she *was* an accomplice."

"Maybe I'm involved, too," I sneered.

"Maybe," he said seriously, and peered down at me with his hot, hostile stare. "Are you?"

I bent down to pick up the larger pieces of broken glass, didn't bother to answer him. "Tell me," I said as I straightened, "why did you let me in on your theory?" I went to the broom closet to find the small broom and dustbin.

He grinned at me. His hand on his hip.

I wanted to throw the trash can at him.

"You want to find out the answers just as much as I do. Unless you already know them. Besides, you like me."

I faced him. "If it *is* me, why wouldn't you turn me in?"

"Would *you*? Turn *me* in? Anyway, it would be your word against mine."

"That depends on who's involved."

"I don't think so. One of them, at least, is sure to be someone you know, someone you trust and have feelings for."

"Not the old men?"

"Nah, not them. They're just the messengers. The men

responsible, originally, for my grandfather's watery grave. But now?" He threw his hands up. "Although, ten to one they're tangled up in this. Maybe they're being blackmailed . . . in return for their help in circulating the new paintings. In return for verifying that the paintings are genuine Crandors."

"But both Zinger and Guardi said they're not; they think they're fakes."

"Remember, though—they left the door open. How much says they'll have a change of heart? They can't be too quick to corroborate the existence of fresh Crandors; it wouldn't be smart—especially when folks figure out their past connection to the artist."

"Oh." I was speechless. He had it all figured out. He argued a case the way a stonemason lays stones, one point at a time, perfectly placed and carefully cemented in the wall of his argument. I couldn't tell my mother, who wouldn't understand in any case.

A knock at the front door interrupted our conversation—thankfully—and I hoisted myself up off the floor. "Get it, will you, Sherlock? If it's Mr. Watson, bring him around to the back door; I need to clean up the glass." I pushed him at the swinging door.

But with a smirk, he reached over and touched my hand. "I've brought you into my confidence"—he grasped my wrist and manacled it—"haven't I?" he said, and whipped me around so that only inches separated us. "As a sign of my good intentions. Promise me now that you'll bring me into yours." He dropped my hand then, like a hot coal, and with his elbow he pushed the door open. "I'm even introducing you to my family," he said over his shoulder. And, as he sauntered out, the brash son of a bitch had the effrontery to wink at me.

Chapter 14

ELSIE

~

*H*aving swept up the glass, I was peeling and cutting carrots and potatoes in the sink, when Hamlet, followed by the two old men, brought his brother around to the screen door. At first when I unlocked the door, I couldn't see the brother. But once it was ajar, the light of the afternoon caught his face and he stood there fully exposed in the shaft of sunlight. At the deep sink where I was working, the sight of him was so startling that, with the razor-sharp paring knife, I sliced my finger clear through to the bone . . . yet I didn't feel anything; I just shook my head, closed my eyes, and sucked on the bloody, gaping wound, expecting that the vision of Robin-Sebastian would disappear when I opened my eyes. Father to Peda, and my lover from countless seasons of the past, just stood there, as shocked as I was, while my dangling finger dripped globules of crimson blood into the sink like gigantic colored raindrops.

"Is this a joke?" I demanded of Hamlet when I finally looked up. I couldn't meet Brother Sebastian's eyes, fearful that it wasn't really him, the Robin of my past, the Robin to whom I had given my life, my love, my soul.

"What are you talking about? Look at you—you're bleeding." Ham came to my side and peered at the wound. "*Badly.* Here, let me help you."

He took up my hand with the hanging finger and held it high so that the bloodletting would cease. "It's too far gone; you'll need a tourniquet. Seb, hand me that dishcloth. Come on, now, quick—she'll go into shock."

The three men clustered around Ham and me while Ham tried to stop the blood flow. Zinger had turned so pale I thought he would faint, and I nodded to Ham, who ordered Droopy, that stooped old man, to lead him to a chair.

"She'll need stitches," he said, eyeing the pulsing membrane as if it were a piece of red meat. "We'll take her to the hospital."

I shook my head, stared at Robin, holding his gaze, afraid this time to let it go. Afraid to talk.

"Get her mother," the old man suggested.

"Uh-uh," said Ham. "She'll be no good."

"Here, I'll fix it," Robin said suddenly, and he gently took my hand from his brother and rocked me while he steeped the cloth in cold water, then bound it to my finger, tightly, until the finger, the hand, and the rag were one. The mess was splotchy and stained with blood, and as the water spread the blood, the entire rag turned a dark purplish-red; nevertheless, the wound was bound and clean for the time being.

I stared at it, wondering why I felt no pain, only a mild curiosity at the situation, as well as a kind of detached amusement. *Brothers?* Hamlet? Sebastian? My Robin? As if waking from a deep sleep, I slumped against Robin's chest, fitting my head under his chin, a position in which I felt at home. I knew that he could feel my weight settle into him in the same way. And, dizzy but thoughtful, I reflected that my Robin secret had nagged at me for years. Peda didn't know who her father was. Nor did my mother know the identity of Peda's paternity. Apparently, neither did I. . . . I wanted to laugh but felt disoriented. Maybe without my secret, I thought bitterly—and tried to move my head from Robin's shoulder, but it felt cemented there—I would have had an opportunity for peace these past few years. Still, for all my speculations and the hot, dark blood that I could see saturating the bandage, I felt surprisingly relaxed lying on this man's shoulder. I was removed from myself, as if I were coasting above my head, as if I were witnessing something that had already happened . . . and so light were my thoughts that they felt like a memory.

Do I tell them, do I not? Do I tell them, do I not? Do I tell them, do I not? The litany of verse bloated my brain until I could think of nothing else. Stitched up, waiting in the emergency room for papers to be filled out. Not focusing. Not caring, even. *Do I tell them, do I not?*

And much later—I knew that hours had passed when I glanced at the bedside clock next to my bed, but I didn't remember how I had gotten home or even having gotten home—that verse still throbbed in my consciousness like a song that you hear from a distance, a song on a speaker that someone forgot to turn off.

"Do we tell them? What do you think?"

Robin's shadow in the doorway resembled a ghost. No face, no features, no curve to his torso. Wrapped in the black shroud of evening, with no lights to outline his presence, he seemed surreal. Was he really there? I sat up in bed and shook my head to clear it, touched it with my sore wrapped finger, and the shock of the pain was so acute it brought tears to my eyes. Similar in feeling, I imagine, to a dive into icy water. No numbness this time, however. Throbbing pain hit me square in the forehead, with my heartbeat anchored to my finger. Holding my hand perpendicular, I shook it cautiously and squinted into the darkness, willing my longtime, long-ago lover to come closer.

He stayed motionless. Silent. And he stared at me. As if something was wrong with me.

"Come close," I whispered.

After a moment, I felt him move toward me; from his body, the stir of cold air on my finger. He perched on the bed, and I could smell him, but it was a milder body odor than I remembered. Then he lay down next to me. I inched up until our heads were side by side. Wet my lips. Stared up into the dark ceiling. Listened to his breathing. Poked at his side until his fingers found my good ones. And lay there for a good, long, still time . . . as if we were mummies.

Until Winter appeared. "What is *this*?" Her voice was strident, frantic. "Peda will see."

Not *How are you? How's your hand? How are you feeling?* I lifted my hand, and a searing pain shot through my arm, up to my head. Leaving the finger altogether. "Aren't you concerned?" I mumbled.

"Of course. But *him*? You just met him. Can't you control yourself?" She was appalled, horrified by her imagined, probably explicit, scenes of our sexual exploits. "Peda will see," she repeated. "Don't you *care*?"

"He's her father." My voice was slurred but low, controlled, and oddly triumphant. *Do I tell them, do I not?* I guess I never had a choice.

"I beg your pardon?" She came into the room, slowly, like a cringing dog, until she reached the bed and looked down at us.

Robin rose, stood up, and held out his hand. Surreal shadows only in the dark room. The two of them faced each other and looked like daguerreotypes . . . and when Robin introduced himself, I started to laugh.

"You knew about this?" she asked incredulously. As if I had played a dirty joke on her. She backed up. "You *knew* it was him all along? Hamlet's brother? *Another* grandson of Crandor?"

"Hamlet's brother? I guess so. I guess he is. But I didn't know, Mother. I swear, I never knew. This is as big a shock to me as it is to you. Probably more so." I started to cry then—I *never* cried—and it made me feel nauseous.

"Get out," she said to Robin, ordering him. Something she never did—she was far more devious.

I started to protest but couldn't find my voice. I let her sweep Robin-Sebastian Crandor from my room until I could get my bearings. And maybe she was right—to give me time to control myself, she said, to give us time together, to give me time to share with her the story of those missing years that I had spent with Robin, those many years that we had forfeited.

Chapter 15

WINTER

⌒ꝯ

*T*he inherent mystery itself: that elusive brightness that flows out of dreams; the brightness that, when we awaken, is already fading from our minds—I still pursued it almost every morning, in spite of my many hours of tortured sleep. Even when I stirred, the morning after I witnessed the fateful reunion between Elsie and Robin, better known as Sebastian Crandor, I tried to will myself back to sleep, to again recapture the vanished brightness . . . until I remembered with a terrible clarity—which forced me to awaken quickly and irreversibly—the downturn that my life had taken. First, the mystery (and hints of fraud and murder) surrounding my painting; second, the mystery (and hints of torture) surrounding the nocturnal screams that haunted my island; and finally, the mystery (and hints of sordid intrigue) surrounding the troubled reunion of my daughter with Hamlet's brother and Crandor's second grandson.

Concerned for Elsie's health after her hospital visit the evening before, I had walked unobserved into her bedroom, thinking that she might be asleep. Instead, to my dismay, I had found her in bed with Sebastian, the brother of that slick young man Hamlet. They didn't notice me at first, and for a long time I observed them from the doorway. I felt like a voyeur. Elsie seemed younger to me, even vulnerable; her lower lip trembled in such a childish way. The man touched her cheek with his finger, tipped up her chin, and kissed her, and then the trembling stopped. I'm sure he was thinking of the other places he would kiss. He seemed to know what he was doing, seemed, in fact, to know her body well. She caressed her own face while he kissed her, so that nowhere could I see one of her features, just the back of his own light-colored, shaved head, which hovered above her head. And then he turned, not toward me but in my direction. The light, however, was dim, and I hid behind the arched molding of the doorway entrance.

Sebastian was not as handsome as his brother. His face was thinner and, I think, less precisely molded. In fact, to my way of thinking, he was a surprisingly plain young man—though some might have called him exotic, with that scar running down his cheek, and with white-blond hair cut so close to his scalp that I could see patches of his tender pink skin. He had an aquiline nose—patrician, some might say—which I noticed when he licked the corners of my daughter's eyes to clear away her tears, and straight-across brows that gave him a fierce look and accentuated his hollow, high cheekbones. To me, far-fetched as it may seem, he resembled a blond Indian. He bore not the faintest familial resemblance to Hamlet. Yet I was intrigued by his fierceness, which belittled Hamlet's wily and debonair good looks and suggested masculinity, rather than Hamlet's oily smoothness.

When I finally showed myself and heard Elsie's confession—that he was Peda's father—I can't say that I was very surprised. Everything that happened that summer was out of the ordinary. My major concern was how to break the news to Peda. Her reaction to the information that her father had come to stay, at least for a while, might undo her. I hoped I would be able to help her.

My own nerves at the time were taut, my appetite nearly gone because of my nights punctuated by screams. Oh, no, the screams hadn't stopped. Every night, like clockwork, the unearthly wails interrupted my sleep, so that no more did I dream unless I was so exhausted I didn't hear the wailing at all, like in those black hours after my confrontation with Elsie. And my waking hours merged into those wavy, relaxed times that no more were relaxed. Jump-up hours, I called them. My eyes were blurry from lack of sleep. My attention span was gone, my concern for my family, my home, myself rapidly on the wane. . . . What could I do?

I avoided Hamlet when I could, made a point to sidestep the experts, those couple of old men who refused to leave, and for old times' sake put up with Clay's slowly staggered presences—I figured his horror at coming across Peda's father would match my own. Nonetheless, I felt no pity for Clay, for he had brought Sophia into my life. In my house, I had made it clear she wasn't welcome, and in time, I was afraid, she would retaliate.

The weather that day, I remember, matched my mood. It was overcast but blustery; chinks of blue sky showed here and there, like cracks in my thick white bathtub. A tumultuous day of brisk, chill winds, and high, fast-scudding clouds. A relief, however, from the month of rain showers that had made the scrub grass greener than I ever remembered but had forced the rising water of the Sound ever closer to my doorstep. I was sitting on my terrace, enjoying the clouds, which parted briefly every few minutes to allow sunlight to flood the flagstone and fall on my face like a cleansing benediction from my nighttime horrors, when Peda ran up from the beach. *Oh no*, I thought, *I'll have to tell her about Sebastian, the man whom my daughter called Robin.*

"What is it?" I asked, staring at the freckles that covered her thin arms.

And then she began to cry, and the unnatural sound pierced my heart with foreboding. For she rarely cried. Her voice had the teasing, smiling quality she had inherited from my father in his winter months. Tears flooded her eyes, blurred her child's face. I drew her to me, and the wet stained my breast, and I felt uncomfortable, until the sun broke through the clouds, sending out a searching ray, sort of like an arm reaching toward us. Peda was drawing big breaths, and when she took her hands off her face, I saw that mucus was running from her nose.

Her words sounded like hiccups in her mouth. "Jake says the only thing worth saying is what you feel, so I'll just say it: I feel scared." Her teeth were chattering, and I held her away from me.

When my doctor taps my knee with a hard rubber instrument and my knee jerks, I always get a queasy feeling. I felt the same way now as I stared at my granddaughter. I supposed that Elsie had beaten me to it and introduced Peda to her father. Cold turkey. No warm-up speech. Nothing to prepare her.

"It's your father, isn't it?"

She looked at me queerly. Rubbed at her eyes in that little-girl fashion. "No," she said, "it's Jake. He can't get up. His eyes are closed, and he lies there and moans, or did. I don't even know if he recognizes me." She scrubbed at her nose, chewed on her lower lip, and stared at me.

I suppose she felt better after tossing me this bombshell. But I certainly didn't.

I got up, took her sticky-wet hand in mine, and didn't even wince. "Come on," I said.

And we walked down to the beach, stepping from one millstone to the other. Even in her dejected state, Peda skipped over the sun shadows on the stones so that neither her toes nor her heels touched a dark line. We made our way down the curved cliff to the bottom of the rocky beach, where we wound our way in between the green-wet, oily boulders where, I imagined, rats the size of cats lived. Above us, on the wind, gray-white seagulls coasted with their mouths open to the air but the force of the wind stole their cries. One seagull, sometimes two, dove below us into the water to snatch silver-blue flashes of unwary fish who jumped from the water in their swim play—up, down, and as they slapped at the water, the gulls caught them on their upswing. A few of the birds held their prey in their yellow beaks while they soared skyward, the others gulped the fish whole, and we watched the still-live ones slither down the long, strong throats of the seagulls.

Where the water seeped into a particularly wide enclosure of some titanic rocks that enclosed us and our view from the outside world, Peda tugged on my hand and we stopped. Digging her heels into the sand, she made curlicue patterns while she looked around us as if she were lost. The smell of moist fish and seaweed and salt and wet sand was overpowering. Peda turned then, craning her neck this way and that, peeking into the crannies of the rocks that looked to me like crevices. Finally, she inclined her head in a peculiarly grown-up gesture toward a cluster of drier rocks, lighter in color than the rest, higher, too, with sharp points shaped like the turrets of a castle.

We tiptoed in between them, at first sidestepping, and I felt as if she were leading me through a high-walled maze in a medieval courtyard. I closed my eyes and put my arms up to touch the rocks on either side. They were sandy and damp, nothing more, and for a moment I was disappointed. Expecting *what?* Only a few more feet, and then Peda turned back to face me when we reached an opening.

"*There*," she whispered, and pointed to a prone figure stretched out under a slab of rock, both of whose formations looked prehistoric. *The original man*, I thought.

Next to him burned a small fire, which was contained by pebbles. What was *that* for? Certainly not warmth. All I could think of was that it was there to protect against the rats and had to stifle a spontaneous giggle.

Jake, Peda mouthed, and put her fingers to her lips, as if she were afraid I would wake him, even though he seemed to be out cold.

She took my hand, and, like a crab, she edged toward him. I did, too, following her as if I were the crab's mate. What were we afraid of?

"He doesn't see people," she explained. It was as if she had divined my thoughts.

"But you tell me stories about him."

"That's different." She dropped my hand, slid down next to him, and laid her cheek next to his.

He didn't budge.

I was shocked by her easy familiarity with him but stayed silent.

I bent over him. Bent over them both, really. And because the huge boulder shaded the sun, the light was faint in the cave-like area—the fire was worthless—I missed the dog entirely. Scarecrow—I remembered Peda had called him that by name—lay in the far corner of the overhang, behind the man. He growled deep in his throat when he saw my shadow swallow his master. I straightened up quickly. "Will he bite?"

"He's not used to people, either." Peda clapped her hands and tried to whistle, importantly, like a grown-up. The dog ignored her. "Here, boy . . . come here, Scarecrow . . . *Scarecrow, please* . . ." She sounded once again like a small child. The dog sidled over to her, stuck his muzzle into her small hands, and licked at them while she pet his smooth forehead.

Jake didn't move. Not an eyelid, not a muscle. And as I examined him, I could see that he was larger than I had first thought; I was startled, in fact, by his old-man-original-man magnitude. Browned by the weather, wrinkled, too, like fine, supple leather, he seemed to exude health. Strange, for someone who couldn't get up. I wanted to touch him so put a tentative finger on his sleeve, as if he, too, might bite. Peda and the dog watched me carefully, as if I might do him harm. Cut him up or something. The man breathed with a rumbling deep in his chest, and it rose and fell, but his eyes, half-open, stared glassily. I wondered if he was drunk and looked around for evidence. Nothing, except for the beauty of the rock pools by the edge of the sea.

You see, where the waves rise with the tide, the pools are left, full of tiny, transparent crabs, green maidenhair, shellfish, old cans, fresh sand. I moved over, crouched down, and sank my hand in their warm shallows, smelled the sea, the white-light bursts of glory about me, and wondered why I didn't have the urge to run for help. Why, of a sudden, I felt so serene. I looked into the pool of shimmering tiny waves, a reflecting pool, its depths obscured by the image of whoever looked into it. Looked back at Peda and her old man and wondered at the fabric of the man's sleeve. Old linen, I guessed, softened by numerous washings, though it looked none too clean. I rubbed the tips of my fingers to mimic the feel.

"How long have you been here?" Jake's eyes were trained on Peda.

His voice was as calming as the shallows of the pool around us, so I felt no panic when he finally spoke, when he exerted such a hold over my granddaughter. Moved closer to him, in fact, slowly, gently, so as not to startle him with my presence. I even felt a surge of envy, because I had always hoped as a lonely child that I, too, would meet such a friend, someone like Jake. Instead, I used to spend hours in forlorn, deserted places like the basement, all alone, imagining that fearful things would happen. Bombs, that sort of thing. Half a century of glass jars crashing down around me.

Peda wound her small, skinny arms around the old man's neck so that they looked like twine. He patted her with his thick fingers, and it hit me suddenly that they looked strong enough to choke the life from boy, man . . . or little girl. Formidable arched cheekbones under thick tangled brows, and corns, protruding like large eraser bumps on his callused bare toes. These were the first things I noticed about the old man, handsome, some might have said, in a seaman type of way, though the skin from his wrist to his fingertips was mottled with age spots, and it was slack, like skin dangling from a fresh-plucked chicken. I averted my eyes, embarrassed for him, for Peda, too, the way she kept her eyes glued to him in that doglike fashion.

The minutes after he spoke were heavy, the only sound in Jake's place the wind and the single, long cry of a gull. I pulled my attention away from Peda and her old man and looked up to see the bird, but the glare of the sun was too strong, so I gazed instead at my crossed feet in their slender sandals, wondering how I should proceed.

But that calming voice, weak as it was, saved me. "How do people with *killing* pain bear it? I wonder. They go into themselves, I think, immerse themselves in the feeling, to blot out the agony. I've tried that, you know, for pain, and once, I believe, I *just* about had it—not *completely*, though. This time, I collapsed instead. Right here." Wet glistened in the heavy folds of his face. Red and scalding in the wind.

He looked up at me with a self-mocking smile, the light from the fire reflected in his dark-pale eyes. Peda's face, I noticed, mirrored his own distress, and she clung to him. Both of their bodies together—that big old man and the child—as they held each other tight like a pair of sails in a windstorm, while Jake's clothes, made of that linen softness, flapped around him like a vagabond's.

I was afraid to speak.

Jake stared out at the sea. "Was I remiss, I wonder, by neglecting my responsibilities?" he said at last. "Once, long ago, at a sale, I watched close to four hundred people rush at the merchandise—dilated pupils, glazed eyes, they had, like body snatchers. Each person wanted to outbuy the other. That was the beginning, don't you know. Afterward, to communicate with nature became my goal, for, like Beatrice, I was marooned in a place unsuitable to my soul."

Beatrice? My lovely lady from my painting? A wave of dread swept through me. Pure coincidence, I told myself. What could I say to this man? He was raving, sounded like a lunatic. The result of a fever? Perhaps I should snatch Peda out of his arms, leave him to his fever and to his ravings.

But he persisted. "Think how wonderful it might be to no longer matter, Mrs. Peregrine. Think how wonderful it might be to no longer worry, struggle . . . or fail." With his penetrating gaze, he stared at me, and I shivered slightly. The beating of the waves reverberated with the meaning of his words.

My palms were coated with sweat. How could this bum on my beach, flapping clothes and all, whom Peda had dragged me to see, echo my thoughts exactly? My unspoken thoughts that I went to bed by, and even rose by . . .

Yet it bothered me even more that Jake had brought up Beatrice—an unusual name in itself, yet even more unusual when pronounced with the Spanish inflection: *Bay-a-treece.* Because if I was honest with myself, I *knew* that this was no coincidence at all.

Chapter 16

PEDA

⁓

At first I was scared to bring Omum to Jake, but I didn't know what else to do. When I left him on the beach, his eyes were open but staring into the air (though I said they were closed), in the same way as the dead bird I had found, and they looked like glass beads. So you understand that when I went to the house to get Omum, I thought maybe Jake was dead. I had patted under his chin and all around his face, and he had the same feel as the seagull: little bones without a pulse.

I wasn't sure if I could find Jake's lonesome place again; he claimed it was soft as a held breath there. On that account, I held mine so that I could find the entrance—and it worked. I found Jake's rocks that looked like they were made of real gold—the shoulders lit up by his fire's orange tongue, which painted the wet walls so that they were dark yellow. And for luck I grabbed a glittering amount of it in my hand.

At the outset when Jake woke up, he talked to Omum, and I stayed so still that a cobweb stretched over my face, but I didn't dare move. I was so happy that he hadn't died from loneliness. When Omum rubbed his shoulders and Jake stared at her with a light in his eye, I played in the Sound and traced salt on my hip and brushed water over Scarecrow's legs, rubbing him to make him feel good the way Omum rubbed the arms of Jake. Afterward, floating on the water, I closed my eyes and let the sun that went in and out of the clouds make warm bursts inside my eyelids.

And when the horn of the moon came out at the same time as the sun, Omum asked Jake about Beatrice. Jake's lined face was half-lit by the setting sun, half-hidden by the darkness of the rock. He had met Beatrice on a windy night right before winter, he said. She was out on the beach, just like we are today, but it was nighttime, and the wind was making her cape billow like a wave. It whipped her mouth and made her eyes water, and Jake stared out at the waves with his hand held up against his forehead.

"It's a flood of memories," Omum said, and he nodded. "They can lead to a great sadness," she said, and he nodded again.

I wiped my nose, and it felt crusty.

"I know a Beatrice, too," Omum said finally.

"There must be a pattern of coincidences, like vibrations," Jake said. "Stacked one on top of the other through life." He watched Scarecrow race with his shadow, chase his tail into the shadows that the setting sun had painted on the wet green rocks.

In the grassy-marsh part of the beach, I yanked long tails of grass out of their sandy beds by their roots and wondered why Jake always talked in riddles that I couldn't understand.

Omum said, "Where do you live? It must be near here to come so often."

"*Why?* Do you think I'm *trespassing?*"

I bit my fingernail, because Jake's tone wasn't friendly. But then, neither was Omum's . . . because there *was* no "near here."

Then Jake said, "Oceanfront beaches belong to the public."

And Omum frowned and dropped Jake's arm. "I didn't mean to imply—"

"Yes, you did . . . but don't look so worried."

"I was worried about *you*."

"Don't. With my boat here"—he pointed in the direction of his long canoe, which I knew was stashed behind another boulder—"I can go almost anywhere."

"You'll be all right to get home?"

He gave her a peculiar smile. "With concentration, I can do anything . . . although I have to admit that curiosity helps. If Einstein could look at his math formulas like poetry, I'm sure I can find my way home, don't you think?"

What did Einstein have to do with going home? How would Jake be able to see with the wind revving up and the dark coming in? Maybe that's what he meant—that anything is possible.

He gave Omum another funny smile. And made a funny noise with his mouth when he got to his feet, snapped his fingers at Scarecrow, and, limping slightly, slogged through the sand toward where his boat was hidden.

"You're sure?" she persisted, and she followed him, plucking at his sleeve with her fingers.

If I had been Jake, I would have been annoyed.

He stopped, stared down at her, looked her up and down. Where were his manners? He didn't even say, *Thank you for all your help.*

Instead he said, "I watch you, you know. Not up close, not like you're a specimen in a fishbowl. But I *have* imagined endings for your journeys," he said. "I read your faces from a distance and see myself, hope for my own future." He paused. "I never get too close, you understand. . . ." He took two long strides toward his boat.

Jake was alone so much, I think he had forgotten how to talk to people. I glanced at Omum. Her face had gone stark white, and she was speechless. Her heart was probably in her throat. She was always afraid, poor Omum. Sure enough, she clutched at her breast.

"You *watch* us?" she managed at last, having not heard the "future" part at all.

"Oh, not in the way you think—I'm no pervert—but I do enjoy observing. From down here on the beach exclusively. I never come up on people's land."

They stared at each other for a moment, until Omum looked away. "I'm glad of that," she said finally. She took a deep breath. "And you're a friend to my granddaughter."

She probably felt sorry for him, thought he was crazy—a lonely, down-on-his-luck old homeless man who had once been a somebody.

"That I am," he said, and pulled his large, peeling canoe from under the rock and pushed it down to the water, where two seagulls were pecking at a crab's rotted carcass.

I looked up at the sun, which was high in the sky, a faded, smiling Smurf ball waiting for night to fall. The wind beat at my chest, and I put my hands up against it. It felt like a soft wall.

"You're not feverish, dizzy?" Omum tried to touch Jake's forehead.

"Not at all; I have spells of weakness once in a while, and then I need to rest, is all, for a time. It's my age, don't you know—happens to the best of us. The child, she's too young to understand." With his eyes tracking Omum's wandering gaze (she had trouble holding his look for long), Jake bent over and put his lips to her wrist where the violet veins crisscrossed.

To me, he then waved, unlocking his arms to catch a fragment of my palmed glitter and sunset.

How did he know?

I opened my fist, which for luck I had clenched tight. And oh, wonder! From his fire under the ledge, I still held in my hand bits of his gold and magical light.

Chapter 17

ELSIE

The next week proved to be the hottest of the summer, and the mosquitoes, encouraged by sweaty armpits and rotting fruit, multiplied, swarming at the windowsills, while on-the-march black, braiding ants advanced up the kitchen counters and the glass-paned cupboards to the ceiling, careful to keep their distance from their smaller red relatives, who moved en masse up, down, everywhere through the torn old screens covering the warped windows.

Every night on TV there were reports of deaths due to heat exhaustion, one station trying to outdo the other. I never paid much attention, of course, but Peda seemed fascinated by the plight of the poor, heat-stroked souls and would sit in front of the screen, biting her nails, while she listened to the gory details of their hardships. When the reporters went so far as to show shelters overrun by animals brought to near death by the weather and the folks who had abandoned them, she tugged on her grandmother's arm, demanding that one of us rescue them.

Despite my clammy neck and my sorely sensitive hand, I felt good, so I put up with her, even encouraged her in her mercy calls to the networks. For her father had come home. And he enjoyed my motherly solicitude, our family togetherness in this old mausoleum of a house, so old, in fact, that we didn't have air-conditioning. I have to admit, I complied with his picture of Rockwellian homeyness and even learned to enjoy it.

I liked to watch Robin interacting with our family; by all appearances, he looked relaxed and comfortable. During his first week with us, mostly he would sit with Peda, gazing down at her head while she sat cross-legged on the floor in front of him and the TV, his fingers opening and closing on her shoulder, as if he couldn't believe his good luck.

And after our late nights together, naturally, under the disapproving stare of my mother . . . well, I'll just say that before he came, I had a vision of myself as a particle in a moldered, stagnant pool, holed up here, you might say, right next to the pulsing sea, with no way out to those rushing waters, obliged to go neither left nor right just sink eventually from lack of light—and life. No more, though—now I'm part of that whitecap surge, too.

During the day, I like to feel with my fingertips where Robin's wide, soft lips, so much like his mother's, he tells me, have nuzzled me the night before on the nape of my neck, just below the hairline. I like to remember the curve of his round, bare cheeks; his thighs; and his large, knobbed root, poised and stiff, rising from his profile. I know, I sound like an idiot—it's a penis, not a root—but for me Robin's smile is my flash of light, and I can think whatever I want to. So much so that I find myself at odd hours closing my eyes, too emotionally exhausted not to allow myself the relief of tears. They roll through the new depressions I have discovered in my face. It's almost more than I can bear, the joy of my lover's presence here. To question it yet would be too cruel, I think.

Robin asked me last night if I could forgive him, for his drug and drinking binges when we were together those long years past. AA, he explained to me, had cured him. But for the first time in a long time, I had a flashback to those vodka-pot rampages. The hard stuff came later. Anger was the least of it—fear was more like it. And my frustration at his will for self-destruction. Banging into the furniture so that chairs put black-and-blue dents all over his body, as if he were trying to obliterate himself. "Self-hate," he whispered to me last night. Thinking he was not meant to be on this earth. "Thoughts," he confided, that he also remembers from his childhood.

Strange, how different Hamlet is from Robin, how self-contained Hamlet is—as if he doesn't need anyone's approval except his own—how self-confident and sure of himself he is, how cocky and wicked, somehow, because of it.

Robin hummed a lot last night, said he couldn't, wouldn't, see me again until his habit had been cured, but that for years he fantasized about our pregnancy, the one he appeared to have ignored when it was actually happening. Awed by the new heart that beat in my belly, under the curve of my breast, my stretched skin made translucent—he had noticed it all but never mentioned it to me. Wished that he could have another chance to prove his tenderness. And then we made love. And he told me my breasts shone like two rare Egyptian obelisks. And he said his blood drummed so hard that he thought he'd explode.

Last night, I remember thinking that Ham would never say such a thing, even if he felt it.

As far as Robin goes, I get it now. For years I held rage in my heart, that he had allowed his habit to seduce him away from me. His addictive love affair with drugs and booze. But if he didn't reach out to me back then, it was because he couldn't see what he had to offer. Robin never talked about his family; I never even knew he *had* a brother. And not until last night did he ever mention his mother except in passing: her features, her soft disposition, crushed under his father's heel.

"Why didn't you tell me?" I asked him when we were fucking. He was pushing so hard that beads of sweat were popping off his brow, and concentrating so hard that he couldn't answer. "That you were related to Crandor, the Crandor of my mother's painting?" (With me he had used his mother's maiden name.) I thought his desire would crumple at my questioning, that he would shrivel at my test, my punishment for his having abandoned me and poor, fatherless Peda, or perhaps for having allowed me to abandon him—a test that I planned unconsciously—but instead the question made him push deeper and he probed with the strength of Attila the Hun. When he finished, he put his soft, brush-like head against my cheek and I felt his heart pounding like a sledgehammer. I could smell him next to me, the warmth coming off his skin.

"I couldn't," he said softly, his dear, serious, straight-browed face next to my own. "It was as simple as that. Telling you would have laid bare my cover, flaunted my failed past. I would have felt like a turtle without its shell."

I could see his silhouette smile into the darkness. "Not much of a shell, was it?" he said. "I thought it was at the time, though—the booze, the drugs."

"I could have helped you."

He whispered in my ear, tickled it with his tongue. "I wasn't ready. I needed to help myself."

Though I wanted to question him further, to interrogate him about the years since I had seen him last, I shivered with pleasure at the sensation of his warm breath in my ear and gave in once more to his passion. More important, I was afraid to break the spell of our reunion, the intensity of his love for me, and the sweet ache I felt at his reinvigorated presence.

Chapter 18

ELSIE

∽

When my mother, the great Mrs. Winter Peregrine, decreed that our standards should be maintained—that in cold weather we should enjoy a fire when entertaining, while in hot weather we should retreat to the cavernous library to escape the heat—everyone obeyed. As such, right after lunch, when Winter's two art experts arrived, accompanied by Hamlet on the tail of Sophia and Clay (invited by Winter, at Ham's behest, to attend a meeting with yet another cop, a detective this time), we all trooped into the library. Rather than meeting on the terrace or the lawn or even the beach, where we might feel the sun and a breeze of sorts, my mother preferred the dark mission oak–paneled library, which was, after all these years, fancy and shabby at the same time, and which, pathetically, boasted only two, very narrow cabinets of books. Old, dusty, disintegrating books. The room reminded me of a decrepit old broad, flat broke and in mourning. Velvet everywhere, which to my mind spelled heat. A tasseled, royal maroon sofa with shiny patches. Heavy, threadbare brocade curtains. And a mammoth portrait of Grandfather George, which hung over the empty, soot-covered fireplace. In pride of place on the mantel stood a mustard-tinted bowl—of great value, my mother claimed—which was cracked and glued and decorated with a faded outline of purple violets. Because the windows were drawn and quartered—as if we were prisoners—the only light fell from a narrow stained-glass window at the peak of the ceiling, and vague ruby and emerald squares leaked onto the worn Oriental carpet, as if all its colors had hopelessly run together. Naturally, after we entered, the dark brown doors were shut tight.

But before Clay closed those heavy, matching mission doors with such finality, I watched the visitors arrive. Trying to form opinions about what might transpire on this heat-soaked afternoon while we baked in my mother's oven of a library. No fans for us, thank you very much, and certainly no air conditioners.

On time, as usual, Zinger and Rip Van Winkle arrived first, ushered in by the great lady herself, who then left them standing so that she could hurry to make her mint-sprigged iced tea. At the doorway, Zinger swiveled on his heels, slowly, like a top, and deliberately examined the contour of the room, up and down, as though it were the body of a woman. Lingering on each object. His eyes were shining behind his glasses, and he rubbed his hands as he made his appraisal. I noticed that his fly was partially open and that his shirt gaped where a button was missing under his bow tie. Next to him, Sleepy-Droopy cracked his brittle knuckles so savagely that the sound bounced back at us from the high ceiling. The man reminded me of a tall crane with staring, shimmery-blank eyes.

"Isn't Ham with you?" I asked.

I felt a twinge of guilt, making Ham put up at the hotel when his brother shared my bed—I knew Ham resented it. I wiped my sweaty palms on my slacks and renewed my door watching. Besides worrying about Ham's mood swings, I was edgy today about the prospect of cops on the premises—considering Robin's past record.

Horatio Guardi stepped in front of the mantel and examined the cracked bowl. "Clay is picking him up," he said. His back was to me, and he didn't even glance at me, just spoke into the bowl as if he couldn't be bothered to look up.

I stared at his stooped back, insulted in a weird kind of way, so that I didn't hear Robin enter the room until he was near me.

There it was: the long scar that ran down the length of his right cheek. I liked the way the indentation felt on my tongue. I reached up, and while Zinger eyed me, I grazed it with my lips, daring him to say something. But he turned away with Robin's laugh, which, for me, was like a return kiss. And then I laughed with him, this quiet man with his observant eyes, annoyed, somehow, that Zinger with the open fly hadn't made a scene.

I sat down, pulled Robin with me, onto the dusty window seat just as Clay came in—blew him off, really, so I wouldn't have to deal with him.

"And how *is* everyone today?" he said. (No one could escape that pretentious *ohhh, noww* voice.)

On his arm, Sophia swept more moist heat—perfumed this time—into the stagnant air of the library. *Jesus Christ—how will we breathe?* Winter was just behind them, holding the tea tray with white-knuckled fists. She frantically moved her eyebrows at me, as if no one else could see.

Of course I ignored her.

But Clay didn't. He dropped Sophia's arm, bowed over Winter's tray, and gallantly grabbed it away from her. "Ah, thank you *soooo* much," he said. "You're *sucha* love."

For whom was Clay acting? Sophia? It certainly wasn't for me. I glanced over at Robin. For him? Nah. . . . But *of course.*

It had to be for the all-powerful Hamlet, whom he had chauffeured over here, according to sleepy old Rip. So where *was* Ham? And where was the cop? I got up, started to wade through the hot puffs of thick air; I felt like a sweaty old woman.

They came in together, just as I was doing my dance— the cop and Hamlet, who, on this hottest day of the year, was dressed in creamy, off-white linen slacks, a raspberry-colored (the newest shade) polo shirt, and a navy blue blazer, and looked cool as a cucumber and even more good-looking than a young Paul Newman. (Robin and I had been binging on old films.) The two men were talking animatedly, their arms linked together as if they were old classmates.

The detective appeared to be in his late thirties, attractive in a cop kind of way. He wore no tie but rather an open shirt that really should have been buttoned up, because it revealed such a massive, simian amount of blond chest and throat hair that at first I couldn't take my eyes off it. When I did, his face was too young, a kid's face, but with a man's eyes—all-knowing, cunning—in a pink, chubby-cheeked, little-boy face. And strangely familiar. When our eyes met, it hit me. Fourth, fifth, sixth grade on the mainland. How I had *hated* this boy!

I looked away and took up Robin-Sebastian's hand, which lay lankly on his blue-jeaned lap. No dressing up for my Robin. But so what? What was this, after all, a board meeting or something? I wondered who would start the procedures.

And found to my surprise that I would. "Won't you take a seat?" I said magnanimously. I swung my arm around the room and looked at no one in particular.

Heard, though, feet moving toward the couch, the armchairs, the bridge table with its two extradelicate but beaten-up side chairs. Hamlet took the most comfortable armchair, of course, Clay the other. On the couch the experts perched expectantly, with Sophia looking like an ornament between them.

My mother sat primly at the bridge table, her hands arranged as if she were about to deal cards. When the little-boy cop pulled up a chair next to her, she didn't give him the time of day.

"What are we here for?" I said, when we were all seated.

Hamlet didn't so much as turn to me—or to his brother. He had been genuinely shocked when he found out that Sebastian was not only my lover but Peda's father. So shocked, in fact, that he hadn't spoken to his brother since Robin-Sebastian had recounted the story of our brief, lurid past and confessed that it had been he, naturally, who had contacted the Getty, piquing their interest in our "Crandor." What better way to get back to me and to his daughter, he wanted to know. The glib Hamlet was for once rendered speechless.

Yet when I started the meeting, antsy-sweaty and eager to be free of Hamlet, Winter, her guests, the cop, and the library, at last he deigned to look at me. "What do you *think?*" he mouthed, glowering.

Then he stood up and, digging into the vest pocket of his blazer, took out another black-and-white photograph of his Crandor grandfather, yet *another* picture with curling scalloped edges. He held it up for all of us to see. "We're here because of *him,*" he said, gouging his finger into the faded image, then tossed it onto the coffee table, where it slid to a halt by the farthest edge, teetering in the heavy, still air. Sophia leaned down and, without touching it, blew it back to the center of the table.

I thought I could feel her breath on my hand, which raised gooseflesh on my neck. I stared at her, squeezed Robin's fingers, then turned my attention to his brother, who seemed to have taken over the meeting.

Who turned toward the boy-cop sitting across from my mother. With her eyes flicking from one to the other, Winter looked like a cornered rabbit.

Ham motioned toward Zinger and Sleepy. "Ask them for the letters," he said. "Order them to give them up."

Between them, Sophia leaned way back. Her bare legs were crossed, and she looked sexy and regal at the same time, and when I saw Ham look at her, I felt my cheeks flush, which had nothing to do with the stifling temperature.

Zinger reached into his back pocket and tugged out a tobacco pouch. He lifted the flap, put his nose down to the bag, and inhaled . . .

Clay edged forward in his chair. As he moved, his khaki shorts hiked up and I made out the bony faces of his naked knees. I wondered if he wore any underwear. In this heat, who could blame him?

The detective stuck out his hand. "Give them here," he said.

Horatio Guardi tepeed his fingers. I clenched my teeth when the old man appraised the cop, but he made no move to hand over the packet. The tenseness of the moment actually hurt me physically, and I cradled my sore arm. At last Zinger slid off the couch, walked up to the cop, and dropped into his lap a bunch of messy, folded papers held together with a rubber band. Meanwhile, with his long fingers poised, Droopy kept his eyes on the cop, who visibly flinched under his heavy-lidded stare.

Clay cleared his throat. "Well, *go on*, man, read them—we don't have all day." He wiped his brow.

Sophia gave Clay a nod of approval, and I looked from one to the other. They matched somehow, he with the diamond stud in his ear, which I knew irritated Winter, and she with her flinging hair, the shape and color of a buzzard's wing. Their darting eyes were the same, too, observing things to which they had no right. But Winter, she allowed it. Their participation in family affairs. Me, too, I guess.

Not wanting to resurrect memories of Clay with me, I smoothed a callus on Robin's palm, closed my eyes, and, for a moment, indulged in a fantasy from our previous night together. It made my mouth feel ripe.

Shook my head then, to clear the vision. "Go on—what are you waiting for?" I said out loud. When I looked up, I found Ham's eyes on me, my mother's, too, her own thin lips pursed and bloodless, which accentuated her forever-hurt, accusatory gaze. At the same time, Ham held *my* gaze too long for comfort. Him and that jittery knee of his.

"Read them, please," I said, and, aching to end this ordeal, turned to the boy-cop, my childhood tormentor, who set the papers on the table before him and carefully took off the rubber band.

"Shall I skim, or shall I read the entire packet?" He addressed the question to me, bypassing Ham and Clay—and my mother, for that matter.

What did I care, for Christ's sake? "*You're* supposed to be the professional."

He shrugged, gave me his nasty, well-remembered grin. "All right, here's something," and from the middle of the messy pile he removed a piece of scrap paper on which a note was scribbled, presumably by the artist. "*I must paint at my own speed,*" he read, then turned the paper on its side, "*and I must keep my work with me indefinitely, to study it from time to time and change it when necessary.*"

It made me feel peculiar, as if Crandor were actually in the room with us.

"If I may ask, to whom are these letters addressed?" My mother's language and querulous little voice irritated me something awful.

"A few to your father," he replied, leafing through them, "a couple to Ham's father. The majority, though, seem to be to nobody. They're meant to be a journal of sorts—at least, that's what I assume."

"Thank you," she said in a husky whisper, and smiled at the cop like she really liked him.

At which his neck turned a deep crimson, and I watched the color wash up his throat, as if someone had tried to choke him. He hid his face in the papers, pretending to study them for a moment, before it began to regain its natural color. Then, without looking up, in a muffled voice that deepened with each syllable—until his speech was audible and distinct—he began to read Simon Crandor's words, eventually getting caught up, as did we all, in the drama he was about to unfold.

"*Within a period of six months, I intend to establish a foundation for my artwork—which will automatically require the corporation that presently holds my paintings (created by my son, my agent, and my advisor) to turn the paintings over to the foundation,*" he read from one paper. He shuffled through more until he came to another oyster-thin piece, which he felt was important. "*The Foundation will be staffed with a board of trustees initially of my own choosing, who will be empowered to seek out worthwhile organizations, such as museums, hospitals, charities, and schools—those who will appreciate, display, and accept my paintings for a small fee, those who will guard their welfare indefinitely—with the caveat that in the event of a painting's 'resale' for profit in an improved market, to other worthwhile organizations, each transaction must be approved by the foundation's trustees, or successor trustees (with proceeds to go to the organization selling the painting). This is my intention. So that the public may enjoy my art, so that the charities and worthwhile causes and organizations may reap the financial rewards garnered from the sale of my art. In short, my goal is to subsidize generations of charities and worthwhile causes while giving the public access to my art.*"

The detective read to himself for a few moments, looked up, then continued aloud. "*My agent; my publicist, Barry Zinger; my friend and advisor Horatio Guard . . . even my son, I think, fear I have lost my mind, that I intend to give away my fortune. No—just the bulk of my collection, as well as any future-generated artwork (excluding sentimental and personal pieces). They think that I am squandering my talent.*"

While his voice remained steady, there was now, clearly, an

added element of emotion to it, which was almost embarrassing. *"If they are correct in their analysis,"* he read, stressing the key words, *"it is* my *talent to squander, after all. I have made all the money that I will ever need. Each of them will be well provided for; each will receive substantial dollar deposits from me. Especially my beloved son, of course, in whose name I have been depositing significant bequests since his birth and, in particular, these last few years, and now months. Also, both Zinger and Horatio will get a fair percentage of the work they have already helped to disperse. I feel confident that all three have been well rewarded by a grateful father and friend, for their hard work on my behalf, their loyalty . . . and their love."*

"As you can see, this is the final paper," the detective said, and held up the crinkled piece for our inspection. "Simon Crandor signed it. Right here." He tapped the autograph twice. "So unless this is a forgery, which I doubt, this is *serious* business—as per Hamlet Crandor's allegation. And justifiably so, in my opinion."

Everyone craned forward, except for Zinger and Droopy. Poor Rip—his eyes had acquired a kind of ghostly shine, like the slick, translucent underbelly of an oyster. There was a hectic flush to his sunken cheeks, and a nerve was ticking on the left side of his temple. The gray hair that didn't stand straight up in tufts; the wisps remaining about his collar and his ears hung lank as seaweed, and for a moment, like Winter, I actually felt sorry for him. Not so for Zinger, who stared at us belligerently, daring us to accuse him of something. *Was* there any proof— any *real* proof—that he had committed a crime? He even wore the ghost of a smile.

"Well, this is something," I heard Clay say, and, as if trained to react at the sound of his voice, Sophia nodded.

"Are these *all* of the papers?" the boy-cop asked Zinger.

"Yeah. What do you think?"

"Is it all true?"

Zinger faced the guy and gave him a look.

"I've done my homework," said the cop. "I guess you didn't expect that."

Zinger's toupee slid to the side a little.

The detective rocked back on the worn hind legs of the bridge chair. "There appears to be a real problem here," he said—I could feel Winter cringe as the legs creaked—"because, you see, this artist fellow's wishes were never honored. He disappeared; he drowned, convenient-like—same as Ham here claims—*before* he could give away his paintings, *before* he could arrange his will, *before* he could dig up fresh trustees, no pun intended." He laughed abruptly, paused to look at his audience to let his words sink in. "*Before* he could subsidize his fine causes and charities. So I see this as a problem. Because the beneficiaries of his artwork turned out to be the three people he disavowed in these documents." He sighed and gazed at the two men on the couch.

I didn't get it—why was Ham making such a fuss when *he* was one of the beneficiaries? Didn't the cop wonder, too? Ham's father was dead, after all. Couldn't the authorities confiscate his inheritance—freeze his funds—if they proved that the money had come to him illegally? That is, *if* there was anything left to freeze. On the other hand, maybe he truly *wanted* to avenge those responsible for his grandfather's death—an issue that was separate, I hoped, from his plan to make a profit from the sale of questionable Crandors (not to mention my mother's supposed original). More than likely, though, he had a scheme of his own and was just using the police. Maybe he figured the two old men would take the rap for the murder—they *couldn't* be the brains behind the concealed canvases (and documents) enigma—which would make *him*, as the only living heir besides Seb (and blameless), the *only* beneficiary. *Just see what you started!* I wanted to say to Robin.

Zinger stared right back at the young cop-detective. "Yeah, well, the courts didn't see it as a problem. You think you're smarter than they are?"

The cop pointed at him, waving his finger at his round belly. "First off, you don't leave the area. Second, the Getty will be informed about the probability of an investigation."

"For what?" Guardi interjected, coming to Zinger's defense at last. "Not for the information in the papers, certainly?" His face was hard, and his voice was so flat that it sounded robotic. "It's privileged information, after all, the unwitnessed voice of a dead man, and, if fed about, as slander, it could be grounds for dismissal in a court of law—that is, if you make this into a case and said case ever comes to that." He paused and locked eyes with him. "Not to mention the lawsuit *I* would initiate."

The detective snorted. "Do you think I'm stupid? I'll tell the Getty only what I deem appropriate for a reopened murder investigation, only what the DA deems appropriate. And you'll stick around because *you two*"—he aimed his pointer fingers at the men like revolvers, "you two will soon be under investigation. And because I think—"

"Who the hell are *you?*"

He went on as if the old man hadn't spoken. "Because I think there is something here to investigate that should have been looked into years back. Because *I* have chosen to take a dead artist's thwarted desires, which are spelled out here clearly, and represent them." He flipped the packet with his thumb. "As far as I'm concerned, these papers are as good as a will. *Somebody's* got to stick up for the dead guy."

The boy-cop didn't seem so young to me anymore.

Old Rip looked at him curiously. "You've studied these papers before, have you?"

The cop laughed, an easy, infectious laugh. He might have been on a picnic, or at a bar, enjoying a backslap drink with his colleagues. "Nope, none of that. But I warned you, didn't I? After talking to my sergeant, I did my homework. Studied Crandor's works, studied his history—got to like him, even—studied his affidavit, and, finally, I studied the man's cause of death. I have his death certificate right here, right in front of me." He picked up a paper and shook it at them. With a smile so wide that his dimples disappeared.

Sophia looked up. "Can you really do that? Reopen the case?"

"Yeah, I can really do that." He gave her a once-over, but antiseptically, as if she were no more than a fish, a passing specimen in a jar.

"You have a vendetta against us? Why, for God's sake? You one of those bored, nightstick-toting guys hungry for power and a cause? Those holier-than-thou dicks who stir up controversy, enjoy confrontation and conflict?" Guardi's face was contorted.

"Don't be an asshole."

Jesus, that should shut him up, shut them all up. I wanted to clap. But a clap of thunder beat me to it. And as we all stood up, as if on cue, the sky outside darkened quickly, the clouds from the windows turned into black, rolling masses, heavy with approaching rain, making the already-gloomy room fall into deep shadow. Another roll of thunder sounded in the distance. And with it came the smell of salty water and seaweed from the unseen, gearing-up-to-storm tossed sea.

Chapter 19

WINTER

~

I had recognized Jake unequivocally from the photograph of Simon Crandor that Ham had thrown so dramatically onto the table, but I didn't know what to do with the information. I spoke to no one at the meeting, ate a sparse dinner alone, and retired for the evening early, praying that nothing would disturb my sleep.

During the night, the rain fell in torrents. Once, I woke up to a shout that seemed to come from the curtains of rain. It was a long calling sound, the animal far away this time, somewhere from across the Sound. Not frightening at all, like those screams from other nights, nor was it alarming compared with the run-of-the-mill night noises, its call so low and so distant I wasn't sure if it was not simply the *echo* of my fear sounding in the surge of my brain. Once, I pushed out my bedroom window to look outside, and a swarm of large, dusty moths, their wings painted gray and brown and black, some outlined with narrow yellow stripes, flew in at me on the rain-drenched air, attracted to the yellow glow of my bedside lamp. I shut the window so fast that some couldn't turn back, and they smashed into the windowpane and ledge, reduced suddenly to pulp—while many of them, I think, flew into the glass deliberately. Mixed with their cindery remains, which stuck to the wet, the rain coated the glass with a greasy film and the larger drops that ran down the panes spotted it with dirty tan beads. It was like a work of art, something that Crandor would have enjoyed. Something he might have copied, taken for his own. I missed our painting, his and mine, so that the enjoyment I derived from a window decorated with moth and rain droplets was particularly poignant, especially when I looked at it with Crandor's painterly eyes, at least eyes I daringly hoped could be his.

In the morning Elsie told me I looked awful, that my face looked gray in the bright light. But even with my thick and swollen eyes, the result of a dearth of sleep, I knew that my pallor was really due to the photo and the absolute realization of who Jake was. I clenched my jaw and stayed silent, biding my time until I could tell Peda about my discovery, which I thought would not come as any great surprise to her.

After breakfast, which Peda missed, I pulled myself up the stairs to her room. Sunlight was pouring through her open window, bathing her bed in a dazzle of fly specks. In the middle of the bed, on her knees in the circle of light, Peda peered out at me from a tepee of sheets. She said, "Morning," then ducked back inside her billowing cloak. What a strange child. Her smile made me want to cry.

From inside her tent, I heard a muffled "Guess what?"

So I joined her on the bed, which creaked and sagged under my weight, and put an ear against the sheet under which she hid. "What?" I said.

She emerged to slide down next to me, swung her bare legs over the side, and banged together her small ankles. "Last night

I dreamed that Scarecrow could talk, but I can't remember what he said." With a bitten-down finger—the rawness of her cuticle hurt me to look at it—she pointed to her collapsed tent. "I went in there so I'd remember better."

"I bet I know what he told you."

She had moved so close to me that I could smell the sweetish kid sweat on her, sucked up from the morning's stagnant heat.

"You do?"

"Jake is Simon Crandor. . . . Am I right?"

She looked at me blankly.

"The *painter*. The artist responsible for my painting, my *favorite* painting, the one the art experts are here to see."

She nodded.

I pulled down my skirt. "Why didn't you tell me?"

"I thought you knew."

I was annoyed. "No, you know I didn't."

She looked sideways at me and tilted her chin at my head. "Not there. *There*," she said, and aimed her curled fist at my heart. "You knew *there*."

I didn't know what to say; I just stared at her until she drew behind me and proceeded to jump up and down on the bed as if it were a trampoline.

In between breaths, she chanted in a singsong voice: "*That's what Scarecrow was trying to tell me . . . trying to tell me . . .*" She slid off the bed then, like it was a slide, and her T-shirt rode up around her bare buttocks. It was wrinkled and in need of a good wash.

"Where's your nightgown?"

"Mom says I don't need one." She flung the shirt onto the bed and ran into the bathroom naked as a jaybird, her arms outstretched in the wing position.

I called after her, "*Peda?* After breakfast, meet me outside so we can . . . *Peda?*" But she wasn't listening. I called again then, into her stirred-up air, *"Peda . . . can you hear me?* I need to find Jake."

Later, when we began our march to the sea—Peda and I—the sun exploded in our faces like a flashbulb, and I couldn't see the sky for the earth. In the lemon-colored haze, even the outline of the water was blurry. When I glanced at my granddaughter, but for the flap of her sneakers flopping against her heels, she reminded me of a ghost floating on a hot current of air. As we neared the beach, the pebbles that had washed up along the shore vibrated in the glimmer of the water's edge, and I felt as if I moved in a trance, for a moment not even sure if I was real. Pinched myself, even, to make sure. Points of light danced on the water as we zigzagged in and out of the rocks. We took off our shoes when our feet sank deep into the wet sand, and, looking back, I noticed that our footprints filled with water and disappeared as quickly as we walked—as if we had never been there at all.

Finally, Peda drew a sharp left and just like the first time halted abruptly, shushing me with a meaningful look when I started to question her.

She pointed. "He'll be in through there."

Nothing, however, looked the same to me. The boulders were different; even the cove itself was different from the last place we had found Jake.

"This isn't the same spot." I looked around and swept my hand after me.

She put her fingers up to her lips. "No," she whispered. "It's *Sunday.*"

Was that meaningful? "Is he a religious nut or something?"

She avoided my eyes. "He comes here *every* Sunday," she said.

I flinched. I hoped he wasn't a bible thumper, this man . . . who, I realized with acute shock, was her great-grandfather.

A greeting. A deep voice behind me, and there he was, the great man himself, ribboned in light like John the Baptist or something, standing knee-deep in water, bending over it and giving a blessing, it looked like, his palms flat on the water's surface, patting it gently.

I squinted into the glare. His face seemed to melt sideways into the curve of the rocks, with the heat; his mouth smeared in and out of shape. I licked my lips, didn't know what to say.

"The whorl of the waves leaves an afterimage on the ear and the eye." He gazed into the water.

Was he seeing a vision?

He moved then, sloshing his way toward us. "Look there," he said, disturbing the water with his big hands. "The surface of the Sound is as clear as poured glass today. You can see all the objects in the sky reflected in the mirror of the water. I'll paint the image, I think. The reflection, I mean."

Considering the lurid yellow light in the sky, I wondered at his words. But, sure enough, when I looked down at the water, the Sound was crystal clear. "Are you all right now? Are you feeling better?" I asked him.

He didn't look much better. His skin threw off a sickly tinge, as if he had been x-rayed too long, accentuated, probably, by the bleached-out haze of the day.

He cleared his throat. Full of phlegm, I noticed. "I'm fine."

"Why do you come here on Sunday?" I backed away from him.

He shrugged. "Isn't it obvious?"

"Not to me."

"But to Peda. And to Scarecrow."

I turned to Peda. "How?"

She had squatted by a large rock and was busy examining a sand crab burrowing into the sand, and another one, too, slightly bigger, that tried to use the same hole. Couldn't make it, so little Peda stuck her finger in the hole and twisted it around to enlarge it, to help the creature make a home—I hoped the two crabs wouldn't kill each other.

"He thinks the rocks here are shaped like a prayer," she said, and slapped her palms together, plaiting her fingertips above them. "See?" She gestured at two of the dark gray boulders that loomed above us.

I nodded, though I didn't see at all.

"It keeps track of the days. That's all," he said, with a slight laugh. His bray sounded rusty, as if he weren't used to making sounds at all, which I suppose he wasn't.

"But the boulders . . ."

"Yes, I told her that. God's plan and all. To keep track of the days, that's more important when you're on your own."

"You're the painter. You're Simon Crandor," I said bravely.

The still water, unmoved by any breeze, seemed to emphasize the unnatural heat of the day, and I wished I could take back my accusation, instead hit the water with Jake. Cool off. Rinse away my bad mood, my tiredness, my fear.

He splashed his way over to me, his big black dog right behind him, and the spray from the salt water flung his presence a long way. A prickly, uncomfortable feeling came over me. I wanted to yell out, *Help!* to Peda, but she was bent over her precious crabs. He stopped where the water stopped, thank goodness, unwilling, I suppose, to take himself away from the coolness.

"Your straw hat casts a checkerboard across your face. Did you realize? It's nice," he said.

I looked up through the lacy pattern of my hat. "Why, thank you," I said, as if we were out for afternoon tea.

How ludicrous. Here we were, this odd old man, sharp-boned, with his thin pelt of salt-and-pepper hair, which curled, wet and matted, on his naked chest, a leathery old painter turned bum who stood in more than two feet of water while he faced me, as if it were a normal occurrence. People met every day for conversation surrounded by the infinitude of saltwater waves; shiny, prayer-shaped boulders; nests of mating, screeching, greedy seagulls; and endless moisture. . . . *God, the moisture.* My hair stuck out from under my hat, and it was sticky, too. I must have looked a sight in this salt-filled, humid air, which I gulped at, taking slow, deep breaths, trying to control my shaking limbs.

"You *are* Simon Crandor, are you not?" I asked again. My voice sounded unnaturally loud, even to my ears, like I was speaking to a foreigner.

"Not anymore." He turned away and gazed out at the waves, motionless as the thick air that enveloped us.

"People can't discard their identity." I was angry. How dare he throw away his family? His responsibilities, his talent. His son; his grandsons, Sebastian, Hamlet; his great-granddaughter, Peda . . . Elsie . . . me.

"Crazed lemmings—one after the other—are said to quit the land and run pell-mell into the sea."

"That's what you are? A crazed lemming?"

"Oh, no, I don't follow anyone. I ran away, though, to the sea. But only once. From my friends and my family who wanted my money more than they wanted me. So I gave it to them. I disappeared. Helped them out, I'd say." He turned around then, and there were wet streaks on his face. "They couldn't have both." He brushed his hand across his eyes, his chin, and down his chest, as if to dispel a long-ago vision. "The thief you must fear the most is not the one who steals mere things. . . ." With the pain of this revelation, his body hunched up in the water. I wanted to help him, but I didn't dare move. "They wanted to steal *me*, make me over in their own image." He stared at me from eyes the color of my father's frozen vodka. I had never seen such eyes, such pale eyes, that seemed to change pigments with the ease of a chameleon. When he lay beneath the boulder, I could have sworn his eyes were as dark as my shelled walnuts.

"You can see that, can't you?"

Maybe he had cataracts? I shook my head. "No. I could never leave my daughter, or my granddaughter."

"Oh no?"

He looked at me long and hard, and then he started to laugh, a low, rumbling laugh, an anguished sound, as if laughter were something barbed that had caught in his throat. And I looked back at him, afraid to move, so that even with the itch that had started on my eyebrow and traveled to my wrist, I stayed still. He didn't move, stared at me just the same, choking on that pained laugh of his without saying a word. My stomach lurched. And my throat—it felt sore suddenly from his sorrow, my own, too, and so violent was my reaction that I covered my face with my fingers so that he wouldn't realize that I sobbed as well.

Chapter 20

PEDA

~

*O*mum has exceptionally small, very white teeth, which
is what I first noticed when I saw her crying. As if she
and Jake were celebrating our coming-together with their tears.
My own eyes stung when I saw them standing side by side, and
I swallowed a few times because I liked seeing them together.
Before this day, Jake would never have come to meet my family,
or even come up to the house. Before this day, he was my secret
alone. He was my superhero; I pretended he was a great warrior. I didn't even know where he lived. Mostly he vanished in a
puff, sort of like Chief Geronimo when he was hiding out. Last
month I saw a movie about the chief, who was said to be the last
great Indian. I used to think Jake lived with the rats in the rocks.
But nobody can sleep there in the wintertime. Because they'd
freeze to death.

I *needed* Jake now. To help me with my father, who, without warning, had suddenly *become* my father. I should have been
happy about that, but the trouble was, I couldn't make sense of

him. He didn't fit in. It was as if he were a figure in one of my coloring books who hadn't been colored in yet: no color in him, no face on him, either, and most especially no smell to him at all. I had tried everything I could think of: every fern and lily I could find, even the crabs I watched. Crab smells were like pirate treasures and shipwrecks covered by castles of sand on the bottom of the sea. They had a secret, sandy tang, while ferns and lilies smelled like our attic, which hid old and delicate things and where I used to make make-believe tea. But my father, he had no smell at all. It was as if he didn't exist, as if he never had.

I needed Jake to help me recognize him—or help me to send him away. Because Jake, like Captain Kirk and Chief Geronimo, held magic in his hand. And he wanted only what was best for me—I was sure of that. Now, for the first time in my life, I hoped that someone else I loved, like Omum, would *listen* to me and learn to know and understand him, too.

Chapter 21

ELSIE

❧

I felt sorry for my mother. Since her painting no longer hung in the conservatory, right above the fireplace, she no longer spent much time on her chaise. The faces of her adored figures had probably become blurry to her—a bare wall, a fading memory, is all. The painting wasn't even *in* the house anymore. The police had taken it away for evidence.

Where Winter spent her time now, I didn't know, nor did I even really care, as I was so taken up with Robin. Maybe I was a hypocrite. But who could blame me? I felt like a starved woman who had suddenly been offered a five-course dinner.

Yet I'd have to have been a complete idiot not to have noticed that my mother no longer nagged or complained or lay around in her powder-puff way. As a matter of fact, her attitude was remarkably, albeit strangely, upbeat, in spite of the lines of fatigue that crisscrossed her cheeks like worm burrows. These crevices had appeared soon after her midnight pacing began, those nighttime hours studded with concentrated glances out her third-floor window (I'd seen her from the patio) while she listened to those animal calls—trembling, most likely—that for the past few weeks had enshrouded our nighttime island. She, who had embellished the sounds, even stuck a supernatural label on them. No, the sounds hadn't let up. But neither had I had the time to track them down. Maybe I'd send Peda on a search. For once do my poor old mother a favor.

And now here we were, congregating in *her* room, while the dreaded Sophia leaned in her doorway. Sophia *enjoyed* the conservatory, *enjoyed* watching me feel sorry for my mother (I just *sensed* it), *enjoyed* studying the men in the room (I *more* than sensed that). "What's happening, then?" she said, bringing her eyes back to rest on mine. "With the other paintings? The *newest* ones?" Her weight rested on one hip, and a smile played around her mouth. And I couldn't help but notice that her bare arms were as muscular as a gymnast's—she *had* to lift weights.

I wanted to say, *It's none of your business*, but because Winter still catered to Clay, I thought I had better keep my remarks to myself.

"The police have seized all the evidence. . . ." I didn't look at her and spoke into the air.

She tried to catch my eye. "What evidence?"

"Evidence that relates to the missing-persons file from thirty-eight years ago, or more, maybe—I don't know. Because of Ham's insistence—Clay's, too, I guess—they're dredging up all the events that led to Crandor's disappearance and taking the possibility of foul play *very* seriously. But I'm sure you're just as aware of this as I am."

I narrowed my eyes, and Sophia laughed lightly, a feminine, fluttery sound obviously aimed at the men in the room. Robin gazed at her with his mouth open. Clay, too; his own lips were parted, his eyes dilated, as if holding his breath. Robin reached for my hands, pressed his wet lips against them, as if to atone for his thoughts.

I pulled away curtly and said to her, "You know what's going on just as well as I do." And wondered again what Clay and Sophia hoped to get out of this whole mess. Then it hit me. *Of course.* Sophia would be the convenient local talent, the *new* art expert, whom the police would go to for advice now that the Getty people were suspects in the case of Crandor's untimely and ill-fated death. She would build a reputation for herself around her discovery of the latest untapped Crandors, and then, as a Crandor dealer, she would make *sure* said paintings hit the art market. After that, she'd be able to call her own shots, work for anyone she chose, even open up her own gallery.

And Clay? What would he get out of all this? He'd bag Sophia with his intrigue—*good luck!*—plus gain social recognition. Doubtless he planned to throw us away, poor old Winter Peregrine and her eccentric daughter. How to explain all this to my mother? Who, in any case, would never believe it.

"Well?" I said again.

With her forefinger, Sophia beckoned to Clay, who immediately joined her at the door. "Talk to Elsie," she said.

Clay glanced at me and turned to light her cigarette. "We don't know anything," he said. "How would we?"

Sophia inhaled deeply through flared nostrils, gave me a brief nod, and waved the smoke away with her silver bracelets clattering.

"Please don't smoke in this house," I said, "*especially* not in the conservatory."

Christ, I sounded as sanctimonious as my mother, whose presence in the room, whether she was here or not, I could feel. The conservatory *smelled* like her. It was the room of an old woman: perfumed and protected, well away from the sea; faded, poufed, and sacheted, just like Winter's head of coiffed hair. To my mind, anything would have given the room a lift, even Sophia's smoke. But instead, I stood up for Winter. I wanted to bang my head into the wall for giving in to her again. And she wasn't even here.

"Thought you wouldn't mind. . . . I mean, your mother's out of range, isn't she?" Clay gave Sophia's neck an encouraging squeeze while he grinned at me. "But no big deal. You don't mind, do you, Soph?"

Sophia stared steadily at the floor, took a drag, and held the smoke in her lungs, finally blowing it out in a hard, steady stream. And then she sauntered over to a silver trophy, a flat, engraved dish, which she used as an ashtray—*how dare she?*—grinding the cigarette out with a vengeance, while she deliberately sought out the eyes of Robin-Sebastian, grandson to the famous Crandor in question. Robin gazed back at her with comradely sympathy and apparent relish, patently missing the undercurrent in the room. *Shit.* She smiled at him and *kept* smiling—*brazen bitch*—shifting her weight from hip to hip and making love to him with her eyes, and he smiled back at her, in love with her charm—*ha!*—ignoring *me*, passing me over as if I weren't even there. Both of them did, in fact—both Robin *and* Sophia.

But then Ham walked over to me, and he had *his* eyes *only* on mine when, with his shoulder, he nudged that woman out of the way as if she were nothing more than a chair. Not in a rude way, but as if she were inconspicuous. And I was glad, buoyed up by his treatment of her, and by his seductive look at me. My cheeks burned, and I took a breath and looked away from him, but not before his hot stare reminded me of our fleeting encounter the morning before Robin had arrived. When Ham had wrapped himself around me and kissed me, so long and deep that even now I recalled that part of him that had grown up against me. Large and rock hard, compared with Robin's tender lips and soft lovemaking—the real thing, unlike Robin's mild flirtation with Sophia, which, in any case, was likely exaggerated on my part.

And which I realized when quiet Robin-Sebastian, with his profound, watchful eyes, saw his big brother check me out, the way my breasts moved as I took a deep breath, the way the tip of my tongue brushed my lower lip, and I knew he was upset—particularly when he saw how I reacted. I could feel him lean forward, his arms and his torso go rigid, his boyish surprise and distracted innocence turn, in those few seconds, to anger. And his face, which normally had a high color, went pale.

The brothers faced each other, and their eyes never wavered, and I wanted to run when Robin-Sebastian jumped up. But, loving the attention, I was too excited. *Punish him!* I wanted to yell. *Throw out your little brother for ignoring me. Thrust hard against me. Go on*, I willed. And he did. But it wasn't Ham who moved.

Robin-Sebastian, my beloved and the father of my little daughter, lunged at Ham, knocking over the antique envelope table in the process, and hit Ham at the side of the head, three flat blows with the meat of his fist heel. Then Ham laughed, which made Robin go mad, and he went at him again, and I could see the sweat that came misting off Ham's face.

"What's this? What's this?" My mother's thin little voice reached us, finally, as if from a great distance—the ruckus had brought her running—and the quivering must have pulled Robin to his senses, for he withdrew sheepishly but with no hint of an apology.

"She's my *wife*," he said. "You knew it; you *knew*."

Oh yeah, I had been married, but for the better, never for the worse. Because the man I had married had disappeared years ago. Which, to my mind (and the court's), had annulled my marriage once and for all. How did Robin have the *nerve* to bring it up now?

Ironically, that was when, unannounced, his daughter opted to appear. With her bare, sandy, and wet feet, which left tiny, gritty footprint puddles on the floor. She looked puny, with a neck like a starling newborn, and her staring, teary eyes that took up a good part of her face. In her hand she held a wad of tissues, and on her cheeks, sand and tears had smeared, making a streaky mess.

"It's all *your* fault," I heard her whisper, with those big eyes of hers trained smack on me.

And then, flicking her eyes between the brothers and me, she hissed, "*You* aren't my mother. You don't even pretend when *they're* around." And she pointed at them. And her mouth spit out, "I *hate* you!" Softly, so no one else could hear.

Just fucking great—she had seen the whole thing. And, as usual, blamed me. There was a shocking hollow maturity in the voice of this little girl, *my* little girl, who, from the beginning, had seemed to me like a reproachful little old woman. Maybe that was unfair. Maybe it was just one part of her. Despite the tautness of her shoulders, which made her seem painfully thin, I wanted to slap her. . . . Instead, I reached out to her with one hand, tried to touch her.

"*Peda*," I begged, and choked on her name, my voice clotted with grief and, I suppose, fury . . . but she stepped away from me and raised that knifelike shoulder of hers against me, like a shark's fin or, worse, an unforgiving barrier against my maternal anguish.

To hell with her. As I pressed the back of my hand against my mouth, saliva ran over my fingers, blending into a couple of forlorn tears, which I brushed quickly away. Out of the corner of my eye, I could see my mother's face sag. Her jowls resembled the poached egg I had cooked that morning.

"Yes," Ham muttered under his breath. "Yes, you told me." His voice rose. "So *what?*" He was clearly embarrassed by his brother's temper.

And abashed—as I was. Looking at Robin in a different light, I could see the newer, little-known Sebastian Crandor, who had kept his persona securely hidden in our previous relationship. Examining him now, as if for the first time, I realized that, unlike his suaver, older, good-looking brother, he, *not* Hamlet, resembled the photograph of their grandfather Simon Crandor. It was in the angle of his body, his carriage and immutable spine, which he took care these days to keep erect.

And, fickle me, I took up his hand and kissed his fingertips, one at a time, as if the altercation had never occurred. Still, I couldn't prevent the anticipation I felt when I glanced over at his brother, and at the prospect of the queasy pleasure of Hamlet's lips and fingers on mine—in love with my own recklessness.

Chapter 22

ELSIE

~

*N*onetheless, when day turned into evening, I was filled with remorse and, skipping dinner, in the dark decided to take my boat out, explore the coves, maybe make my way to Manhattan blind: skirt the barges, the swells, and the stink boats by sail and moonlight. *Feel* my way into the city, which would force my senses to pilot my brain, free up the emotions that had compelled me to the boat, to the Sound, and to the water in the first place.

Erase the look on Peda's face when I had kissed Seb's fingertips, erase those words of hers that I had heard faintly but distinctly during the melee and afterward—more of a shock to me than her father's snarls had been when he went after Hamlet. "It's all *your* fault. *You* aren't my mother. I *hate* you," she had hissed. The rhythm reverberated in my head. *I hate you, I hate you, I hate you.* I put my palm up to my forehead and squeezed the beat pounding in my brain. Such venom from such a tiny child. Erase the vision of her and the thought that maybe I didn't know her after all, that defenseless little body. Maybe she hadn't meant it; maybe those words had just popped out in the heat of the moment. I pictured the tip of her rosy tongue, snagged between her front teeth, and the expression reminded me of a pup's, one that I had seen once in a pet-store display, with a hungry look in his eyes while he watched people go by.

So I ran toward the beach through the steaming air, away from the spillage of light, and with each step my sneakers made squishing noises on the millstone path. In my hand I clutched my earphones; I wanted to listen to music while I drifted on the waves. At the jetty, I lowered myself down the ladder onto my father's old wooden rowboat. The green marine paint on its sides was peeling in great flaps of soft, curling sheets, which in the fog looked like iridescent skin. One oar was floating in an inch of water on the bottom slats of the boat and rolled with the waves, banging into a rusted water pail that lay wedged against the only seat. In the boat, I grabbed the oar Indian-style and paddled around the sea wall, looking for the other oar, which, after a time, I found stuck between two cattails in the salt marshes. Struggling to free it, I leaned way over the side, watching a reflection of light at play in the water. Tracing the light to the shore, I could swear it came from a small fire on the beach, which with a slight wind gust either flickered and died out or was blotted out by the fog, which had noticeably thickened. So brief was my glimpse of the fire that I attributed it to my imagination and went on with my chore until I had the missing oar onboard and wedged in its oarlock.

As I rowed out into the open Sound, I told myself it was so much better to offer oneself to the harsh elements, so much easier than dealing with one's family. Establishing the rhythm of rowing, *one-two, one-two*, gave me a sense of control, with no mission in my life except to survive. A law, I believed, greater than any one disappointment.

So that when I heard the scream, the scream that I hoped I also imagined—not a result of Winter's fearful description—I rowed faster. And faster.

Helll . . . p! . . . Helllll . . . p!

And from my mother's island the call chased me as I made my way toward the blurry lights of Manhattan. Sweat welded my underpants to my skin, and my crotch itched madly, but I wouldn't, *couldn't* stop. I rowed in time to the motion of the waves, sinking and rising, exhaling, inhaling, with each stretch and arm movement. So simple, when you think about it—the waves the ocean's heartbeat. *Everybody deserves a second chance, don't they?* I adjusted the volume on my iPod to blot out the screams, rowed strongly, and closed my eyes against the furry darkness, the vastness of the ocean and a line of clouds that seemed to divide the dark sky from the inky water.

Patsy Cline's "Crazy" came on, and I swayed to the tune, pushing against the oars to stem the tears that bubbled onto my cheeks, rolling down so fast that I was finally forced to lay up the oars. I thought it was a stitch that Cline could produce such a sharp emotion in me, refusing to believe that the sobs I tried to stem were born not from the dead singer's words but from my small daughter's rejection of me—which was nonnegotiable. Tried and indicted before proven guilty. With a final, self-pitying nod of farewell toward Peregrine Island, I turned the nose of the old boat into the soupy fog and dug into the rising waves with my heavy oars. "Was she right? Was she right?" I whispered into the mist. The sprays of cool water hit hard against my bare flesh, and I shivered under the barrage.

"*Jesus Christ*, what is it with you?" I said, and stopped my mad rowing. Forced myself to leave the topic of my daughter and concentrated instead on her father, which, I guess, was not much better, but at least it put a stop to my pathetic crying jag.

While I thought about Seb, I rowed gently, remembering

him as he polished the glass on the boat that I had rented for the summer, the boat I had wished I could have but hadn't been able to afford. My water-skiing boat that slept four. Seb, squeezing that dripping, hole-ridden sponge filled with suds over the speed cruiser's sharp lines, all the while cherishing me with his gaze— too much too often—steam rising from where he scrubbed the fiberglass while down on his knees, rinsing the bubbles away with a spurt from a hose, the overflow that clung to the golden hair of his legs and his arms . . .

And that white tan line at his throat. Winter had fantasized our fucking. By her tight lips and teary, reproachful stare, I just knew it. As if I had committed the sin to end all sins. His marks on me in daylight, the way he had bruised me with his desire. If only she knew what I had done to him. What lay on his body underneath the layers of rumpled cotton he normally wore.

Ham knew, too. But I liked that. I enjoyed his jealousy. I enjoyed his touch, so much so that my breath, I found, was suddenly caught tight in my chest. Ham's body, in its nearness, which radiated such heat and promise. When, the week before, he had run the speedboat aground with a dull, muffled thud, he had turned to me, with his face in profile, and I had thought he was in pain from the tenseness of his jaw. And when he had pushed the boat off the rock, it had veered wildly, tossing on the waves like a buoy, and he had flailed with his oar, missing the water completely. But I didn't care. Because when Seb's back was turned, he bit me on my shoulder and all I wanted was for him to draw blood.

You see, while Seb walks straight, upright as a mast, when his natural inclination is to slouch, Ham's gait is easy but purposeful and sure. I know exactly who he is: an ambitious, self-centered man who brooks no excuses for his behavior. He is exactly who he claims to be, and if you don't like it, screw you. When he touches me, I feel the promise of his ambition; when

Seb touches me, it is almost as if someone is walking over my grave. Because I am never sure who is making love to me: Robin Tavelli from Vermont, or Sebastian Crandor.

In those Vermont days, I never asked Robin about his family. I was curiously uncurious, just so grateful to have his arms around me in the middle of all that snow. I wanted to leave my family behind and assumed that he did, too. I had dreamed of ways of being as unlike my parents as possible. The divorce, the hurt, the superficiality of my mother's life—I wanted to forget it all, even my dead grandfather, who had put together the architectural nightmare in which I had grown up. At best, the house was transient, a temporary structure that could be swept away in a flash by the power of the ocean opening out and out and out beside it.

I stopped rowing to contemplate the thought of forever waves and looked out to study them around me, searching the horizon for the Manhattan lights, my journey's beacon. But the milky fog had become too opaque to see through. I stood up, hoping to get a better view, and waved my arms like a seagull flaps its wings, trying to push back the dense air until I could find the island of Manhattan, but it proved impossible. As impossible as the realization that I was lost, with not one demarcation to guide me, either to my destination or back home.

To still my nerves, I started to repeat the names of nearby islands, like an incantation. But I thought my voice sounded pitiful, so I stopped, reminding myself that Winter had always told me to value myself. That if I thought highly of myself, then so would everyone else. I had taken her at her word. But now no one else was around to see me strut. To see me row bravely around in circles.

A flash of light on the horizon, cutting through the white air like a comet, stopped my circling. Wiping my cheek with the back of my hand, I peered up, following a fork of lightning to the water in front of me, where it swept across a quarter of a mile, parting the thick mist with the beauty of a speed skater. Followed by a clap of thunder. And then again, at intervals of about three minutes, until all around me was lightning and thunder that mixed with the sudden onslaught of a driving rain, and so hard was the tattooing on the water that my vision was cut to maybe one foot ahead of me. My eyes smarted from the strain of seeing; my eyelids prickled from the pressure of the drops. Which went on . . . and on . . . and on. Until my heart hurt, too, its beating as wild as the raindrops through which I couldn't see. And I felt so lonely that I sent up a prayer to a god in whom I didn't believe. Daring him to help me. Daring him to help me find my way home. Why is it that people never perceive the underlying violence of nature?

"Which way is home?" I screamed. "Which way is home?" Expecting God to appear, to raise His head above the water like the bloody, decapitated head of John the Baptist. Expecting a sign from Him to prove to me that fairy tales are real, that *He* is real. "Just a simple question," I begged, realizing in my heart that it was a question most people spend their lives trying to answer.

The rain stopped then, like an answer, as abruptly as it had started, and a mist as thick as cheesecake replaced it, engulfing me and my rowboat. Way thicker than before, only this time the black sky was gray like the water and I couldn't tell where it began and the Sound ended, except where I sat, and I trailed my fingers in the water to make sure of its presence.

Got out my crumpled pack of cigarettes after that. The damn things were too wet to light, but I sucked on one anyway, like a kid sucks her thumb. And I looked out into the forever of waves and dark sky, emerging between torn patches of cloud to join, from the water, the rising mist.

Until I saw the mirage, which I swear was a man's head,

moving toward me through the mist like a prophet, his face covered over with a beard that, except for his eyes, hid all of his features. I could just make out his torso as he paddled along—rigid as an Indian warrior, he seemed—with his bottom half sunk into the hollow of the old canoe. And in front of him, at the bow, a black dog sat on a high bench, as if he were another person, a compatriot of his out for a Sunday ride. Staring at the water—that's what he was doing.

"Hey, here I am," I yelled. I stood up and waved my hands over my head while the boat seesawed madly. "Over here. . . . Over here! Can you see me?" I swayed to the rhythm of the seesaw. My leg muscles tightened, and I felt strong suddenly. Back to my old self. Like magic, capable of anything. "Here, here I am!" I yelled. "I'm over here. Directions! Can you help me with directions?"

The prophet's head turned toward me in slow motion. I wanted to sing. Finally, he changed courses and paddled right at me, not swiftly, but at a steady, strong clip, yet no expression crossed his whiskered face, no acknowledgment whatsoever. The dog, however, that was a different matter. He sent staccato yips my way, followed by a ferocious tail movement, which the man did nothing to contain.

When the canoe came up alongside me, I could tell that the man's whiskers were an illusion. Besides a kind of scarf, which hid his mouth and nose, it was his old age—creases I saw up close. The eyes were startling, too, translucent, as if he had surfaced from the deep . . . or the dead. I was looking for a miracle, wasn't I?

"Follow me," he ordered. Whispered it, really, so that I had to strain to hear him, but his whispering seemed appropriate in the mist.

"You don't know where I want to go," I blurted out. Not, "Hello, how are you, thank you for saving me."

"You want to go home," he said, and fluttered his fingers in what I assumed to be a northeasterly direction.

"Peregrine Island. Do you know it?"

He didn't answer, just turned his boat around and threw his chin where the bow pointed.

"Now," he said. "Before the fog gets worse." And those strangely dark yet translucent eyes flickered over my face.

How much worse could it get?

I sat then, arranged myself to follow him, with my heart clapping erratically. What if this man was a murderer, a rapist, a serial killer? I felt my pulse beat almost out of control and took deep breaths. Danger, after all, is what I used to seek. Why not now?

I rowed, he paddled, for close to an hour, and still we were nowhere. With no land in sight. My trip out had been nowhere near an hour. Forcing myself not to panic, I stopped finally, yahooing at him to do the same. He didn't stop, however, so I resumed my rowing, faster now, in order to catch up. Not once did he turn around. But then, neither did I, except to follow his direction, my goal post, a muted red, pointy spike at the end of his canoe, which became my guiding light in the fog.

Plus the dog's face. Every time I turned around to follow the red goal post—I was rowing backward—the dog was staring at me as if his life depended upon it. He was grinning at me—he had moved to the foot of the boat—and I don't think his eyes ever left my back. He never once missed a twist of my head. Waiting for me to react, I guess.

Eventually, my forearms began to ache and I called out to the man. No answer—what a surprise. My mind adrift, my head nodding, I wanted so much to close my eyes. Wanted to tell this to the bearded man without a beard. But we moved on through the waves, leaving no trail in our wake. I might disappear forever. Even so, this rowing, it occurred to me, felt far better than sitting through Winter's holiday church services over on the mainland. At least I'd go out doing something I liked.

Then, like another vision, a small, narrow beach appeared, and it was like none other I had seen before. Mammoth, square-cut boulders hung over it like a shelf. Curiously, the tiny beach was cut off by about a foot, maybe less, of swashing water. At low tide it probably receded so that the water dried up. Maybe the storm had caused the beach to flood.

The man didn't seem to mind. He pulled up on its dark, wet shore, got out, kicking away bits of driftwood and debris, then motioned for me to join him.

With one thrust of my oars, I pulled up on a sandy knoll next to him, scraping the bottom of my boat badly, and hoped I hadn't torn a hole in its old, peeling shell. I sat there then, letting the sweat cool on my skin, wondering what was going to happen when I left the safety of my boat: if I would survive, if the tiny beach could survive another violent rainstorm. I eyed the old man, who stood up against the backdrop of the deep, dark boulders, under a sky that had suddenly grown a few stars. Stars that looked like seeds thrown haphazardly, burning weakly through the muddy gray haze. Underneath them, a scudding cloud reef, ringed with rose, announced the beginning of dawn.

The old man pointed and shaded his eyes against the metallic sky, squinting as if he couldn't see well. "Home is on the other side of those boulders," he said. "You just have to climb them."

How could I trust him? . . . But how could I not?

I crawled out of my waterlogged boat. My sneakers were wet, and I shivered, cold in my dried-up sweat. Stared at my savior, an old, old man with bare, skeletal legs, though I could see clearly that knots of muscle still clung to his bones. Combing his hair off his forehead with the fingers of both hands, he started to come toward me, and I, brave woman that I am, backed up.

The dog, yapping, moved in line with me, as if we were dancing. Crouching down, his butt high in the air, he stared at me. Bounced up and ran rings around me and crouched again. Yapping.

"This isn't my island," I said. White breath steamed from my nostrils.

He touched my elbow, and I flinched, so he gripped it and pushed me in the direction of the boulders.

"Climb them," he ordered, "and you're home."

I looked up at him and noticed that one of his bottom teeth was broken.

"Who *are* you?"

It was more than odd that this old man, this John the Baptist look-alike with the dancing dog, had appeared through a storm to save me, then had led me to this reef. He was unshaven and dressed not unlike the surfers of California, but much more raggedy-like, yet his speech was affluent, so rich, in fact, that it reminded me of a humanities professor I once had. It also brought back vague memories of my grandfather. Not to mention my dad, who prided himself on his speaking ability.

"Who *are* you?" I repeated.

He propelled me over to the rock. Shivering and stiff from the boat, I felt like a sidestepping crab. He let go of my arm when I lagged and looked at me curiously, as if he wanted to laugh. Maybe he'd make his move now. Throw me on the sand. Rape me, this old man.

Rough-like, with a rasp in his throat, he asked, "Does it really matter?"

And then he walked away, his feet turned out and his back as straight as a spear—though I thought the effort cost him dearly. Left me without a backward glance. As if I didn't matter. Got into his canoe and paddled off. The dog in the prow, as proud and rooted as a carved icon.

And so I climbed over the shiny kelp at the foot of the boulders, then hauled myself up so that I was spread-eagle over those slick rocks, even put my cheek down on the barnacles and slimy snails that covered them, my nails scratching to hold on, and bleeding after a while, so as not to slip down. And I cursed that old man for sending me on a wild goose chase. I'd be here through eternity. Pictured myself on the rock, naked as a Tahitian, destined to live out my days eating the snails I scraped up and talking to the seagulls. Hauled myself up and up and up while I fantasized. And then I reached the top.

Pulled my tired limbs so that I straddled it like a sack over a mule. . . . And there it was, its loggia in the distance: the curves and spires that my great-grandfather had tacked onto his house. High up in the pink rim of the cloud mass, which intensified with the sunrise, erasing all traces of rain from my night spent out on the water.

Bending then, so that I could move my neck but not lose my balance, I glanced down at the other side, at the Sound swallowed up by the heavy haze that still hung over it. Just barely could I make out the waves and the tide through the feathers of steam that rose from it, but nowhere at all could I catch sight of the canoe.

Chapter 23

WINTER

~

From where I had stood next to Sophia, I had seen it all when I entered the room: the flirtation that prompted the fight. My daughter, the alley cat, who enjoyed her games with men. She had faced me, the bitch—I don't like that word, but in this case? How could she have turned out this way?

I had just wanted to relay a message, that's all. Give everyone the afternoon to prepare themselves for the meeting today. Because on my ancient answering machine, whose tape tangled, even ripped much of the time, was a garbled message from the detective, announcing his now-imminent arrival, along with the sergeant from his department. "To submit our findings," the man had said, "and to return your paintings." The officer had then ordered all of us to be present at twelve noon today—family, friends, art experts—advising us in the same cordial but formal tone that whoever needed a lawyer should invite such counsel to attend. Yet who could I have called at this late date? And why would I even want to? Scare tactics, that's what these people used. I had seen the same thing on *LAPD*. "Strongly suggested," I believe were the man's exact words, followed by his ardent wish that I was feeling better than I had been when we had last met.

Hearing that I had been feeling bad, of which I had no inkling, made me now feel worse, as I sucked in lungfuls of damp, heavy air while I waited for him and his fellow officer to arrive. It was a record day of heat in the Northeast; the violent rainstorm of the night before had done nothing except to raise the humidity and the degrees. In my opinion, we hadn't seen the last of the storm: dirty, leftover water filled the air. It was the residue, the grit, that was the problem.

Especially in the closeness of the library—the one room in the house that I have *always* hated. So I put Sebastian's offering of lilies in here because I felt the same way about them. Both the library and the flowers remind me of death and departure. No one with any sense brings lilies, except to a funeral, and the room? Its dank, dark, and oppressive atmosphere gives me claustrophobia. But Elsie likes it. She was always impressed by her father—"my daddy," she used to call him, and still does—which I think annoys Peda as much as it does me. This was his favorite room. The room in which he liked to entertain and impress people, and so for his daughter I keep up the tradition. "Use it for the guests," Daniel decreed, satisfied and smiling, whenever we entered together, even though he consistently knocked off my happy-to-please-him arm if I touched him.

Dismissing my sadness and those disturbing feelings, which usually I can't for the life of me shake, I snapped to attention when Elsie entered. "Moth . . . *er*," she said. "*Winter!*" Wasn't she overusing my name? Hitting me with it to make a point . . . like her father used to? "When are they coming?" She looked at her watch. "Aren't they late?"

Careful not to touch the orange pollen tongues of the lilies, which would stain my rose-colored silk, I plucked one flower from a stem and squeezed its yellow petal, studied the fluid that moistened my thumb, then put the perfumed fingers to my nostrils and inhaled, extra careful not to challenge my daughter. For years I hadn't heard from her. She had never thought of *my* feelings. Then one day she had just appeared, bringing the youngster in tow. I was thrilled to see her, of course, to take her in, welcome her home as if those years had never existed. But why couldn't she ever think of *my* feelings? Some things, I think, never change.

"Are they?" I answered. "I don't know. I imagine they'll be here soon."

"Who's coming?"

She spoke more calmly now—maybe she felt remorse? Did I actually sense some long-ago tenderness in her voice? Or was it only wishful thinking on my part?

I took a breath and pretended to examine my nails. They'd grown too long, I noticed. "I honestly don't know," I lied, and looked around at the Getty men, at the unshaped anxiety that stiffened their shoulder muscles, watched Zinger cough and spit into his outstretched palm, watched Ham pace, concern tightening the skin across his face. The news from my answering machine seemed to shimmer in the air like electricity.

It occurred to me that we couldn't hear the doorknocker from the library, with its fish-tank interior, so I hurried outside. Maybe the entire police force, as backup, was waiting for us in the sun. But no one was there. My nerves were almost as frayed as Zinger's.

Half an hour went by, and still no one appeared. Five minutes more, I'd give them. And then what? With this promise, which I knew I wouldn't keep, came a pounding. We sent Peda, of course. Who, at the outset of the questioning, I would ask to leave. She knew too much. So did I, for that matter.

The secret of Jake was lodged in my throat like a fragmented chicken bone. Waiting for the police, waiting to see who had come to interrogate us, I felt myself sweating. I held my head in my hands. Should I expose Jake as Simon Crandor? What if he refused to come forward? And, worse, what if all this was a figment of my imagination, fostered by Peda's fantasies?

When I looked up, the big cop, all in blue, the one who had come the first time to talk to us, filled the doorway. When he saw me stare at him, he flushed and looked down at the floor. The young detective, done up in a charcoal pin-striped suit, accentuated by a dotted burgundy-and-blue silk tie, pushed past him, and the blushing policeman's ruddy cheeks reddened further. All business was detective Todd Kalina, introduced formally today by Hamlet Crandor, as if the two knew each other well. To everyone else in the room, the blond detective held out his hand.

Nevertheless, I was relieved by the men's almost-comic appearance: they reminded me of Sancho Panza and Don Quixote. In retrospect, I guess I shouldn't have expected the chief of police (despite Todd's ominous phone message); after all, in the court archives, Crandor had been dead for more than thirty-eight years.

"You took so long to get back to us, I thought the case was closed," I said boldly.

Everybody in the room gawked at me—as if I never opened my mouth. And, to be truthful, even I was shocked at my audacity.

The detective stroked his soft, beardless chin while I listened to the stepped-up rise and fall of my breath. "Nothing like that," he said at length. "We had to finish our homework." He gave me his best Trident smile. "Me and Joe-Ivan here." He thrust his elbow into the cushioned arm of his sergeant, who grinned inanely at me. "Your story needs closure, but *we* needed time."

Horatio held up his hand. "*What* story? Over a forty-year-old case? For which you couldn't find any evidence? What gives you the right to delve into people's private lives? Detain them? Harass them? I warned you before . . ." His fingers shook violently. "I'm tempted to sue you, goddamn you, sue your goddamned department."

I put my hands against my lips and closed my eyes.

"He's got a point, you know," Zinger said. "No one can demand our records, our files, worm their way into our lives like this. There's a privacy law; it's *enough* now." Zinger's face was red and glowing, the pores wide open, slick with oil. I gagged from the imagined smell of his sweat. From looking at him. From listening to his grating, urgent voice. He sounded like a worked-up evangelist.

Elsie half rose from her seat. "If anyone else had been on this case," she said, "it would have been dropped by now."

"Maybe." A little smile played on the detective's face as he looked at Elsie, and for a second I felt a guilty surge of nervous exhilaration. "It was unfortunate that you got *me*, then."

I rubbed at a spot on my dress, concentrated on its outline. Controversy made me uncomfortable.

Clay strained forward, fingering his ascot. "You told these fellas not to leave Connecticut. That's all. While they did their job. What harm? I, for one, want to know what you've found out, if anything."

His voice always had that dramatic ring to it. But he was right, good old Clay. I would have said the same thing. *Get on with it*, I wanted to say. *Leave us in peace.*

I smiled at him, careful not to make eye contact with Sophia. Her wrists were lightly crossed at her knee. In one hand, she held a wineglass, which she tipped slowly back and forth. Clay had poured her the wine, I assumed. I wondered what she saw in him, his slicked-back hair, comb lines and all, his diamond earring, and his air of sexual fluidity (I had always questioned his sexual preference, not caring, really—though of course I didn't like it if he cottoned to both sexes).

The young detective went to the center of the room and spread wide his hands. "There was a note in the papers," he announced, "one we all missed at first, in which an anonymous informant named names. Those responsible for sabotaging Crandor's wooden sloop, the one he so diligently restored."

I looked over at the two old men—Zinger made a lot of noise when he breathed, but now he sounded positively frightening.

How could those two experts, or the cops, have missed such an incriminating document? I didn't believe it, not for one second.

Todd focused on Zinger's face. "Crandor's assailants drained the gas from his motor, the note claims, so that it would have been impossible for him to make it back to shore before a storm hit. And no oars. But, worse, apparently the drain plugs were removed and the bilge pump was compromised, so that any leak would have sunk the boat almost immediately anyway." He walked back and forth as he talked. "A calculated plan meticulously thought out and executed by the culprits. For months, these people watched the weather, mindful to urge Mr. Crandor out on the Sound when a storm was imminent. Crandor was a dynamite sailor so thought nothing of it." He looked over his shoulder at Guardi. "I'm told it turned out to be one of the major hurricanes of the century—the night that Crandor disappeared."

A conveniently found document? Was Todd bluffing? Maybe. Because, despite the obstacles he faced—the inordinate amount of time elapsed after Crandor's disappearance and the delays trying to obtain information because of it—he had turned this case into a personal crusade. To prove his theory, to *convict*, to kindle his notoriety and establish a reputation for himself, until he turned his name into a household word—*this* is what I thought he was after. For he thoroughly enjoyed the public eye and the power of his role. *We* were his ladder to success. And Ham was helping him. But *why?*

I fanned myself with my hand and looked around the room. Zinger licked his lips with a smacking noise, blew sweat from his chin, and ran a hand down his belly. Horatio's skin looked waxy; swollen plum patches hung beneath those slits of eyes, with which he gazed at the young detective, level and threatening, at odds, I thought, with his fragile constitution.

"Go on," Sophia urged. Her fingers with the chipped nails pulled at her red-lacquered lip.

Shafts of dusty light raked the walls, blinding us with the glare, so that the window looked like a mirror.

"Wouldn't the man have known better then to go off in a storm?" Elsie said at last. "A storm that was predicted? No one is *that* stupid."

"He trusted them, I guess. Didn't pay attention."

"Are you accusing *these* two men?" Clay asked. He grinned and flittered his fingers at them. "A man who wears felt gloves to read the paper? And another who can't keep his hair on? *These* are your assassins?"

Detective Todd smiled. Ignored Clay and fixed his eyes on Ham. "Men I now need to question. Maybe even arrest. Your father was the other one."

"He's dead," Ham said. He drained his wineglass. "But of course you know that."

"On the other hand, who's to say the *real* Crandor placed the notes behind the picture?" The cop turned back to Clay.

Elsie looked annoyed. She was right: this was turning into the cop's version of a cat-and-mouse game. "Where is all this leading?" she said. "Can't you test the age of the papers? Can't you identify the author by the writing?"

"We *did*. The paper is *presumably* authentic. And no, the note was *typed*."

"Then find the typewriter. What do you mean, *presumably*?"

Todd snorted. "A typewriter today is a dinosaur—most of them have disappeared. As far as the paper goes, no one can say for sure."

"So that still doesn't prove anything. And, as you say, *anyone* could have placed the documents there. This whole thing could be a setup, instigated by someone to mislead people like you, throw you off the track." Elsie stretched her arms above her head, then slowly turned her chair around to face Sophia.

The big cop shuffled his feet, started to say something. But Todd put his hand on his shoulder and answered Elsie himself. "Oh, yeah . . . there's a setup here . . . but, thanks to the brains behind it, I can finally exact retribution for Crandor: I can prove that forty years ago there *was* foul play. And that these two men, with the help of Ham's daddy, *murdered* him, murdered Mr. Crandor. As to the *setup*, most likely one or two of you in this room have worked out a scam to throw new pictures into the marketplace for a wad of dough. If there are a few casualties in the meanwhile—an exhumed tabloid, a missing body, a sordid murder from half a century back—well, so much the better for publicity." Todd threw his arm at the seated experts, at Ham, Clay, Sophia and Seb, Elsie . . . and at me. "How am I doing so far?"

"That's what *you* think," I mumbled to myself, energized for once by my secret. A secret I was finally and absolutely sure I hadn't imagined. A secret of which I was absurdly proud.

The young man turned in my direction. *My God, he heard me.* But it was toward the door he turned, to where Peda stood, appearing as silently as a spirit-wraith. She sneezed loudly—her calling card; a strand of mucus swung from her nose. Her pointy face reminded me of a snapdragon, one that closes and opens with the prodding of a finger, or with the atmosphere. Today, like a snapdragon, her face was closed tight, so tight that

I couldn't read her expression at all. With her arms buckled into her armpits, she chewed on the inside of her lip and examined something invisible on her toes.

Seb rose. "Well, I think that's enough. After all your hype, you have no *hard* proof . . . of anything." At the sideboard, he poured himself a glass of iced tea, swung the bottom of the glass in circles to stir it. When drops of the drink splashed onto his shirt, Elsie stepped in front of him to blot the spot with a tissue. The two dipped their heads together, and his hand slipped around her neck.

And that's when Ham strode over, grabbed a glass, and threw some bourbon into it, relishing the pained look in his brother's eyes.

Elsie placed her thin fingers over Seb's square-nailed ones. I had to look away then, embarrassed by the intimacy of the two hands. Embarrassed by the currents of hostility between the brothers, and my daughter, who egged them on.

The young detective stood up. "On the strength of the 'hard' proof you think I lack, notwithstanding, I'm taking these two men in," he announced.

When Zinger cried out, "On what charge?" the cop confronted him and Guardi . . . but Ham whirled and spoke rapid-fire into Todd's ear before he could answer.

The detective's eyes tightened. "This guy wants to vouch for you," he told them. "Take you under his wing, so to speak."

Had Ham and Todd rehearsed this? Why would Ham do such a thing? Out of loyalty to whom?

Todd eyed the two old men, smiled at them out of one side of his mouth, as if his other cheek were numb. "For the time being, you're free to go, on Ham's and your own recognizance . . . thanks to Crandor here." With that lopsided smile still frozen on his face, he glanced at Hamlet—like he thought he was crazy . . . or maybe ingenious. "Who is vouching for you out of loyalty to his father, also named in the note . . . as long as there's no state hopping."

"This could take years," Horatio said, "the way *you* work."

"That's tough, isn't it?"

Horatio Guardi cleared his throat, began to cough. It was a hacking sound. "When, then?" he asked through the cough.

"Before the end of the summer. When I can get your financial statements, and your background checks are complete. If we find anything. . . ." Todd shrugged.

"There never *was* a body, and you *know* that. Where's your proof? A paper written by *whom*? You're taking the word of a *ghost*." Horatio laughed, hiccuped.

Todd smiled so widely this time that his pink gums showed, then leveled his gaze on the old man. "I guess you could say that: I'm taking the word of a ghost." He winked at Ham, who pointedly averted his eyes. "But make no mistake: take *my* word for it, Mr. Guardi, there *will* be convictions."

"Is that a threat?"

"I promise you closure by the end of the summer. Interpret it any way you like."

If he wanted to scare us, he was doing a good job of it. Because I was as positive as I was sitting here that the two men's financial statements and their background checks would *never* check out. Plus, I was sure that the cop knew it, too. And after he got through with them, well, then he'd go after Clay and Sophia, expose their small-town hopes at making a killing off fresh paintings on the art scene. By the end of the investigation, it would be my turn, too. They'd find *something*—I was sure of it. Maybe for covering up for Jake.

Ham leaned over and, with painstaking deliberation, brushed an invisible piece of lint off Elsie's arm.

Seb drew in a sharp breath. He took hold of Peda, who stood by my knee, and brought her close. In lieu of Elsie, probably. Because of his brother's behavior. To repel the visions of his penurious, dead father. For something uncorrupted to hold on to. He gripped her by her tiny, wing-boned shoulders and leaned her back against his front . . . as if to keep her from running away.

Chapter 24

ELSIE

~

After the meeting, we ran into each other on the driveway, Ham and I. He found me with my binoculars, spying on a small, slow-moving boat that I had discovered far out to sea. When he appeared, curious to see what I saw, I was peering through the branches of one of the wind-bent sea pines that screens the driveway and Winter's overgrown gardens from the Sound. Soon, we two peered together at the boat and its splash of paddles. He shaded his eyes, studied the sunlight flashing off the water, and rubbed my shoulder, and, after a while, we laughed together.

He said that he felt good when he was with me. Took a deep breath of the close, ninety-degree air, the briny smell of the Sound, and added that the pillows of air around us, which reminded him of the hot and cold patches in a pond, made him feel alive. Then he threw his arm out toward the distant lighthouse, an expansive gesture, as if he were embracing the scene before him. "It's like a mirror," he said of the water. "The other day, when the wind was up—remember?—then the waves were capped in white and they rolled in like thunder."

Jesus—he changed personalities as rapidly as the air puffs. In his present mood he reminded me of Robin, his younger and gentler brother. He had also obviously forgotten that this is where I live—every morning, every evening, I see transformed saltwater scenes; sometimes the changes are so fast I don't even notice them . . . but it's never because I don't want to. The Sound is in my blood. I stared at him but didn't reply. Just blushed and concentrated on his features. Behind him, the pink and raspberry astilbe acted as a frame for his well-built good looks, and I had an urge to photograph him, right here in this setting. Keep this picture of him fresh in my mind.

Apparently he had the same idea, for his eyes stayed on my mouth for the longest time, waiting for me, I assumed, to help him describe the oncoming craft and the man who sat at its helm. But the more I strained to look out to sea, trying not to imagine his lips on mine, the blurrier the picture became, until the man, the boat, and its passenger had all turned into a watery blob.

"The police called me in on the case," he said flatly, finally switching his gaze from me to the boat. He kept his eyes on its path, which was expanding as the boat inched its way closer to us across the vast stretch of dark water.

Through my binoculars, I could now see that the vessel was a canoe. And I could see a man's back, and what appeared to be a bearded head bent with effort, his paddles raising, then dipping. A gull in the boat's path lifted suddenly, wheeling and screaming in the hot stillness.

Ham's warm fingers touched my shoulder and spread out, slid down my bare arm. With his fingertips, he traced the blue veins on the inside of my forearm; I shivered, thinking that this was not a place that anyone toys with. Moved away from him and pushed through the twisted pine branches toward the beach, the boat, and its passenger, who, I hoped, was in fact the old man who had guided me home.

Ham held the branches up over my head, so that the path took on the aura of a dark green arbor.

"So what?" I said. "You think I give a shit if you fraternize with the cops?" I stopped so abruptly that he ran into me and the branches whacked me on the left side of my face. Biting back tears, mad at him for the sting, for him just being him, I kept the branches at arm's length. "Why are you following me?"

"I just wanted you to know. The police contacted *me*, said I'd be an invaluable tool. We've established a solid case against Zinger and old Horatio. Don't you want to hear the rest?"

I shook my head, appalled at his smugness. Didn't he realize that with his collaboration, he was enabling the cops to smear the name of his own father? Condemn him for murder? Without a trial? Dead men couldn't defend themselves. Didn't he *care*?

He blocked my way, shoved me against a thin, thorny trunk. With my toes I dug into the warm sand, then scratched one ankle with the toes of the other foot. Considered kicking him in the groin, which, truth to tell, was a large, soft-tight target that I had noticed earlier and imagined brushing up against.

I pushed at him hard, but with my thrust his grip on my arms tightened so that he hurt me. When he moved his thumb, I noticed that he was making bruise marks. His breath had quickened, along with the pressure on my arm, and his eyes took on a dark glaze.

"What do you see in my brother?" He shook me a little and flicked my cheek with his index finger, moved his face down to mine so I could smell him, feel the heat of his breath on my cheek. "There's no accounting for taste, is there?" he said.

I slid down the trunk. But he slid down with me, so that together we landed fast on the sand beneath the arbor of misshapen trees. He flattened his hands and ran his palms up my bare calves, my knees, to my thighs under my shorts, and then he reached under the band of my panties, his fingers deftly following my crevice, and I felt my flesh weaken, turn too soft to move when he carefully opened it, releasing a heady waft of my own warm, trapped air.

He unbuttoned his pants. "No . . . ," I said, not really meaning it. Hating myself for my weakness. My throat felt constricted, and my voice sounded so hoarse it surprised me.

He laughed then, a hard-edged sound that made me move, try to pull myself up on the tree trunk. But he yanked me down, so hard that a splinter of wood pierced my palm. And it bled, and he sucked it, licking away the small flaps of skin around the wound.

I couldn't help myself, I told myself later on. Couldn't slow my breathing long enough to take control. And hated myself more than usual, if possible.

Afterward, he lit a cigarette, expelled the smoke in a cloud, and looked at me long and steady through the smoke without saying a word. Ground it out before it was done, drove the fist of his right hand triumphantly into his left, then tossed off his sandals and ran across the sand, striding forward, setting down one perfect foot after the other with the confidence of a tightrope walker. And I watched him. Disliking him more and more by the second. *Of course* the cops would have buttered him up; they *needed* him, counted on that ego of his to feed them information.

"So?" he said, a small crack to his voice when he rejoined me. As if he were an inexperienced boy asking for my approbation.

My muscles ached from their own pent-up tension, and I stretched, squinting against the haze, trying to find again the old man and his boat.

"Why would you cooperate with the police?" I asked for the second time, hoping that now he would incriminate himself.

He shrugged. "Why not?"

"Why do you want to persecute old Horatio? Or my mother? Why do you want to drag your father's name through the dirt?"

"My father's got nothing to do with this." Ham turned away, strode over to the beach again, so close to the waves that when he turned to face me drops of seawater spotted his sunglasses. "I want to know who's making the fakes. I've got a *right* to know. That's all. Or if they *are* fakes."

"What for?"

"So that nobody makes money off my family." He paused for a moment, watched me carefully. "At least not without me getting a piece of it. I thought I told you that." He took off his glasses, rubbed his eyes with his fingers. When I didn't answer, he looked at me from under his arched eyebrows and ran a finger over my lips.

"Fuck you!" I said, and reared back.

"Well?" he prodded. He smirked a little. "What's wrong with that?"

The beach was the color of muslin. The only sound came from the water smashing onto the shore. The sky looked like rain, and the air was heavy. It felt like his breath, like the essence I had smelled coming from myself. And it made me sick. Thunder rolled in the distance, and the sun hid behind the clouds. And I started to walk away. Like a billy club, my binoculars swung from my hand and hit my leg with each step.

Ham ran after me. "Where are you going?" he said.

I turned, stopped dead in front of the weed-filled leucothoe beds a level up from the beach. Almost of a height, we confronted each other.

There was a long, strained silence, and then I whispered, "What is it that you think you see in me?"

He stared at me, uncomprehending.

"There's no accounting for taste, is there?" I said, and walked away.

On the terrace, the sky erupted with hail. Hard pellets like mothballs rained down on me, and I ran for the house, watching the tiny white balls bounce almost three feet off the ground. The last I saw of Hamlet was from the swinging screen door. He was standing below the terrace, under the bullets of hail, stock-still, and staring after me as if he had lost his last friend.

I wanted to tell Seb about the salty, worn man, how he had found me lost in the night. About his shiny black dog. And about this day in the afternoon when I had discovered, far off in the Sound, the same old man, who looked as if time had forgotten him and whose voice I remembered as low and sandy yet in some way peculiarly comforting. I wanted to describe in detail this person who had saved my life. All this, I hoped to share with Robin-Sebastian, in order to eradicate Hamlet's presence from my person.

How one brother (Ham) could bring out such an unpleasant streak in me, while the other (Seb) spawned only sweetness and loving feelings—at least now, if not in Vermont—was beyond me. Why I felt the need to live on the edge—to seek out ruin, to enjoy sex generated from danger, to sail blind into a night storm, to pick scabs raw so they could never heal—this, also, I wanted to discuss with Robin. Though of course I never would.

So I sat and waited for him in the kitchen and watched the hail let up until it turned into a soft rain, and then the rain paused and the air was suddenly quiet, full of moisture and the overwhelming wet smell of heavy, drenched sand and dead fish and raw, teeming sea life. I licked my lips and tasted salt, listened to the silence give way to the drone of mosquitoes, and, as night spread across our island, a dark blanket dotted by flashes of starlight, in the dark I concentrated on my hot breath and the red runaway sun, and the sound of moths batting against the screens.

But Seb never came. Dinner came and went, and still no Robin-Sebastian.

At nine o'clock, barefoot, I tugged open the side screen door, made my way down the dark and narrow stairway, and from there followed my daytime path around the house onto the terrace. Under the willows in the back, a grounded spotlight shone up from the biggest tree's base to the shivering umbrella of leaves and disappeared into the cloudy, starry midnight-blue sky, blissfully free of rain. To the tempo of the foghorn's toll, I ran down the millstones to the water and then, since it was low tide, walked out to the end of the breakwater, which was strewn with debris from the afternoon hailstorm. Leaning on a half-immersed boulder at the tip of the breakwall, I listened to the foghorn . . . and then I heard that mewling shriek again.

I couldn't imagine anyone screaming for so many nights. It sounded weaker than the night before and certainly nothing over which to lose sleep. A cat maybe, half-drowned or starved. When I looked over my shoulder toward shore, I swore I could see something skulking, but it was probably nothing more than the ghostly light bouncing off the frothy, wound-up waves. Still, I decided to take a look, maybe save the poor thing if I could find it, whatever it was, and rescue Winter from her terror and night sweats.

But minutes later it wasn't the vision that brought me back to land; it was the fire I saw onshore that drew me, flickering from the same area that I had seen from my boat. And so bent was I on following it that I forgot about the wailing cat, which, if I were honest with myself, had scared me almost as much as it had scared my mother. Well, not quite, but enough to make me move fast and with more determination than if I were out for a morning jog.

The fire reminded me of the old man, and as I came closer, its intensity seemed to grow. I wanted to thank him, find out his name, find out how he knew *my* name, how he knew where I lived.

So I hurried toward the light, the wind from my running-walk blowing my hair out behind me. It felt good, the dry breeze a relief after the days of humidity and heaviness. But a spongy beach made my toes and my heels sink deep, and it was hard going for a time, so that I had to take deep breaths while I watched vapor come from my mouth.

The fire had petered out by the time I reached it, probably from the force of the wind; a few old cinders were left, nothing more. I called and waved my arms and stood around next to it for a while. At last I made out a man hurrying in my direction, coming down, it seemed to me, from the terrace. Shorter, bulkier, than the old man, and not as hunched over. Robin, the man looked like, from the span of distance in the dark.

I went to meet him, and we came together near the inlet, near the shallow whitecapped waves, near the swirling patterns of moonlight on the water. By the flush on his cheeks, I could see he was upset. My own face, too, felt hot.

"I saw you today," he said. "With your binoculars . . . with my brother."

He put his head to my hair and inhaled beneath my ear, tickled my neck when he pushed away a damp tendril. "I smell him on you."

I lied then. Told him to get lost. That he had a hell of a nerve accusing me of something I wouldn't do. Placed my palms to my cheeks so that they wouldn't redden more, so that he wouldn't see. But he didn't argue. He accepted my lie. With his beating heart against my telltale cheek. And I felt immortal, jubilant that I could do whatever I liked, have whomever I liked, live with one foot always on the accelerator.

His eyes were filling up, I could see, and I could further see that he didn't want me to see it. Despite this, I dried the wet beneath his eyes and licked his tears off my fingertips.

Just above the elbow he grabbed me, hurting me, which somehow helped. Closed his eyes and shook his head without opening his eyes, and I just knew that he knew. With his sturdy, blunt fingers rubbing my spine, I leaned back against his open hand and thought of the pale blond hairs that covered the backs of those hands. He exhaled kisses against my eyelids, and when he spoke of his love for me, his voice was ragged. His sandpaper beard scratched my cheek, and I winced. And he caught my eye for as long as I could stand it.

"Come on," he said, and pushed me a step toward the beach. "Come on, see the fire I made."

"It's not the old man's?"

He stared at me with his hand on my back. "What old man?"

I shook my head. "It's not important."

There was a long pause while he searched my face.

"Your fire?" I reminded him, feeling sweat spread under my arms with the prickly heat of my conscience.

He took my hand and led me down to his cinders, where he applied a lit match to pine kindling he brought from behind a rock. As the kindling took, we lay down on the sand next to it, our heads pillowed by smooth rocks, and looked up at the crescent-shaped moon directly above us. When a cloud for a moment ran over its brightness, eliminating the shadows on the water's foam, Seb raised up on his elbows to look into my eyes. With his face hanging over mine, he said, "I started all this . . . with the painting, you know."

"I know," I whispered.

"I just wanted you back. And Peda. When I called the Getty, I called anonymously, but I didn't think about Ham. I knew their people would have to contact my family eventually; I assumed that Ham would tell me when they called. I mean, we're the only ones left. But I should have known better." His voice was bitter.

I touched his eyelashes with my tongue, and he jerked away. They tasted salty. I wanted to kiss him but was afraid to.

"It never entered my mind that Ham might come here without me." He wouldn't look at me, then rolled over so that we weren't touching and stared out into the black vastness of the ocean.

"I never thought there would be all these complications: the letters, the extra canvases . . . my brother's greed." He turned back and rocked on one elbow, sank his eyes into mine. He wasn't talking about the paintings; he was talking about his brother and me.

"It's not your fault," I said.

I wanted to tell him it was *my* fault, that somewhere I had gone bad, I wasn't worth his effort. Started to vocalize my words of self-hate, when a scream that sounded like *Help!* interrupted me. That animal again.

Helll . . . lll . . . p! Closer than before, and terrifying because of its proximity.

Despite the August heat, I started to shake. Robin-Sebastian and I jumped up at the same time. He threw his shirt over me and covered my eyes with his hand. Me, the liberated woman, cowering under the shade of his outstretched fingers.

And then again, that noise, that eerie cry for help. *He . . . lll . . . p! . . . Hell . . . lll . . . p!*

And I stumbled against him, digging into him so that he would hold me upright, and we made our way up the bank, the quickest route to the house, leaving his fire to disappear with the incoming tide.

But it wasn't the noise, the *he . . . ll . . . p! helll . . . p!*; it was my shameful cries into this man's neck that frightened me most of all. Because I hid my eyes from those screams so that I blotted them out altogether, horrified because I was suddenly, painfully aware that what I blotted out temporarily would never withstand the test of time.

Chapter 25

PEDA

I used to think that Jake was a god. From on top of my rock castle or from inside my sea cave, the one that fills with water when the tide is high, I used to wait for him. Sometimes for hours. With my hands in my pockets, swatted by the wind, my big toes digging their way to Australia. If I was lucky, birds on long stilts made a parade in front of me. From my lookout on the rocks, covered with tiny, drying-out flies that rose, like me, with the *whoosh* of each white-capped wave. At low tide I liked to crawl like an eel, lie flat on my stomach at the ocean's edge, with inches of water under me, and stare straight ahead past New York to Africa, while I waited for my old man and Scarecrow, Jake's shiny black dog with the plaid collar.

But I don't think of Jake as a god anymore. Yesterday, when I learned different, I chewed the inside of my mouth until it felt almost as sore as the deep gash felt on my forehead when I first met Jake, on that early spring morning right after I fell from the rocks.

Before I changed my mind, however, as usual, I spent most of the day waiting for him on my waterbed, floating under the tick of the hot sun while screeching gulls wheeled around me, dive-bombing for those unlucky fish whose silvery scales caught the sun's rays, and with it the birds' fishing eyes. Back from the waves, I pictured a mighty fish-god to the rescue, magnified by a millionth of a millionth percent, and he looked to me just like Jake. And because of my love for him, I felt my chest tighten, and I swallowed hard, and my tears blotted out the waves, the blue sky, and the fish-god.

And then Jake appeared for real, and his shadow over me blocked the heat from the sun. I reached up my arms, and he leaned down, so close to me that his face seemed to fall apart, and I saw only the inside of his eyes, dots swimming around in them just like the darting fish with the silvery scales. He was awesome.

For a while we sat side by side on the highest rock; it was as if we were glued together. And we talked about everything. We sang songs, and fat drops fell from the corners of his eyes. I watched him and wiped my own runny nose with my sleeve. He pointed out the beauty of the rock beneath our feet. I was the only one besides him, he said, who understood its perfection. I pulled a purple piece of ocean glass from my pocket to show it to him and polished it with my thumb.

And asked him why grown-ups—mainly my mother, I confided—were so hard to understand.

"What do you mean?" he said.

I told him about the time I had found my mother on the beach, lying with her knees raised. In front of Omum's friend Clay, who sat, glaring-like, at a clump of wet, curly hair that sparkled between her legs. I told him at first I sat very still, trying to pretend like I wasn't there. Then I snuck another look. The hair on my mother's body was dark, not like the hair on her head, and kinky, kind of, but pretty up against her naked body, which was the same pink and white as the inside of a conch shell. Anyway, she turned on her side and saw me looking at her. So did Clay, because I saw his mouth quivering while he looked at her wet clump. But she didn't get mad; she didn't do anything except wave at me. And her long breasts waggled when she waved. So I just waved back and left. But it made me feel funny.

Jake bent down to peer into my eyes. "Why?" he said in a soft voice.

"Because she shouldn't have been there with Clay. About a month later, Sebastian—you know? I told you about him—he came to visit. Besides, Mom isn't interested in the same things as I am."

Jake nodded and said he could appreciate my feelings. That was all he said. But I knew he understood.

And that's when we saw the three swans swim by, their long necks arched, pulling their heads way down under the water, looking for food, same as those gulls do. So I skipped my flat, polished stone across the water at them. They turned to look at us, then pushed themselves out of the water and they lifted off like three planes, using the Sound as a runway. When they reached the air they flapped their wings extraloud, to tell us, *Told ya so. . . . Told ya so.* Because two of them carried small, silvery fish in their beaks. Still alive and still flopping about as those big old swans flew up above us. I could see the eyes of the two fish as clear as I could see Clay's wet middle finger, shimmering, as he had held it out for me to look at when my naked mother waved at me. But I didn't tell Jake that part.

I slid down off the rocks then, scraped my shins so that they bled but paid no never mind, and for Jake's sake, Scarecrow's, too, I did cartwheels on the wet sand so that my palms and fingers ached, and I left big handprints for the waves to wash away. Scarecrow followed me, barking at my flashing hands, although, truthfully, I wasn't very good and I fell a lot, and then he licked me all over my face with his scratchy tongue and I laughed and Jake laughed, too.

Before Jake left, with Scarecrow in his canoe, he kissed me on the cheek, the first time ever, and then he said, "It's a strange thing about family: you spend all your days trying to get away from them, and then they're all you really want."

I didn't get it, but I guessed he was talking about Elsie and me. I didn't *want* my mother, though, and I thought he knew that. So I ran along the breakwater, willing him to come back so that I could tell him, but in the marsh, when I saw him row into the grasses and park his boat in a swampy bog, I hid behind a sand bar.

What was he doing? Why wasn't he going home? Above his head, a plastic bag floated on a wind puff and rippled like a jellyfish, and I wondered if he also thought it looked like a jellyfish. I wanted to ask him and decided to show myself, picturing his look of surprise when he noticed me. But when I saw him haul on knee-length rubber boots, which I had never seen before, and step out into the muck, and motion Scarecrow to follow him, and Scarecrow with difficulty half swam and half walked in between the swaying mustard-colored grass, his head bobbing up and down when he took swim strides, I crouched way down so that Jake wouldn't see me.

The sun cooked the top of my head. My heartbeat melted through my ears, and I wanted to get out of the sun, but I didn't dare move as I watched Jake and Scarecrow climb the embankment to our lawn and the millstones in front of our patio. Hadn't he told us he *never* came up to people's houses? Right behind Scarecrow's long, licorice-stick tail, with which he beat the air ferociously, swarms of peeping wrens dove and swam in the warm wind gusts as if they were following the old man and his dog. When Jake neared Omum's house, I stood up. I didn't think he could see me anymore. Besides, he didn't turn around. I squinted at the house, which in the heat looked like a melting chocolate bar. Scarecrow, on the yellow-green lawn, raced in circles and chased his shadow. I leaned way back and did a hula hoop, trying to imitate him with my own shadow, but against the water's glare I caught only my toes.

Like a bandit I snuck after them then, hunched low and scurrying up the low hill, from one broken-branched locust tree to another. Once, I hid behind a bunch of Clay's dying sunflowers, their poor, droopy heads heavy with seeds.

Where was Jake going? I held my breath until I couldn't stand it. At the side of the house Jake stopped and, without a care in the world, threw a lime-green Frisbee to Scarecrow, who leaped way up for it while it floated just in front of his nose. Didn't Jake care if anyone saw him?

All of a sudden, he whistled at Scarecrow, who dropped his tail and ran to Jake's heels, and then he sat down, like I did, to wait. Wondering where his master would go, watching him closely as Jake turned around like a lighthouse beacon whose rotating eye keeps watch from out in the middle of the Sound.

Eventually, Jake walked away and he and Scarecrow disappeared into the rhododendrons by the side of the house. There's a path there, grown up with weeds and runty start-up trees, that leads to the front driveway and to another side path, which is even more weed-filled, that goes to the old carriage house and stable, now a garage, although no one uses it, and a falling-down garden and tool shed. I ran to follow, shading my eyes and tiptoeing like an Indian. At the rusted gate that separates the garage courtyard from the rest of the property, Jake stopped, unhooked a twisted nail on the gate, and, to my surprise, because it had never opened before—we always lifted it—the gate swung open, hanging from one hinge and rocking as if it might break.

I wanted to clap but jumped around instead so that I

tripped in a gravelly hole and fell down. I lay there for a moment, rubbing my side, my sore ankle, and my watery eyes. When I looked up, Jake and Scarecrow were gone.

Again I followed them, limping through the one-armed, rickety gate. And my heart beat madly, my melted blood thumping so hard in my ears that I almost didn't hear the shuddering of the warped, paint-peeled door at the back of the garage. A door I had always been afraid to enter. Omum had told me that it led into the old tack room, that it was spider-filled, haunted, and full of bats. *Don't go in, don't go in*, I wanted to yell—to warn Jake, just like Omum had warned me. Before it was too late.

Especially when Jake never came out. But I waited for him there, in front of the old carriage house, until a thin lavender streak of light showed up in the west on top of the sky.

After that I went in. Holding my breath, biting my lip and tiptoeing. So soft on my toes, I never woke Jake at all. Watched him, is all, lying spread out on a narrow bed, asleep with his mouth open as if he might catch flies. Those that were left, anyway, that hadn't gotten stuck in the sticky strips hanging from the one window. Clean as heck, the room was, no sign of bats anywhere, or spiders. Just old Scarecrow, who lay flat, too, with his four legs stuck out straight on the sway-backed wood floor, his wet black nose pointed straight at me. Wagging his tail. Looking at me as if this were an everyday thing—me coming to visit sleeping Jake in my omum's garage room, all cleaned up now, and living there, it seemed to me.

I wanted to cry. But I swallowed my tears and examined the plants in clay pots that lined the pine walls and the other ones hanging from long wires from the ceiling. And the rocks lined up on the deep sill under the window. And between the plants, paintings, in baskets made of fishing line and grass, and a fishing creel that was filled with crayons and tubes and more spools of fishing line. A kitchen to my left, shiny, waxy, glowing with only one pot on the take-it-with-you cooktop. And Jake with his mouth open to my right, lying on a flat bunk, round wire glasses slid down to his nose tip and an open book on his stomach. The pages were stained, and the writing was too small for a regular eye to see. I had an ache to hug my old Jake and, starting toward him, whispered, "Hello." Scarecrow started, too. But the "hello" died out on my tongue. Because the smell of him was different this time, his wild, salty beach smell gone and in its place only soap. Except for some fine sand he had forgotten to wash off on one cheek, which I had a desire to wipe off for him.

I know the answers to lots of things—what makes flowers open, where Scarecrow likes his tickles, why I will never die— but as much as I tried to come up with an answer this time, I just couldn't figure out why old Jake would come to spy on me and my family.

When I tiptoed out of the cleaned-up old tack room, Jake's eyes were still squeezed shut and his breath was whistling and he never even knew I had been there. From the Sound came the far-off spluttering and humming of a boat's motor, coming up from the New York City direction. I wanted to run out to it, to greet the Jake I instinctively thought would be driving the boat. Then I looked over toward the bed where he really was and vowed on Omum's grandfather's grave that I would never tell another living soul Jake's secret.

But with my vow, I also knew then and there that for me, Jake had lost his awesome, magical power: he was no more of a god than my dad was, my omum or my mom was, or even I was. Looking over at him, I screwed my eyes tight and held my knuckles against my eyeballs. But against my fingers the tears, hot, sticky, and liquidy, leaked through anyway.

Chapter 26

ELSIE

When Seb placed my naked feet across his lap, he said, "There's more to this than you're telling me," fixed his eyes on mine, and began to stroke my toes.

"I don't know what you're talking about." I sat up and stared at him. "God, that feels good."

Kneading my instep as if it were clay, he looked down to concentrate on the massage. "Then enlighten me: Why is your mother giving a lunch on Sunday?" He raised his head. "And why did she invite those Getty people if she's trying to get rid of them?"

"I know as much about it as you do," I said.

When I began to hum, he threw his hands in the air, and my feet fell onto the hot sand like discarded trash. "I don't believe you," he said. He got to his knees and rotated to check out the beach exposed by the outgoing tide, to better see the planks of pier railing still standing after the last squall.

I moved next to him so that our shoulders just grazed, but I didn't look at him. "Okay," I said. Together we stared up at the sky, which was beginning to deepen into bands of pink and red. An outcrop of stars appeared through the dark red, blown in with a breeze that swept the hair off my forehead. I pulled the wisps behind my ears and thought about how to break the news to him. How to tell him the truth.

"Do you remember the night I took my boat out in the storm and got lost?"

He nodded.

I dribbled warm sand through my fingers. "You know the old guy who steered me home . . . the one with the haunted eyes, who spoke in riddles?"

Seb gave a short laugh. "Haunted eyes and riddles? How melodramatic." He leaned back and twisted so that he could look me in the eye. "What does this old guy have to do with your mother's lunch?"

In front of us, the twilight swallowed the bay until only a thin layer of vapor defined the water. Splashes of light bounced on the waves from the newly risen moon.

"Can't you be patient?" I said, and took his hand. I tickled the palm, moved it down my cheek to my throat. "That guy changed my ideas on life."

Seb snorted. "In such a short time?"

I pushed his hand from my neck, stood up, and moved a step away to stare at the ribbons of fog that had begun to drift across the Sound. When I turned back to him, I caught a flash of my own reflection in the silver-gray current. His, too. I held him in my gaze, and he dropped his smirk, adopting a hangdog expression.

I stamped my heel into the sand. "I'm serious, you know."

"Yeah . . . sorry." He was starting to look bored. "So go on—tell me."

"Well, the old guy, he reminded me of Captain Ahab. You remember—from *Moby-Dick*? He didn't talk much, but when he did, he spoke in riddles and I didn't understand a word he said."

Robin-Sebastian rose and, stretching, reached over to clasp my shoulder, which he tried to massage. "So what?"

I jerked away. "Well, I get it now."

"Get *what*?" He sounded annoyed.

"When Ahab found me, I told him that the island had disappeared; I was *sure* of it. I was fucking scared, too. . . ." I stopped, eyeing him.

"Go *on*," he said. "I wish you wouldn't use that language."

I rolled my eyes. "I told the guy that I knew every inch of the Sound, even blindfolded, but this time I couldn't find my way home. And *he* said that sometimes things take on disguises, but that they *never* disappear."

"So what's the point?"

I turned my face away. If he didn't understand, I certainly wouldn't tell him.

"The old guy also had a black dog with him, who wore a tartan collar, and the dog seemed almost human."

Seb looked at me curiously. "Peda's old man," he said in a low voice.

I nodded. "And when he and the dog left in their canoe, his voice followed me across the water and into the house." I hesitated. "You won't believe it, but I swear I heard his voice in the kitchen."

"Your imagination is bigger than the whale's." Seb grinned and fondled my neck.

At least he had gotten that much right—the whale and Captain Ahab. Maybe he just wasn't letting on.

"So what's the big secret?" He stared down at me. "The lunch," he prodded.

Why did he have to be so curious? Could he sense what was coming?

"Last night Winter told me a story that you'll find just as hard to believe."

He raised his eyebrows. "Try me."

"Winter thinks that Jake, Peda's old man *and* my Captain Ahab, is also Simon Crandor." I stopped and took a deep breath. "As well as your grandfather."

"Oh, *come on*. You, too?" He dismissed me with his hand, and sand granules blew into my face. "What are you playing at, you and your mother?"

Overhead, some gulls beat their wings at each other, and for a minute I didn't say anything.

"I think she's right . . . my mother," I said finally.

Seb clasped my wrist, and when I tried to pull away, his hand banded itself around me like a cuff. I could see the pulse in my fingers begin to throb. He dipped his head so that his face was only inches from mine.

I found myself studying him, comparing his tanned skin with Jake's, whose elbows were darkened to tar pitch, comparing the features of the two men, young and old, which, when dissected, seemed to me uncannily similar. Or maybe I just imagined it?

"Why do you think that?" he said.

Look in the mirror, I wanted to say. *But you already knew it*, I wanted to say. *You felt it, didn't you?* I wanted to say.

"My grandfather's *dead*," he said. "It's a *fact*, that boating accident. My father"—he let go of my wrist and straightened up—"he made him into a goddamned saint. Ask Hamlet."

Seb was moving onto the battered pier as he talked, and then he stopped and rested his elbows, which I noticed really *were* as dark as his grandfather's, onto the splintered railing. He bowed his head.

"Hamlet's in on this, I suppose?" His words fell into his hands.

"Maybe the old man just wanted to come back, like you did."

"I wasn't dead."

"How the fuck did I know that?" I threw the accusation at him with all the force I could muster, from *years* of stored-up anger.

He pretended that he didn't hear me. "Besides, you forget I instigated this whole thing. The reason I'm here—the reason Ham and those Getty people are here—is because I primed them; I got them interested in the painting in the first place. If what you say is true—by some incredible coincidence—how would Simon Crandor, alias Jake, alias Captain Ahab, *know* to come here, too?"

I shrugged. "How the hell should I know? That's probably what this lunch meeting is all about."

"Is Ham in on this?" he asked again.

"How could he be? You said so yourself."

"My brother manipulates his way into a lot of things. Look what he's done with those paintings and those papers. *He's* the one who called the police. He probably made this whole thing up—and now he's gotten you and your mother to believe it."

"For what reason?"

"Money, power, what else? Bring the old man back—real or not—show him off, bring out new works of art, that sort of thing. For God's sake, look what he's done with you. He brags about you to me, describes those long thighs of yours, talks about the magnetic attraction between the two of you."

I couldn't deny it, of course. And, when Seb described our attraction, for a minute I actually pictured Ham's brilliant white smile.

In the moonlight, the lines of Robin's, alias Seb's, face were carved deeper, dug out like Jake's, and his expression when he looked up from the rail mimicked the soulful look of Jake's big black dog. I joined him at the railing, and he ran a hand down the back of my head, making my skin prickle, pulled me close while his fingers played lightly with my hair.

"I'm sorry," he said after a while. "For everything. For the booze, for the drugs. For your years of trouble." He closed his eyes and raised my hand to kiss its hollow, then ran his fingertips down my arm. "We'll get to the bottom of this," he whispered.

I felt a rush of blood to my head, leaned against him while I pondered the familiar sweetness that spread between my thighs. The only noise came from the toll of bells that I recognized from the lighthouse, and they made me feel inexplicably sad. I pulled my old Robin, my new Seb, down to the sand, where I softly stroked under his shirt with my nails until I felt a shivery response go through his body, until he freed me from my shirt and my shorts, and he his. I swished my bare breasts against his chest, my mouth moved across his day's soft stubble, and the taste of his sweat mixed with sea salt stayed on my lips.

It was as if the anger had been sucked out of me with his lovemaking. When we climbed up the millstone path, hoping to make the house before the nightly wails started, I didn't tell Seb that, of course. But I felt so good that even my voice had changed. It was low and porous now, and my words blew away in the wind like sparrow feathers, and in the shadowy light Seb put his hand up to my cheek and stroked it, because after a while he noticed the change, too. Even the dampness in the air had evaporated so that the stair railing, usually moist and warm, felt dry and cool to the touch now. At the kitchen door, the broken gutter that had always annoyed me because it provided a conduit for a constant stream of trickling water tonight seemed soothing, and the door's olive-green paint, which had been scratched away to reveal badly scarred oak, seemed inviting, instead of sorely in need of repair. As the door closed on the tolling bells and the sound of the tide and the sea air, I even felt compassion for Winter, admiration, too, for having the guts this coming Sunday to confront everyone around her table. I didn't think *I'd* be able to pull it off, and that was a hell of a thing for me to admit. Maybe now I could look at my pint-size daughter without seeing her GET LOST sign spit-painted across her forehead or thinking that she had her fingers crossed whenever I appeared, wishing that I would disappear in her steamed-up mirror . . . because I really *didn't* want to be the person she feared I was.

To see if we could prove that Jake was positively Seb's grandfather—or not—from old pictures of the young Simon Crandor and his family, we spent the rest of the night in the attic, studying photographs and newspaper clippings that Sebastian had discovered in his brother's briefcase, and others that I had dug up in our family papers. Hidden-away-in-the-attic papers of my family that had never held much interest for me before.

The only light we had available to us came from two small, chipped, Wedgwood-blue porcelain lamps that I found hidden behind an old chest and that we now placed on the remnants of an unraveling, dirt-gray petit-point rug—with a raised rose design of faded pink and yellow and white buds—the work of which convinced me that the rug had once been luxurious. On it we sat facing each other with the pictures in between us and the lamps on either side of us, bare now of their disintegrating parchment shades, which we removed to install one-hundred-watt bulbs in place of their old fifteen-watters, hoping that they wouldn't blow when we discovered that the wires were velvet-covered and decaying in spots, not to mention the plugs, which were hanging by threads.

On top of the pile, a large photo—back to front with writing on it—slid onto Seb's lap when he plugged in one of the lamps. "Well, wouldn't you know—*there he is*." Seb read the inscription, and then he clenched his fist.

I picked up the offending photo, which he had let slip through his fingers. "Who is it?"

"The reason I moved to Vermont." He stared into the black dormers. "Me as a child . . . with *Jonah Crandor*."

Father and son were holding hands. "How can you blame someone else?"

"*You* did." He paused to look at me, accuse me. "You *do*."

Did I? I didn't know. I examined the picture. A small boy with an ordinary-looking man, distinguished in an old-fashioned way, with an underslung jaw, piercing eyes, and a mustache. "Must have been tall," I said out loud.

"I suppose." His gaze went back to the black rafters and the round dormer window that outlined the black night. Too cobwebbed and too dirty to show stars, too dirty to show anything at all.

"Turn it over," he said. "Read the inscription."

"*To Seb*," I read, "*with love*."

"Ironic, isn't it?"

"I think it's kind of cool."

He stared at me. "What are you talking about? Cool?"

I tried to touch his hand, but he got up.

"Where are you going?"

He leaned against a wardrobe, scrutinized me for a moment. "I suppose I owe you an explanation."

I frowned. "You could say that."

He hovered over me, rocking from one foot to the other, going from a pink to a yellow bud on the worn rug. "For years—"

"Sit *down*," I ordered.

He slid down next to me, struggled up on one elbow to watch my expression. "Before I met you, I tried to find something meaningful in my life. Something I was proud of—you understand?"

I decided that he hadn't changed a bit; he still didn't give a shit what I thought. "Maybe," I said. It was all about *him*, same as always.

"I wanted something so that my father, Jonah Crandor, would be proud of me: a scored goal at a soccer game, my architecture degree, whatever. But I never got his approval. Just the opposite. I'm not saying that it was right or wrong; it's just the way it was."

I frowned and turned my face away. I couldn't stand the self-pity.

But Seb went on, selfishly oblivious to my discomfort. "The old man locked himself away after my grandfather disappeared," he said. "He shut down completely. Eventually, he never came out of his room at all, drank himself to death. In the early years, he would surface for meals, I remember, and talk about the great Simon Crandor and his art legacy. He deified him. *Literally.* We had no Christmas, ever; we had 'father worship.' Sometimes my father would scan Hamlet's homework, but it was on rare occasions, and then only to discuss his son's A's and the fact that the great Simon Crandor would be proud of him. *Me*, he ignored. You see, I didn't *get* A's. It was as if I didn't exist. Hamlet said it was because I reminded Dad of his father—physically, I mean—but so what? That should have been a *good* thing. Of course *now* I understand. I shoved his guilt in his face; coexisting with me must have been a living hell for the old man—every day he was forced to see his own kid who reminded him of his crime, made him puke it out of his memory, and made him want to die.

"Anyway, it got to the point where the only thing that made *me* feel good was booze, too—floating away on vodka from Jonah Crandor's world. . . . Like father, like son." Seb laughed, but it wasn't a nice sound; it felt like a slap. "In time, coke, too—as you found out. Because the feeling that my father gave me—inevitably my brother did, too—was that of being nothing at all. And you know the rest." There was a short silence while he wiped his eyes. "You know what I'm saying?"

No, I didn't know what he was saying, because in Vermont I had never asked him about his family—I suppose because I didn't want to talk about my own. And now, well, he just made me mad. It had taken him less than five minutes to turn everything to shit.

"There's nothing worse than really believing you're nothing." Seb tipped my chin back, forcing me to look at him. "You know, *really* believing it. It's no excuse—I'm aware of that."

His eyes skimmed my face, and I looked down, ashamed for my killer thoughts. Poor fucking guy.

"Funny, though . . ." His gaze found the black hole of the round window. "When I ran away from home, from that feeling of being nothing, you know, the feeling didn't disappear. It was stronger than ever. That's why I think the drug thing got out of control. But that's all beside the point. The point here is that for Jonah Crandor to write this inscription is hypocritical— it's pathetic."

I tried to smile. I wanted so much to lighten the mood, bring it back to what it had been before he found the photo. "You don't feel like you're nothing now, do you?"

Seb gave a short laugh—that grating noise again—and took my hand, wove his fingers in between mine. "You know better than that, Else. Come on, let's look at the rest. Find the great Simon Crandor. I think he was in his forties or fifties when he died. Didn't look at all like Jonah; he was rounder, gentler."

Feeling guilty, I moved away from Seb self-consciously . . . . tried to arrange the packet of papers and photos so that the few we had of his family were in one pile, mine in the other, and the unknowns in still another. There were mighty few Crandors.

"Look at my grandfather," I said, and my hand shook. "Winter's father." I pointed. "And there's *his* father." We peered at the two faded figures in the shiny old photo, and Seb massaged my two palms. "Use the magnifying glass," I said, and I took my hands away from his to give him the glass, after which he bent over the photo to examine the dated old man beside my grandfather—the man who had developed Peregrine Island.

"He's wearing a pocket watch, and I think that's a cigar cutter," Seb said, and rubbed the image with his forefinger. "There's a sort of locket on the watch chain, too—"

"Where's Simon, I want to know."

He handed me the photographs that he had separated from the pack, three of which had been taken of Simon Crandor at different ages, photos Hamlet had brought with him to Connecticut. To learn about the relative whose painting he had come to study . . . or steal?

Next to them, I smoothed out a newspaper announcement of Crandor's death, above which his picture was pasted—the same picture, it appeared, as one of the photos we looked at. The one with him in glasses, a gentle, indoor man with a high forehead. Clerky. Nerdy. A large man, but soft and round-faced, with deep-set, crinkly eyes. Someone I would have liked but with whom I would have had nothing in common. Nor would Seb, I assumed.

"Look at this one," he said, pointing to a still-younger Crandor. A good-looking guy with a smooth forehead and the same little-boy grin as Seb.

I looked from one to the other. "Do you see it?"

"There's a resemblance, I guess."

When he smiled, I put the picture next to his jaw and compared the features. "You look a great deal alike," I said, "but I don't see any likeness between the man in this picture and that old man out there." I raised my thumb in the direction of the cobwebs and the sea. "Not in any of these. This guy's smooth— no calluses on his fingers, no lines on his face, even the older one. If anything, he gets smoother and more round-faced with age. More tissue-papery. My mother must be wrong. Maybe we only *imagined* that you and old Jake looked alike. Maybe we only *wanted* you to."

"I told you." Seb looked disappointed, and I touched his cheek.

"You have me," I said.

He laughed drily. Got up and tried to pull me with him.

But I stayed put, refusing to budge until we had gone through the last bunch of papers, in the unknown pile that we had almost thrown away. "Please?" I said. "It'll only take a minute."

He squatted next to me while I dealt the pictures out as if we were playing poker, discarding them on the floor after we glanced at them. "It's getting late," he said after a few minutes. "It'll be dawn soon."

"Just one more," I pleaded, and dealt the last old photo with a flourish, the clearest picture of the lot, it turned out, as if it had been taken yesterday, cleanly preserved after having been hidden under the junk in the attic.

A picture of young, happy faces, arms interlocked while the seven, maybe eight, smiling people posed for the camera. In front of my formal, potbellied great-grandfather was my grandfather, a healthy, younger man as big as life, and next to him was a much thinner Simon Crandor with the unmistakable chiseled features of Jake—this time, the resemblance was indisputable—and next to them both was the woman Beatrice, who looked adoringly into the artist's eyes, her back against the hungry, smiling stare of a green but determined-looking Horatio, bookended by a young, grinning Zinger. In front of them all stood a boy, smirking into the camera, while his father, plainly Simon Crandor, with his hand on his shoulder, held him still so that the boy couldn't torment the dog and the girl child by his side, who played with something—at first I thought a rope but on closer inspection decided it was jewelry. A necklace? No, it was smaller, thicker, more like a cuff or a bracelet, but the girl clutched it so tightly to her belly that even with the magnifying glass I couldn't, for the life of me, be sure.

Chapter 27

WINTER

∾

*I*n the bright sunlight, two cop cars waited next to the lilac bushes and the shimmering, silver-leafed poplar trees. From behind the geranium tubs, where I watched them, I felt like a criminal, spying on these policemen, who, from each patrol car, stared silently out at the patches of shaded, weed-filled lawn directly in front of them. But I didn't dare move. I didn't want them to see me while I waited for the detective and his sergeant to arrive. Why the backup, anyway? Obviously, Detective Todd was expecting trouble to come out of my lunch.

When he had called on Friday, he had said said he wanted to see me immediately, along with my family, friends, and visitors. "For what reason?" I asked. He explained that after our last meeting he had delved into the art experts' records—as he had said he would—only to find, as he expected, that most of them were falsified. He had then taken the two men into custody— which I was stunned to hear—but because of their advanced age, the department had decided, for the time being, at least, to release them once more on their own recognizance, as well as Hamlet's. Maybe their "time being" was over now—hence the presence of the two patrol cars. "The law," he had assured me on Friday, would "deal with them appropriately. You can rely on that, Ms. Peregrine." I was too surprised to offer him yet again my married name, which, after the divorce, I hadn't used much anyway. Instead, I pictured this boy-cop placing his palm to his heart in the manner of a zealous Boy Scout. With this vision in mind, and with the finality of his statement, I impulsively invited him to lunch. Of course he prevaricated, at first telling me that our meeting would be brief, no more than ten minutes at the most, while he questioned us. "One of you *must* know more than you've let on," he said. "There's no need for socializing—I prefer a sober setting." But when I asked him to bring along Sergeant Joe-Ivan—I figured the more witnesses at our interrogation, the better, *especially* if the witness was another member of the police department—it piqued his curiosity, and he then agreed to attend my Sunday lunch—as long as the guests included the individuals he planned to question.

You see, I needed time. To organize my thoughts, to hire a lawyer if necessary, in order to reveal the *real* Simon Crandor to the world *before* the cops took the two old men to jail for foul play—or, worse, for premeditated murder. Although I didn't *like* my "alleged" Crandor experts—for that matter, neither did I like Hamlet Crandor—I felt I owed them this much. At least they wouldn't get the death penalty. It never occurred to me that if Jake had wanted to show himself he could have, and would have, long ago. How could I convince him *now* to expose himself? Without a doubt, he wouldn't want to help the two nemeses who had conceived and coordinated the scheme for *his* demise.

It was Peda who did it. She refused to accept Jake as her great-grandfather. And that was intolerable to him. Because

Jake had grown to love Peda and he longed to spend legitimate time with her. She *knew* he was the painter Simon Crandor. That he had been—past tense—her superhero. But she could not understand how this weathered, scruffy old man—whom she thought *she* had discovered, living among the rats in the rocks—could be related to her. "Why would you make up such a thing, Omum," she had demanded, and then she had stomped her foot, "when *I* introduced him to *you*?" As if *I* were a liar. She would not accept Sebastian as her father, either, for that would mean, as Jake was his grandfather, that *both* of them, in the end, were related to her.

Nevertheless, *I* could not understand her sudden wish to be rid of the old man. And Jake didn't know how to explain himself to her. It was the only time I heard him short on words, when I went to find him—and find him I did, with Scarecrow's help—under the boulder where on that blustering day I had first caught sight of him. I could make out the same fine grit of salty sand on his cheeks. Yet this time there was a tightness of pain around his eyes when he admitted to me that maybe *this* was his opportunity to rejoin the world as Simon Crandor.

"Peda," he said, his silvery eyes misting, "is never afraid, so why should I be? Every day for her has a taste—no, a breadth—of possibility, so why not for me, too? Why not for both of us?"

And all I could think of was that for Peda, until now, Jake had been *her* hero, the man who had given *her* the possibility, the responsibility, even, of a life—once shaded and lonely—now filled with sun and anticipation. It was because of *him* that the timid and sour child whom Elsie had brought down from Vermont no longer existed. And now their roles were reversed.

When the detective and the cop finally arrived, I was surprised to see that Sergeant Joe-Ivan was dressed in civilian clothes. Polka-dot bow tie and all. In his crisp white shirt and seersucker jacket, he looked quite dashing. A tad embarrassed, too, because he kept glancing at his superior in the same way a boy throws covert glances at his father. But the detective again pushed past him, dodging his big belly and deliberately avoiding eye contact with him. Todd looked as if he were going to a polo game or a parade or a yachting event. White slacks, striped tie, blue jacket, hair slicked back just so. And the sunglasses—they would have wowed any poor, unsuspecting female. For Elsie's sake, or maybe Sophia's? I had given him the guest list, after all, although naturally I had omitted Jake.

"Of course you'll be a bystander," I reminded him when we shook hands, "just like you promised."

Again he agreed, but not happily, when he signaled poor Joe-Ivan, who in turn nodded vigorously, swearing not to participate in the conversation until after lunch, after which they would be free to start their questioning. Both of them were dying to find out why they had been invited, what confidence I planned to share with them. I studied Todd's face, wondering if he had a clue. He was not a stupid man.

Because the sun was bright, not too hot, yet just enough to bathe my legs in warmth, I led the men on a walk around to the conservatory door, where I hoped to find Peda and call her in for lunch—before I went for Jake, who was waiting just below on the beach. I cupped one hand over my eyes against the glare of the sky, which was a robin's-egg blue, when I saw Peda standing on the plank swing that was tied to the limb of a Scottish pine. A spike of sunlight lay on her shoulder and made her sweat-curled, sun-bleached hair shine like spun gold. She swung up into the sky and tapped her tieless, sockless sneakers together, an anachronism under the smocking of the pale yellow baby dress she wore. Elsie's doing? Where *was* the woman's taste?

When Peda joined us, I saw that she was holding her breath and sweat was spreading in half circles under her arms, staining the pretty yellow, turning it to a sick brown-green. Had Jake told her he was coming to lunch? Had her mother? Elsie was the only person who knew; I had confided in her the day before, swearing her to secrecy. Why I had told her was beyond me—maybe I wanted to feel close to my daughter, share with her a secret I relished before I let it go.

From the front door, my guests trailed in, all of them terribly curious about why they had been invited to Sunday lunch. Elsie led them into the dining room; I did not want any socializing before lunch. The end of the table overlooked the Sound through triple-hung windows that ran floor to ceiling and were built into an arched wall, so that, like a compass, at the head, one could swivel in his or her chair to find the best view. I left that seat empty, placed Peda to the right and me across from her.

When Elsie saw the seating, she lifted one eyebrow but didn't say anything, just stared at the feet of her poor, ribby daughter. "What do you have on, Peda?" She pointed at the sneakers with their dirty, trailing laces, holding her finger there . . . then, still glaring at her daughter's feet, moved her hand slowly upward until it reached Peda's wet armpits.

She didn't mean to be cruel—though sometimes I truly wondered if she insulted people for the fun of it—but her voice carried and the guests coming in looked away. Peda tried to smile, but her lower lip trembled.

Her father came to her rescue. He bent over and hugged

Peda to him so that she seemed like a rag doll, threads of her moist hair plastered against his cheek. Seb's white sleeves were rolled up against his tanned arms—no Sunday dressing for him—and he looked relaxed in a way I had not seen him before, especially when he tipped his head back and laughed. In response, a tentative smile appeared on the child's wet-cheeked face.

Frustration can often feel like hatred, I think, and I could see just that emotion mirrored on Hamlet's face when he looked at his brother. None of his plans had gone his way—at least not yet—and I knew he blamed Seb. I was sure he also wondered about the luncheon, although, to give him credit, he acted like a gentleman and never questioned me. Maybe he had an inkling, though? Maybe he and his detective friend had conferred, for now he asked if he could sit by him—not a very gentlemanly thing to do at a luncheon party. But he asked in such a charming way, and he looked so debonair in his dark blue jacket, that of course I acquiesced.

Following Hamlet into the dining room, round-shouldered Horatio Guardi balanced himself between the chair backs with his cane. He looked as if he had aged ten years from the time of his arrival on our island—only a few weeks ago, but it felt like an eternity. To him, too, I gathered. His face was haggard, thin and papery around his eyes, and he blinked as if he were emerging from a deep sleep. He stopped, and with one hand he leaned heavily on the back of a chair, while with the other, his cane swaying, he blotted a watery drip that vibrated on the end of his nose. Dandruff covered his shoulders.

Fanning myself with one hand, I tried to usher in Zinger, who was patiently taking small steps in the wake of old Horatio. And behind them, Clay and Sophia lounged in the doorway, both smoking cigarettes. Why couldn't they get moving? Not even Elsie had sat down—she was chatting away with the petite Sophia, who, rather than looking at Elsie, stared at herself in the wall mirror until I had to turn away from her obvious self-pleasure. She never smiled; her face, in fact, looked blank—except when she looked at herself. Maybe I was being unfair, because she was dressed in such rich garnet colors and her coloring was so vivid—she had on dark crimson lipstick as well—that she made my athletic, makeup-free daughter look almost waxen, despite the pale blush to her cheeks.

I didn't try to rush anyone, not really, because watching them in their luncheon clothes gave the occasion a solemn air, which I sort of relished. And I enjoyed taking in the fresh white tablecloth, the array of peach-colored roses in its center, against the high windows that looked out on my grandfather's millstone steps that rolled down to the Sound.

That is, until I saw Clay smooth his tie and then expel cigarette smoke in a cloud through which he looked defiantly at me. He knew I didn't allow smoking in the house. To make matters worse, when he stubbed out his cigarette, he leaned toward Sophia and imitated my flapping hand and then very softly mimicked my voice in a high falsetto, which I suppose he thought I wouldn't hear.

That was it. I told them to sit down or they could all leave. My voice sounded strange to me, loud and ugly, as if someone else had spoken, an actor out of a play . . . or maybe from one of my dreams. And then I left, slamming the kitchen door behind me. I could hear their murmuring. Maybe they thought I had finally lost my mind. I could imagine them questioning Elsie— as if she would tell them anything.

Chapter 28

WINTER

*W*hen Jake and I entered the dining room, I heard a collective gasp. At least, I thought I did. After that, I was sure that everyone stopped breathing. But maybe that, too, was my imagination, because, after all, how could anyone be expected to identify Jake as Simon Crandor before they could get a good look at him?

Except for Peda, of course, who I thought would be thrilled to see him, especially here, as she had been nagging me to invite him to the house since the first day I had met him. But when I asked her to escort Jake to his seat, she acted strange, in a way, until Scarecrow thrust his wet snout into her stomach and momentarily brought her to her senses. Her eyes appeared too large, too dark and unblinking, in her small face, and against her knobby shoulders, Jake's hands appeared too large. She looked like she was trying not to cry. Enormous tears popped up anyway on her spiky lashes, glittered on her cheeks. Maybe she wanted him all to herself? Or maybe she *really* didn't want to accept him as her great-grandfather. . . .

As I waited for the time bomb, for someone to recognize Jake, my hand shook so violently I couldn't control it, and my breath was so shallow that I felt light-headed. *Would* anyone recognize him? Obviously, age and time and heartache had changed him. His cheeks were camouflaged by a beard shadow, his skin had browned to the color and consistency of a dried-up poplar leaf, and his tall body was hunched and hardened by the elements. But he still boasted a high forehead, and, while wrinkled, it crowned the same aquiline features that I had recognized in the old photo. He filled the room, this big, gaunt-faced man in his faded clothes, with a calmness that I didn't find threatening, and that I hoped, therefore, no one else would, either. And I was right. Clay stood up to introduce himself, followed by Hamlet and Sebastian. The two old men, though—the cops, too—they just stared.

I was appalled by the fast beat in my throat, and as I watched Jake sit down, I leaned back to release some of my tension. . . . Who knew what might happen?

"Heel," Jake said quietly, and the dog fell in by his side.

Until now, no one had caught on, but out of the corner of my eye, where I discovered to my horror that a tear of my own had crystallized, I noticed that Horatio Guardi's cold gray stare had become hot and scratchy red—as if he had a disease—and he held a trembling, blue-veined hand in front of his eyes, as though they hurt. Or to block us from his view—I couldn't tell which.

Zinger prodded him on the arm. "Hey," he prompted. And then, nervously, "Horatio, what's the matter with you?"

At which point the wheezing started. And the old man's eyelid rolled down over one of his blood-filled eyes—it looked as if an artery had burst—and his slack mouth drooped down even farther. He pointed with one long, skinny, quivering forefinger. "*You,*" he said in a strangled voice.

Zinger glanced at him and then back at Jake. He sat for a moment, stunned, then coughed and choked, spraying bits of saliva and bread all over my fresh white tablecloth.

Horatio couldn't catch his breath, and I wondered if I should call for a doctor, even an ambulance. But the sergeant had jumped up to help—maybe this was in his repertoire—and started to knead the old man's shoulders. Upon which the nattily dressed detective whispered something to him. Abruptly, Joe-Ivan dropped Horatio's arms and ran out fast, as fast as he was able, considering his weight. Nevertheless, he returned quickly enough . . . with an oxygen mask, which he then applied, attaching it to the head of poor, wheezing Rip. I hoped the old man wouldn't die from the shock of seeing reincarnated Simon Crandor.

Meanwhile, Zinger looked like he had been hit in the face, his jowly, sallow cheeks a kind of custard color. He didn't try to help his friend, and he didn't look at Jake. With one hand he stroked the stem of his water glass, and with the other, using his thumb and index finger, he strangled the stem of his fork. Small bubbles of spit formed at the sides of his mouth.

My other guests stood up, silent and waiting, bent over the table, most of them, their eyes riveted to the oxygen-masked man, except that every few seconds they'd peer at the hunched stranger with the beard stain who sat at the head of my table. The fan overhead blew warm air around us, and the waitress from the catering service poked her head in the door to ask when I wanted her to start serving. I waved my hand at her and glanced at Clay to see if he had noticed my wave, if I should try to wipe the black cast from his face. But no, his eyes were riveted on Jake, too, like a snake ready to strike. It gave me the chills, that look.

After a while, the cop, Joe-Ivan, took the oxygen mask off Horatio Guardi and the old man slumped back in his chair, deflated but breathing normally again, though one red-rimmed eye, I noticed, still drooped dangerously. His mouth, too, trembled, and his lip was pulled down as if he had nothing to keep it up. But in a voice that was frighteningly calm, he mumbled something to the room, so low that we could barely hear him, *"It's Crandor, isn't it?"* The expression in his eyes, if one ignored the distortion of his lids, was terrifying because it was so impassive.

It came to me then that the notion of death was all around us here, floating in the warm, fanned air, and I shivered because I suddenly felt so cold—a strange sensation that mimicked a fever on a hot day. I'm sure that everyone else felt it, too. As if his announcement just couldn't be. No one but spirits come back from the grave.

I watched the cops sit up in their straight-backed chairs. Hamlet, except for a little ridge of muscle that flexed along his jaw, stiffened as if he had been shot through with electricity. Otherwise, his face might have been frozen. Opposite him, his brother eyed Jake blankly, and then his pale blue eyes clouded. He glanced at Peda, who was frowning at Jake with great concentration and whose face was dirty and tear-stained, with little runnels along her nose, and Jake gave her a smile that looked to me like an injury on his face, it was so hot with concern.

"Oh, shit," I heard Sophia say, and she clasped her hand to her mouth when she saw Jake look over at her.

The silence after that was more powerful than the windstorms that come in from the Atlantic. I forced myself to speak finally, seeing that neither Elsie nor anyone else was of any use at all.

"We'll have lunch now," I said inanely. Smiled, or tried to, but my lips bunched into a tight, crooked line. The sun, I noticed, was pouring in through the windowpanes, illuminating the dust that hung in the air. My eyes were stinging, and my throat felt clotted. In this atmosphere, who would want to eat? Who *could* eat?

"Oh, great, I'm starved," I heard Clay say quite distinctly, but it was as if he had spoken from the bottom of the sea.

I glared at him and saw that his face was purple-red—I hoped from embarrassment. And then I realized that even as I hated him for his obtuseness, it is human nature to be fascinated by the terrible, although we might hide our eyes from it.

Still, as if he were contagious, I slanted my own eyes away from him and from the brightness of the window. . . . What had happened to my great plan?

Jake stood up and moved over to that brightness then, to the window, where a long streak of sunlight engulfed his torso. I had to squint to see him. He dug his hands into his pockets and appeared to contemplate the southwest view for some time, after which he tilted his head at the table to consider his grandsons and his long-ago friends who had turned on him.

"So," he began, "time can mean freedom, don't you think?" He sighed deeply, eyed Horatio and Zinger, and then lapsed into silence, while the room, along with its rooted occupants, waited. "It can free us from our beliefs," he said at last, "from our animosity." He ventured a half smile at Seb and Ham, neither of whom returned it.

It was obvious that he was thrilled to see his family: his two grandsons, the great-granddaughter whom he could finally acknowledge. I saw how he looked at them. Still, how could what he said be true? Time churned the seasons; every month I lived seemed to be shorter than the last one. And yet my appetite for new days, I found, never ceased, no matter how much I had a dread of time itself, of aging. . . . Maybe I didn't know what he meant.

Ham stood up, flailing his arms about like a wild man. "What the hell are you talking about?" he shouted. His eyes were killing eyes, and they frightened me. "Where have you been all these years? Who do you think you are, coming into our lives at this stage?" He looked around to find his brother, who stared up at him, glassy-eyed, and then he sat down abruptly.

Taking deep breaths, he tried to compose himself. After a few seconds, eyes narrowed, he met his grandfather's argentine stare and, with an executioner's studied calm, he said, "Where were you when we needed you?"

I could see that Seb was shocked by what Hamlet had said, but I wondered what shocked him more: the cruelty with which his brother had attacked their grandfather or the revelation that the self-confident Ham might actually *need* someone.

I joined Jake at the window, touched the old man's shoulder, and felt tremors coming from him, his vibrations so violent that they reminded me of an overheated engine. From the sideboard, he handed me a glass of wine and the burgundy sloshed onto my fingers.

Jake sank down into his chair. Next to him, Scarecrow, groomed for the occasion, slept with his nose between his paws. Jake looked steadily at his oldest grandson. "You seem to have a perverse desire for an argument"—his voice caught—"just like your father."

Ham stared at his grandfather for a long time, not saying anything. Then, with his fist in his palm, he rose, leaned over the table. "How dare you . . ."

Jake never took his eyes off Hamlet. "Your father tried to kill me," he said quietly. "How could I forgive him long enough to gather up his fatherless boys after he died? You were grown after all, capable, in my view, to care for yourselves." I was quite certain that I saw tears fill his eyes.

"I made mistakes," he went on, "particularly during those

years." And he replaced his hostile attitude, controlled as it was, with a more kindly tone. "*Learn* from me," he pleaded. "It's not too late; everyone makes mistakes."

He seemed to be asking for Ham's forgiveness. Maybe for everyone's in the room.

"You made a hell of a lot of mistakes," Ham said harshly.

"I wouldn't say that," Horatio Guardi interjected. "Simon Crandor was the most honorable of men, the most talented, the most fortunate, a man I envied for his future, for his talent." The old man's face was a terrible mask, his breathing ragged. With a relentless motion, he massaged the bridge of his nose.

Jake studied Horatio over the rim of his glass as if he had never seen him before, as if their lives had just joined, as if their past was just that, a thing of the past. "I felt like I was being buried alive under that future," he said to him. As if he owed him an explanation.

Zinger laughed berserkly. "Guess you were, at that." His eyes were sunken behind dark circles, strands of his hair flattened by needlepoint drops of sweat in the bands of his scalp. He wasn't looking at Jake but peering past him into some distance of his own. "We wanted to make you *great*. You understand? Your passions were futile, you'd be gone soon enough, but your *art*—that was something different. To work without the benefit of reward? To sabotage *our* work? Why'd you do it, Simon? Why'd you make *us* do it? We wanted to preserve your art." His voice rose to a fever pitch. " Your drawings, your paintings, your talent. Can you understand that? We wanted to make you *great*." He laughed like a hyena. The poor, crazy little man. "We *did* make you great." He sat back, a splayed hand on each knee, which he pounded with each burst of hilarity. He was so hot he had a slick of oily sweat where the bottom of his upper arm lay against his cushioned rib cage and another where the underneath of his chin met his fleshy neck.

"Shut up!" Horatio Guardi hissed.

Painful heartburn seized me. I hadn't eaten anything yet. My plate before me, laden with crabmeat chunks, nauseatingly pink and fleshy and incandescent, made me feel even sicker. The mayonnaise had congealed between the endive in small globs as shiny and perfectly symmetrical as Zinger's drops of sweat.

Jake replied calmly, "No one can own a piece of art. You can own the maple, you can own the oils, but you can't own the gloss of the pearl, or the voluptuousness of the milk-gorged breasts, or the arrival of the spring -geese. Or the parade of the carriages, or the—"

"Do you know what my name is? Do you *know* who I am?"

"Of course."

"What is it, then? What's my name?"

"Zinger."

"You never called me anything *but* Zinger. No one ever did. I have a first name, too. Know what it is?"

Jake reached across the table as if he wanted to touch Zinger's hand. "Oh, yes, I remember. I've been remembering all these years that Barry Zinger wanted me dead so badly that he and my beloved son, Jonah, along with my best friend, Horatio Guardi, arranged for my death at sea."

Old Rip looked up, his face colorless as chalk. Neither had he touched the food on his plate. I wondered what the waitress must think. Nobody except Clay was eating. Not even Peda.

"Jonah could never get over what he had done," Horatio said quietly. "He lived his life behind a wall of guilt that he took out on everyone around him. From then on, every day was rough on him." Horatio glanced over at the cops, gave Detective Todd a mirthless grin—more of a grimace—which the young cop didn't acknowledge. I hated to think what *he* must be thinking. "I never saw Jonah again—my only godson."

And the only son of Simon Crandor, I wanted to remind him. I swung my head to look over at Jake. He must have been thinking, *What about you, Horatio Guardi, my best friend? What about* your *guilt,* your *hell, the part* you *played in your plan to do away with me?*

Guardi's face appeared desperate, pent-up, as though it would burst. As though he had heard Jake. "We wanted to make you immortal," he said. "Otherwise, your work—with your good causes and your intentions—would have faded; you wouldn't have been represented in major museums. No one appreciates a benefactor; your life would have amounted to no more than a pipe dream."

"So what?" Sunlight slanted across Jake's plate, the lettuce leaves wilting under the heat and oil. "I suppose that I'm satisfied with less than most men." He stared into the Judas eyes of Horatio Guardi. "Men like you."

"Are you? Then why are you here today?" Tight-lipped, Rip stared back at his old adversary, his onetime best friend. I wondered if he saw Jake as he used to be or as he was now. "For revenge?" Under the table, his hands, freckled and puckered, were twisted together. "You can't prove anything." He glanced over at the young cop. Guardi's face was so pale it looked powdery, but his forehead was smooth and delicate and wet with sweat under the thinning front hair, which shone with an unhealthy glow in the bright light.

I supposed that he thought Jake-Simon relished this reunion. How wrong he was. After all these years, the poor man was used to his solitary ways, a man who took pleasure in his own company; a man I had to *beg* to come to this luncheon, which, I knew, he thought would be a grim and heartbreaking ordeal.

No one talked while coffee was served. Jake, I saw, accepted a cup of tea, then sat hunched over it as though he could escape into it, with his shoulders drawn forward, elbows on his knees. Nevertheless, for all his isolation, his eyes held a remembered scorn—I saw Zinger bite his lip in recognition—and he sipped his tea with a surprising delicacy, again recognizable, I'm sure, to his old colleagues.

"My family . . . ," Old Jake said suddenly. "I came today for my family." He looked at Peda, who all the while had been stealing glances at him from across her dessert plate. But now, sinking her spoon into the vanilla ice cream on her strawberry shortcake, she avoided meeting his eyes.

Her attitude took me aback, but I was too preoccupied to give it much thought. Clay, conversely, had never once taken his eyes *off* Jake's face. I recognized that expression. His lips looked glued together, as if he were planning out his future and how Simon Crandor would fit into it.

Without warning, Ham sneered, "*Your* family? Who's *that*?" His face looked ugly and contorted.

"Could I say something?" Seb asked. He turned to his grandfather, his arm curled over Elsie, who I saw move slightly toward him when his hand skimmed the back of her neck. "After insisting that your art go to organizations for the betterment of mankind, for public consumption only—years ago, I mean—how could you then have gone into seclusion and hoarded the *rest* of your life's work?"

"How could I not have? If my son had been found out, he would have been indicted for attempted murder." When he saw the question marks on their faces—it had been years since Jonah Crandor's death—and the digging looks from Jonah's two sons, he said, "And after his death? It was easier just to do nothing. I guess I was cowardly."

"You wouldn't have had to turn him in," Ham said.

"So that he could try it again?"

"Ah . . ." Ham stopped here, turned slightly, and stared out at the sky. He let several seconds pass. "And you knew that these people"—he swept his hand around the table—"and my *father* orchestrated your murder?" His tone was insulting. "*How did you know?*"

"I knew. Just accept it at that."

Ham shook his head and crumpled his napkin into a ball. "He was a serious man, my father, a man who liked to explain things to me; he wasn't a murderer. I don't—"

Jake looked at him sharply. "I'm glad to hear you loved him."

"I don't think—"

Jake slapped the table. "Ask *them*, then." He waved at the two old men and laughed, a short, hard, abrasive sound that gave me goose bumps. "For a long while, I didn't paint. I contemplated; I meditated; I survived—a hard game for those without."

"Are you a fucking saint?"

At that, I heard nervous laughter and turned to locate its source. Sophia, two small dots of red on her cheeks, looked like a child caught with her hand in the cookie jar.

"Maybe it would be more appropriate to say I hid, I went into hiding, because I was scared, and because, frankly, I didn't know what else to do. I moved from place to place, and after a while, I painted again. Stored the pieces, which I was never very sure of, mainly because of my frame of mind. Also, my work changed. I couldn't paint the same way anymore. After a few attempts at sentimentality and a lost-long-ago life full of hope and laughter—*the dining-room scene of the happy family immediately came to mind*—I started to paint by my conscience, heavy of heart, rather than by my memory." He put the tips of his fingers to his forehead. "And I wondered, still do, if people would care for the finished pieces. But before I die, this time, that is"—he glanced at Horatio—"I have every intention of offering my work, near gratis, to the public."

"What will you live on?"

"What do you think I've *been* living on? If I have enough

money to survive by doing odd jobs, by selling minor works—prints, drawings, such as that—that's all I need."

Ham averted his face. "No one will believe that you're Simon Crandor, back from the dead."

Jake frowned into his plate. "I worry about that, too." He looked up and gazed at the faces around the room. "I thought that this was the right time to reveal myself." He swallowed. "For my family . . . but also for my art."

"You have a great-granddaughter," Seb said.

"Oh, yes . . . I know, although I must admit it took me some time to piece the puzzle together. While I followed your lives—Seb, Ham . . ." His voice softened slightly, and he turned to glance at Seb, and then at Hamlet, who at once pointedly looked away. Seemingly undaunted, Jake continued, "You boys moved around a lot. In the end, though, life doesn't need a blueprint. It's charted out already; we just aren't aware of it." He stared at Peda. "My soul mate," he said. "She gave me the courage to face you today."

Peda, I noticed, still wouldn't look at him.

The old man gazed at her with a twinge of sadness. "Things will change now, but I hope not too much." He let his hand drop onto Scarecrow's head.

"You're goddamn right they're going to change," an authoritative voice cut in. Detective Todd stood up and elbowed his sergeant, who struggled to get to his feet.

When I tried to speak, my mouth was dry. "You promised," I said. "You said you would wait until after lunch."

The baby-faced detective pretended he didn't hear me. "You'll have to testify." He moved over to where Jake sat and stood looking down at him.

Jake pressed his hands down on the edge of the table, as if he would rise, too, do what Detective Todd dictated, but he stayed where he was. "Oh, no," he said. "No deal."

"Get up; look at them," the cop ordered. His voice was low and shaky. He pointed at Horatio Guardi and Zinger, clasped Jake's shoulder to make him turn, make him acknowledge the enemy.

"Yes," Jake said curtly. "Look at them carefully. Do they look dangerous to you?"

I heard Zinger say, "It *hurts* when you look at me." And when he caught me staring at him, he rubbed at his gray eye sockets.

And Rip, well, his anger had left him like water evaporating through a sieve, and he was weeping, silently gulping air through his wide-open, flaccid mouth, a peculiar sight with his thin, parted haircut. A pathetic figure who could have been a fragile old woman, or a stork, or a broken-down old man, like he really was.

"Look at the three of us," Jake said, addressing Todd and Joe-Ivan. "All of us. We're a generation who has run out of time. I don't think your law will be able to accomplish more than the Almighty, to whom these two—as well as I—will soon be consigned."

The detective pointed then and, bending over the table, pushed his face close to Jake's.

"Stop it," I said. I felt my shoulders tighten. "Leave him alone. If we need you, we'll call you. To prosecute them, if necessary." I angled my head at Guardi and Zinger.

My daughter came to stand behind me, Seb with her. And Sergeant Joe-Ivan, well, he purposely moved away from Todd and settled his hand on Jake's shoulder. I hoped the boy-cop wouldn't fire him.

Except that Peda made the detective forget all about Joe-Ivan—at least for a moment. Because this child, who throughout lunch had intentionally avoided Jake's glance, anchored herself to him now, clinging to his arm and swinging from his chair until he had to pay attention to her. Fidgeting, I thought, like a spoiled brat because it had been such a long lunch hour. But no, when the old man faced her, she wrapped her arms around his neck and confronted Todd on his behalf.

"Do what she says," Peda told him, and reached out with her free hand to Jake's supporters and me. "He's not only Simon Crandor; he's Superman, don't you see?"

The detective eyed the child. In a peculiarly high voice, he said, "*You* don't count," then leaned down into her smocking until his nose was a fraction of an inch from hers.

Who did he think he was, talking to a child like this? Behaving like this?

Elsie, who had slid back down in her chair, stood up so quickly this time that the wineglasses shuddered and a few fell; red and white wine spilled, and the smears on the tablecloth resembled diluted dribbles of blood. I thought she was going to hit him.

But Detective Todd moved too fast, slipping away to stand at the back of his chair, from where he addressed the table. "I can't let this go, you understand. Not by a long shot." After which, with his pinkie, he summoned Joe-Ivan, who followed him obediently to the door.

On a parting note, Todd warned, "There *will* be repercussions."

But Joe-Ivan winked at Jake, I saw—for everyone else to see, too—and at Peda he cast his eyes heavenward.

Chapter 29

ELSIE

~

The police left at last, leaving my family and me to our own devices. "Of course, we'll have to report this," the hotshot cop said on his way out, informing us that there would be serious ramifications upon the release of Jake's story, and that *we* would be held responsible. But that was okay with me, because I was sure that Jake could take care of the situation— managing his reappearance was a snap, given all he had been through. He was a man of magic, after all.

So Winter and I moved into the conservatory, where it had all begun, with Jake, the two old men, Hamlet, Sebastian . . . and Clay and Sophia, who I hoped would soon leave. But not, unfortunately, I discovered, until they had had their say—determined as they were to represent the "new" Simon Crandor in the art world and in the media.

"We'd like to represent him. . . ." They wasted no time. But Sophia didn't ask Jake-Simon Crandor. In her smoky voice, she turned to me, as if I were the end-all, flicking her weasel look between Winter and me.

"Well, holy fucking shit," I said under my breath. I didn't want to give that stony-faced bitch the time of day, so I looked at Clay, whose face had turned a deep pink.

At the same time, my mother put her hand over her chest, to help her breathe, she said, because the air felt like soup, but what she really meant was that she couldn't stand my language. You see, she hates my swearing, hates the *fuck* word the most . . . and whether it's uttered in a whisper or a roar makes no difference to her. Maybe she's right—I don't really like it, either.

Hamlet flared up, speaking heatedly. "I'm sure my grandfather would like to become reacclimated, acquaint himself with his family, and then there'll have to be an accounting, an inventory of all his artwork—his *entire* collection—taken by *objective* appraisers." He scowled at Clay, skipping over Jake's raised eyebrows.

All oil and obsequiousness, Clay turned to Jake. "Well, Mr. Crandor?"

When Jake faced him, Clay, true to form, dropped his eyes and bent to wipe an invisible speck off his shoe, while watching him through his eyelashes. It struck me that Clay was always watching. Watching and plotting. Like a spy.

Sophia gave Jake one of her taut little smiles, the kind waitresses give when they bring menus. Looking for a big, fat tip later on. She wanted a fat tip, that's for sure—from the celebrity Jake. He'd make her famous, all right. Rich, too.

I hoped the smile wouldn't influence Jake.

"Represent me?" he said. "You could help, I suppose, but the paintings aren't to be sold all at once, of course. Maybe some dispersed for a prudent amount, to cover expenses, to—"

"What do you live on?" interrupted Clay. "Do you mind my asking?" His eyes were big and innocent.

Hamlet cleared his throat. "He's already told you. Besides, it's none of your business."

"Look at me—do I need much?"

We all turned to stare at this new Jake, the old Simon Crandor long buried. He looked like a bum. A beach bum, a Superman of the waves, just as Peda had described him, a salty old ratter-tatter eccentric, a bare-bones man. But I thought he looked vibrant, too—although Winter would probably disagree—and he seemed pleased with himself, as well as self-confident. Look at the way he had put Hamlet in his place. And let's not forget the time he had led me home in his boat.

But I wanted Clay to leave the old guy alone. Clay made me mad, the way he was ass kissing. So I blurted out, "Why are you always so interested in other people's lives? Why don't you get a life of your own?" I couldn't believe I had said it; it's what I'd wanted to say for a long time.

"What do you think I'm doing? It's for me, for her—him, too, naturally."

"Yeah? Well, that's what happened to Jake the last time: greedy people trying to take a piece of his action." I glanced at Zinger and Guardi, but their eyes were glued to the floor and the ceiling, respectively.

"You know me better than that." Clay looked hurt. Shook his head at me like a big dog. Poor guy, his nose was dotted with oily black pores, which I had never noticed before.

Sophia narrowed her eyes at me, tilted her head. She lifted one foot, held it out in front of her, and studied her sandal; shiny purple polish the color of translucent upchuck shimmered on her toenails. Her bare legs looked sick white—porcelain, perfect doll's legs—against the dark color of her dress.

"We want to help you, Mr. Crandor," she said breathlessly.

I'm sure you do, I thought. The fit of her sleeveless, backless silk challenged the imagination, and I'm certain she knew it.

"These days, it's *Jake*," he reminded her.

"Okay, *Jake*, then . . ." She hesitated a moment, pulled in her breath, and said, "We'd like to help you reach your public, share your work with the world, just the way you want."

"That's right," Clay agreed.

"I'm not that much of an egoist."

"I didn't mean to imply . . ." Her hair, which was cut in slabs, swung across her face as she talked, stirring the air and in the heat sending out an overripe, swampy smell that made me feel like throwing up.

I could see Winter drifting, just bobbing along, and wondered what it would take to make her jump in, help save Jake from Clay and Sophia. Then again, maybe he didn't need saving. Jake's lack of speech didn't mean a lack of thought. *He can take care of himself*, I told myself.

Jake said, "No, of course you didn't." He looked tired. "Little by little, maybe . . ." His voice trailed off. He sighed and pushed his glasses onto his head, a gesture that startled me, it was so different from Jake the old salt—so intellectual, somehow.

"Maybe you're rushing him," Seb suggested. "Maybe it's too soon."

Ham stared at him, looked away defiantly when he saw me give Seb a thumbs-up.

Upon Seb's suggestion, Sophia's mood shifted and her eyes took on a darker cast. She threw looks at Clay, who nodded thoughtfully, and said, "We'll begin whenever your grandfather wishes, whatever is good for him." His voice was stiff but obliging. Still, he could never take no for an answer, this guy.

Therefore, when he started to go on anyway, in order to arrange a date to actually *meet* Jake, to go over the canvases hidden behind Winter's painting—"And by the way," he said, "when did you paint them, Jake? And how in the world did you ever manage to install them behind the painting? Very clever, if I may say so"—I fixed him with a stare that silenced him . . .

and prodded my mother into proclaiming at long last that it was time for non–family members to leave.

So Winter told him outright, in a loud tone, as if she didn't have any manners, but I didn't care, because Clay didn't have any, either. I rejoiced, actually, when I saw Sophia pull him up off his chair.

And he acquiesced because, as Sophia reminded him, despite Ham's and Seb's interference, she and Clay were the closest avenue the reincarnated Simon Crandor had, or was likely to find, for representation. As Jake himself had said at lunch—Sophia was speaking to Clay in a low tone behind her palm, *damn, did she really think no one could hear her?*—the old man hoped to incur the public's trust before he died, worried that no one would believe the paintings were truly his, especially since his style had changed so dramatically. Who better to convince the public of the authenticity of Crandor's artwork than ordinary citizens like them—members of the art profession who had personally witnessed the man's resurrection? Certainly, no one would believe a grandson who had everything to gain financially.

"Remember, the man wants to be accepted by the public," Sophia cautioned Clay in an even louder whisper, charging, "You wouldn't want to risk losing this new Simon Crandor, would you, Clay?"

Risk getting on the wrong side of this man they hoped to tout as the man of the hour, this artist who they believed would generate millions—no matter *his* intentions. They had lucked into the hottest story of the year, probably of the decade: a painter risen from the dead, a painter on the level of a Picasso or a Monet. Even bigger. A legend in his own right already.

"Wait until the press gets a load of this," Sophia murmured, again loudly enough for me to hear through that curtain of hair of hers. "Wait until they see Crandor's *new* paintings."

She tickled Clay's ear with the tip of her tongue, and when she breathed into it the words "we've hit the jackpot," I saw him give her a toothy smile.

It was a good thing Jake didn't hear her—the old man might have regretted having ever come forward. Luckily, he was busy talking to Zinger, Guardi, and Winter, and his back was to both Clay *and* Sophia. Still, in time he would take care of them—of this I was sure.

Sophia's pronouncement, however, seemed to satisfy Clay, and he walked with her to the door, where he rudely demanded, "Aren't *they* coming, too?" Meaning Horatio and Zinger.

"Not yet," Seb said.

He had been watching Jake carefully, and I was proud of him for his solicitude, for standing up for this man who, unknowingly, had been the cause of his shattered childhood.

"My grandfather wants to talk to them in private," he stated.

And though Seb used this ruse to urge Clay and Sophia on their way, so indeed *did* Jake plan to talk to his old colleagues in private, I learned—and, for that matter, the rest of us as well. Nodding, laughing, he had discerned that the two men were still terrified of him—with good cause, I think, because they believed that he would sooner or later change his mind and turn them in. And us? Well, when all was said and done, I suppose that he felt obliged to us, to this new-sprung family of his, who were entitled to hear his story . . . but, even more important, I sensed that *he* needed—at long last—to pass his story on to us.

Chapter 30

WINTER

∼

*T*o question the artist about my painting had always been a secret desire. But now that I had my opportunity, I wanted first to find out how the man had gained access to my house. Had he forced his way in? Did he have a key? How did he manage to place the new canvases behind my painting? The letters, the papers? And *why*? So, after Clay and Sophia left—thank God—I simply asked him.

"The painting," I said. "How did you do it? How did you manage to put those canvases and letters and papers behind it? And *how* did you get into my house?"

"Which question should I answer first?" Jake gave a quick laugh, letting my questions hang in the air like large, heavy balloons.

Elsie frowned at me while Peda touched Jake's arm with her small hand, patted the dog with the other. And the two art experts just stared at him, in a silence as oppressive as Jake's grandsons' mutual antipathy.

After a long moment had elapsed, Jake said, "I'll show you; it was as easy as carving a stuffed turkey." And he turned my repossessed painting around so that its pouch faced us, then gently pried open the torn sleeves. "I have to say, though, the backing didn't look *this* bad when *I* got through with it—then you didn't even notice that the painting had been tampered with."

"When did this 'operation' occur?" I asked. The *temerity* of him.

He didn't react to the sarcasm in my voice but rather, with an expressionless face, answered flatly, as if he were on a quiz show, "I hid the letters and papers years ago—when I returned from the dead, so to speak. *After* I recuperated from my injuries—which, by the way, took an extraordinarily long time."

Jake focused then on Zinger, who lowered his head between his knees. The breath coming through his nose was raspy. "Why?" Zinger asked. He addressed the floor.

"Why did I hide the letters and papers, or why did my injuries take a long time to heal?"

"Why did you hide the papers? How would I know about your injuries?"

"Isn't that a stupid question. . . ." Jake was bitter, but then, who could blame him? "Don't you *want* to know what happened? Aren't you curious?" He shook his head. "Just a little?" He looked from Zinger to Guardi, neither of whom would meet his gaze. "My old wooden sloop," he said softly. "She split in two, you see. We hit something—an uprooted tree trunk, I think—that acted in the way a javelin targets an enemy. Took it right in her chest. It was just too much for the old girl, with her filling up with water so fast." Jake sighed, examined his fingers, looked up, and stared again at Guardi and Zinger. "Water, you ask? I held on for hours. *Hours*. And much later, when the time came to examine the remnants, not quite half of her left after the storm—pieces of preserved wood, pieces that saved my life, you know: the keel, the shredded canvas, the leftover parts of old *B and J* . . . You remember, don't you, Zinger? We named her for Beatrice, and for my son"—he caught his breath—"for my son, Jonah." Jake kneaded his eyelids with his knuckles. "I got help"—he exhaled, ran his eyes over Seb, whose eyes were overflowing, to Ham, who was riveted to his grandfather, his forehead damp with sweat—"when I realized that the drain plugs had been taken out manually. I had inserted them myself, you see, so I knew they were fixed. We discovered the fittings had been loosened, too, even broken. The shackles, the pins . . ." Jake's voice was hoarse. He massaged his temple and squinted up at the ceiling. "The bilge pump had been tampered with before the storm. Had to have been for her to have taken in that much water so quickly. You know how careful I was with her, Guardi. Polishing, rebuilding, always checking. Treated her better than . . ." He swiped at his runny eyes. "I was *so* determined, you know? To get that water out. I believed in the sturdiness of her, just never saw that trunk coming. The hulls burst open, and she split. Just like that." He bit his upper lip. "Inexcusable in a real sailor."

Zinger raised his eyes to Jake. "But you're okay now, Simon—look at you. You're here, in good health, and with your family."

With blurry eyes, Jake smiled at the little man. "In good health?"

Zinger wet his lips. Dropped his eyes and hunched his shoulders. He resembled a caterpillar, a slug shivering into itself when threatened.

I found it curious that neither Zinger nor Horatio Guardi thought to inquire about Jake's injuries. Assuming that either man still had a conscience, that is. Instead, I saw fear etched into their faces. No dignity left there at all. I would question Jake later, in private, with my daughter and my granddaughter by my side, maybe encourage Jake's two grandsons to join us.

"I'm glad about that, truly," Zinger muttered to the floor. He turned to Horatio Guardi, who nodded. The old man's fists were clenched; his mouth, too. And his eyes, they were hard to look at because they shimmered, I thought, with years of unshed tears.

The tick of my heart beat in the heavy silence. For once, my daughter, next to me, was quiet. Sitting at Jake's feet, Peda reached up to take Jake's hand. And, across from her, Seb and Ham moved closer together, overwhelmed, I felt, by the story of their grandfather. One . . . two . . . three . . . four. I cleared my throat . . .

Zinger glanced at me then and said pensively, "What did you aim to do with them, anyway?" His voice was soft, and we had to strain to hear him. "All those letters and that affidavit? They didn't come to light until now, and *that* was only by accident."

Jake stared at the multiple wounds in the painting's spine. "What makes you so sure it *was* an accident? Winter's father used to tell me that if you're patient long enough, life has a way of evening the score." His voice sounded strained. "But don't worry—although for years I wanted revenge, as I told the detective, I have no intention of testifying against you now. I feel it's no longer necessary. Husks of old men are we, punished enough. If possible, I make it a practice never to break a promise. Had you forgotten that about me?"

As I listened to him, my throat felt scorched and tight. *Of course* he had known my father, but obviously better than I had thought. While his deliberations were his own, he spoke in a similar fashion.

Half turning, he leaned toward me, bending like a palm, as if he had heard my sentiments exactly. As if he could see as well as I could the specter of my father that suddenly stepped between us.

"I've had the key for years, too."

I thought back to when I had last changed the locks. Never, as far as I could remember.

Jake leaned down farther, so that his face was disconcertingly close to mine. "Your mother gave it to me," he said gently.

"I beg your pardon," I said. My smile froze on my lips, came out in what I imagined was a grimace. "She's been dead for years."

He nodded. "Nevertheless, you've examined the painting, haven't you?"

What kind of question was that? I *lived* with the painting. Those people were with me every day. My eyes welled up.

Jake moved from my line of vision, turned the painting so that the familiar figures enveloped me. I concentrated on the image of the child, as if she might save me.

"Here, look here." He stuck his finger into the woman, Beatrice of the black braid.

Though my eyes were blurry, I saw Horatio rise, saw him join Jake so that both men gazed down at the canvas, flooded suddenly in the light of the setting sun. The two of them were standing so close together that one might have thought them friends.

Stooped, distorted, old, and plainly tired, Horatio Guardi squatted down in front of the painting, like an old Indian sent out to die. His lips had turned as purple-black as prunes. And as wizened and dry as the fruit, too, the lips told me that something was terribly wrong.

"I thought I'd be a priest when I was growing up," he whispered. "My prayers were profound and pure. In my dreams I was celibate, an aesthete. Until I saw Simon's Beatrice one morning in front of the church in town, with her red cape and her voluptuous, protruding lower lip, red as the cape she wore, wet as the ocean we lived near, and I fell into a fever of wanting her, which has never to this day left me."

It was as if he were delivering his confession from inside that very church, just there at the golden glow of the booth's window, to Jake and to the rest of us, the juried congregation who would mete out his punishment.

With sudden ferocity, he said, "*You* loved her, but I loved her more, didn't I? Even though George Peregrine ultimately won her." The old man was cupping and uncupping his hands, and the sound of the rubbing, the old-man dryness, jarred me. "I know she thought highly of you and nothing much of me. Pitied me, mostly, I guess. But in the end, what difference did it make? The two of you, always going off alone like you did. You and your Shakespearean quotes. Because, after all, she married *him*, didn't she?" He looked up and stared at Jake.

What was the man talking about? He was incoherent.

"To blame the past," he continued, and his mouth twisted resentfully, "she believed *that* to be the weakest of failings, but in this case I couldn't help myself." Horatio looked down, frowning, at the back of his hands. "I've always hated you for treating me as if I were nothing, for making *her* believe it. You and George—so smug, so talented. You got everything you ever wanted, even her." He tried to pat, maybe grab, Jake's arm, it was hard to tell which, but his hand wouldn't reach far enough, so that the brittle fingers worked like squid's feet, milky blue veins overlapping the scored knuckles.

"We never . . . *I* never—"

"No, I know you didn't, at least not on purpose, but you *felt* it, didn't you—you and George—and, therefore, so did she."

Tears burned in my eyes, and I knew if I tried to talk, my voice would break and I would cry. Zinger was walking around in circles, with his hands clasped behind his head, and the two brothers for once were silent. Peda went to stand in between her father's knees, his tan, white-sleeved arms clasped tight around her waist, while Ham, in an ironing motion, smoothed his linen slacks with his fingertips. Elsie, bless her jaded heart, put her arm around my shoulder, put the other hand on top of mine to stop me from stripping more leaves off the fern that stood next to me. There was a blanket of green around my chair where the leaves had dropped, and I leaned down to pick up the slivers one by one.

"No wonder you tried to destroy him," Elsie murmured.

Horatio Guardi didn't answer, just sat there, rocking and rubbing.

"My mother's name wasn't Beatrice," I finally managed. "And the woman in your picture," I pointed out, "doesn't resemble my mother, the image I have of her here . . . or here." I tapped my head with my fingers, then placed my outspread hand on my heart. "For that matter, your Beatrice doesn't in the least resemble the photos I have of my mother." The echo of my child's voice reverberated in my ears. And I couldn't stop my tears.

Elsie grabbed my hand, and though her palm was moist and sweaty, it was a welcome diversion, for which I felt absurdly grateful.

Jake bent toward me. "At the time—those many years ago—I painted your mother how I saw her, how all of us saw her. She was very young, remember, unused by the world. But I was the only one who called her Beatrice, at least that I'm aware of." He glanced at old Rip. "We quoted Shakespeare to each other—hence the naming of the two boys; Jonah happily took my suggestions." He waved at his grandsons. "Beatrice, by the way, is the niece of Leanato, who married Benedick in *Much Ado About Nothing*; Sebastian, the brother of Viola in *Twelfth Night* and the brother of Alonso in *The Tempest*; Hamlet, of *Hamlet*—presumably, you know."

"Always the brother," Sebastian breathed.

After a long pause, I said in a near whisper, "What about my father? Where does *he* fit in?"

"He was my best friend until your mother died. I never saw him again after that; I guess in a way he blamed me—he was the jealous sort. But before that, we were the best of friends; all three of us were," he amended, looking at Horatio. "And all three of us were in love with your mother. I painted her quite often, until she died. . . ." I could hear the distress in his voice. "Guardi here, he lusted after her, and your father . . . well, he married her."

I didn't want to probe more deeply—not yet, not now. Except for the identities of the child and the men in the picture—these names I needed to know. But I had a feeling I already knew who they were, that I had always known. "Who is she? Who's that?" I asked. I pointed. "And the men?"

He looked at me strangely. "Why, it's you. Didn't you know? See the bracelet you're holding? A cuff, you call it? Wasn't that your mother's? And if you look *very* closely, you'll notice a tiny locket around Beatrice's neck that she claimed belonged to George's father."

Of course. Though it was difficult to see, *at least* I should have recognized the cuff, monogrammed and, I remembered, with a sense of shame, worn, with my mother's initials—how could I have missed something so revelatory precipitating such an obvious but poignant and rare memory of my mother?

Elsie dropped my arm, went up close to the picture to examine the child and the mother's figure, and gasped. "I should have known it," she said. "There are some photographs . . ." She stopped and glanced at Seb, who grinned at her.

"And the two *men*," Jake said, his unblinking, translucent eyes pinning me to my chair, "your father . . . and me, of course. The two of us, we were *always* behind your mother." He smiled at me, and then he coughed into his hand.

"Oh my God," I said. I covered my eyes with my hands. How often had Jake returned to this house with me unaware?

As if he had caught my thought, he said, "I returned here

only twice. Once after the boat accident, to hide the letters and my testimony for the eventual day of reckoning. And the other this spring, when I realized that Horatio and Zinger, even Hamlet, perhaps Seb, if I were lucky, would arrive sometime during the summer to assess the painting. Remember, I had bird-dogged the lives of my grandsons; I shadowed them, hoping to one day connect with them." Jake smiled shyly. "Anyway, when I learned they were coming," his eyes skidded from one grandson to the other, "that's when I inserted the newer canvases." He gestured at the picture on the floor. "Both times I stayed in the carriage house, in the same room I used to occupy when I visited your parents. Always alone, I might add . . . then as now." He wiped his eyes and glanced at me.

"My *own* wife, as you might *not* know, died in childbirth, after which your mother . . . well, she was infinitely compassionate. The child, my son, he stayed in the South. Never a real home there, though." Jake turned toward Ham, who, bearing forward in his chair, locked eyes with him and tried to smile, which, with heartfelt recognition, the old man clearly welcomed; then he looked up at Seb, whose lips, I noticed, slightly trembled. "Maybe *that's* why . . ." His voice weakened as he stared back into the picture's painted fog and the misty faces that he had drawn so long ago in my family's likeness.

Why was he rambling on about *his* family when *my* heart was skittering so about my own? Did Peda's Superman of the waves, the great Simon Crandor, actually feel remorse for the son who had tried to kill him, his own father? Did that excuse the boy? Put the onus on the father for his remissness toward his son, his estrangement toward his grandsons? The rift this behavior—or misbehavior—had spawned that was at last to be mended . . . not in my book, but then . . .

Look at me. All these years, I had been oblivious to my *own* family, those living, as well as those represented in my painting;

I had been conversing with a family of ghosts, living with spirits behind the painted faces as my everyday companions, spirits who had helped me weather my life, yes . . . but I never knew it.

Or did I? Because I was suddenly struck with the certainty that reality—just like a dream—in the end is inherently, *only* how you interpret it. Jake and Peda, even Elsie, had taught me that.

Chapter 31

PEDA

After the discovery in the conservatory, I lost my sense of smell. It happened this way. In the evening we decided to go onto the terrace—that is, Jake and I—but Omum threw a fit. Because of the nighttime screams, she was afraid for us to go outside. And I became *very* upset. So, to remind me, and to remind Jake and Sebastian and my mother and Hamlet and even Zinger and Horatio Guardi, she acted out the scream, waving her hands around, trying her best to sweep our objections away. "*Helll . . . p! Hel . . . ll . . . p!*" she cried out. And the fear that I heard in her voice scared me, too—scared Scarecrow so much that he put his tail between his legs and hid behind me—because, to tell the truth, we had forgotten all about the screams.

Thereupon I told Jake I couldn't go outside with him—I had to think fast—because aliens had moved into the boulders on the beach. Hadn't he seen them cavorting? I asked. "You can *smell* them," I said. I was *sure* of it. And that's when I really started to believe the story I had made up. "They smell like raw potatoes," I decided. "That *must* mean that they exist. I mean, if you really think about it . . ." I remember I nearly choked then, my voice so low that it turned into a scratchy whisper—I had found *him*, Jake, King of the Waves, Superman of the Sound, in the same way . . . and just look who *he* had turned into.

"Well," he said at that, touching my shoulder and peering into my face, "then we'll have to go out and find the aliens ourselves." And he made me swallow my fear with his look, and he took me by the hand, and with the other I screened my eyes with three fingers, but because I trusted him, I followed him. Omum threw another fit, but she let me go because Jake inspires trust, she said.

We went to the end of the island in the twilight, walking slowly, just the two of us, until we reached the end of the point. And there, standing by itself, proud neck bowed before a fan of brilliant, rainbow-colored, spotted tail feathers, was the biggest bird I have ever seen, motionless and peaceful under the stream of a moonbeam.

"It's a *peacock*," Jake said very softly, "a lost bird, who mimics the sound of a human voice, interpreted by some as a scream when he opens his beaked mouth. All those nights, it wasn't an alien after all . . . or a deer or a tortured child. It was just the misunderstood song of a peacock."

To the water's edge we walked then, so we were right next to the big bird, who didn't twitch, who regarded us curiously yet didn't seem to care that we were there. I edged closer to Jake anyway, and when he stopped, I snuggled under his armpit. I felt his body heat, and he stroked my hair, and he seemed mighty to me.

He fixed his eyes on the peacock. "Peda, there's a Greek myth about a giant named Argus," he said, and his forehead creased, and I felt him thinking hard.

"Like you?" I wanted to know.

"Oh, no." He crouched down so I could look directly into his face. "Argus was a giant with one hundred eyes who was killed by a god named Hermes. But do you know what?"

I shook my head.

"Before long, the eyes of Argus transformed into spots on the peacock's tail."

I whispered into his ear, "Like our peacock?"

"Just like it," he said. Jake's cheeks glistened, I believed with melted teardrops, and I touched the stickiness with my fingertips. Using my shoulder for support, Jake stood up then, rickety-stiff, and he looked at the big bird, who seemed so alone on the water's edge, and when Jake finally spoke, it was as if he spoke to *him* and not to me. "Fortuity, coincidence . . . or is it fate?" he said. I could barely hear him, and puffs of his breath sailed on the mist. "Do you see, Peda? After all this time, one hundred omnipotent guiding eyes granted to us, miraculously presented on the face of a peacock's tail."

And I craned my neck to study the peacock, to see the face with one hundred eyes on the peacock's tail, and I swung Jake's hand so that I would never lose him.

Jake smiled and he gazed down at me. "A bird is all it is." He added sadly, "Who was stranded by the waves, like me."

Then, like *magic*, the stream of the moonbeam lit up Jake's eyes in the same way it had the peacock, and, for the longest second, the peacock and Jake seemed to me to be one and the same.

ACKNOWLEDGMENTS

*I*f you have lived on or near the water—a river, a lake, the ocean, the Sound—you have come to appreciate that it can be the heartbeat of life. Once, during a hurricane, I watched the water rise and advance toward my home, and I realized that there was nothing I could do to stop it. No one could. I mean, man can stop a battle, an invasion; he can fly; he can send someone to the moon; but how can he stop a tidal wave? We evacuated. And I understood then that while the ocean—in this case the Long Island Sound—gives life (in a multitude of ways), it can also take it away. And I thought it was such a privilege to live there and to witness. With that came the inspiration to write *Peregrine Island.*

If you have discovered art that you admire, that you love, I believe you may have grasped the mystery of a soul—in some wondrous cases, yours as well as the artist's. I believe this happened to me with a nineteenth-century painting by Luigi Loir, a painting I held in such high esteem that it gave me the vision to write *Peregrine Island.*

My thanks go to Robert Emmett Ginna, Jr. for his wise, once-upon-a-time advice on plots and detectives and cops; and to my patient copyeditor, Annie Tucker, for her talent and expertise. Many thanks also go to my publisher, Brooke Warner, for her energy, advice, wisdom, capability, and patience, and to Cait Levin too, as well as to my publicist, Meryl Moss, for everything they did to make Peregrine Island come to fruition.

Finally, and most especially, my gratitude goes to my wonderful family: first and most important, my very tolerant and loving husband, Neil; my sister, Elaine, always ready on advice when I need it; my children—Antony, Jeremy, and Alexa—for their love and support; Ann, my publishing compatriot; and also Carie and Gael. To my writing partners, my extraordinary dogs, Mini and Mighty. And lastly, to little MacMac and Luca; my gratitude goes to them always, as they continue to make me laugh, showing me in countless ways that life can be so much fun.

ABOUT THE AUTHOR

*A*s a journalist for *Vanity Fair*, *The Huffington Post*, *Holiday Magazine*, and *Greenwich Review*, Diane B. Saxton covered everything from torture victims to psychics, animal rights activists, exotic travel, and movie producers.

A new chapter opened up for her after interviewing Amnesty International US founder Hannah Grunwald. Alarmed that the stories of incredible and influential lives such as Grunwald's could be lost as the Greatest Generation passes, Saxton began capturing their histories and compiled them into a 1,000-page biographical collection, which became the inspiration for her next novel. She brings the same gift for storytelling with illuminating subtext to her debut novel, *Peregrine Island*. Saxton divides her time between New York City and the Berkshires, where she lives with her husband, dogs and horses.

SELECTED TITLES FROM
SHE WRITES PRESS

She Writes Press is an independent publishing company
founded to serve women writers everywhere.
Visit us at www.shewritespress.com.

Portrait of a Woman in White by Susan Winkler. $16.95, 978-1-938314-83-4. When the Nazis steal a Matisse portrait from the eccentric, art-loving Rosenswigs, the Parisian family is thrust into the tumult of war and separation, their fates intertwined with that of their beloved portrait.

The Black Velvet Coat by Jill G. Hall. $16.95, 978-1-63152-009-9. When the current owner of a black velvet coat—a San Francisco artist in search of inspiration—and the original owner, a 1960s heiress who fled her affluent life fifty years earlier, cross paths, their lives are forever changed . . . for the better.

Things Unsaid by Diana Y. Paul. $16.95, 978-1-63152-812-5. A family saga of three generations fighting over money and obligation—and a tale of survival, resilience, and recovery.

A Drop In The Ocean: A Novel by Jenni Ogden. $16.95, 978-1-63152-026-6. When middle-aged Anna Fergusson's research lab is abruptly closed, she flees Boston to an island on Australia's Great Barrier Reef—where, amongst the seabirds, nesting turtles, and eccentric islanders, she finds a family and learns some bittersweet lessons about love.

Fire & Water by Betsy Graziani Fasbinder. $16.95, 978-1-938314-14-8. Kate Murphy has always played by the rules—but when she meets charismatic artist Jake Bloom, she's forced to navigate the treacherous territory of passionate love, friendship, and family devotion.

Water On the Moon by Jean P. Moore. $16.95, 978-1-938314-61-2. When her home is destroyed in a freak accident, Lidia Raven, a divorced mother of two, is plunged into a mystery that involves her entire family.